The Shipped Trip

NC BARTON

THE SHIPPED TRIP
FORTUNE FALLS BOOK 4

NC BARTON

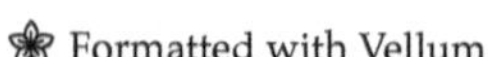 Formatted with Vellum

CHAPTER 1
CHLOE

My fingers pick and pull, trying to untangle this mess of yarn in my lap. This massive tangle of knots that leads nowhere. This hopeless mess of threads.

I took up knitting when I moved back home as a way to distract myself from my disaster of a life, but I can't find the end of the yarn so I can just start.

Dammit!

I throw down the yarn. Enough.

My eyes flick to the drawer where for years, I used to keep my leotards and tights. I bet I still have a couple in there. It might feel nice to…

My phone lights up with a text.

Ruby: You coming over for Margs and Meg night?

The clock on my nightstand shows it's already past six. Shit. If I don't leave now, I'm going to be late.

I text back.

Me: On the way. Can I bring anything?

Ruby's reply is instant.

Ruby: Just your sweet face.

Then a few seconds later.

Ruby: And hot chocolate.

Slipping into my boots, I put on my coat and call out to Dad, "See you later."

"Have fun, peanut."

Despite the downright chilly March air, I ride my bike instead of borrowing Dad's truck. It's nice to feel the sting on my cheeks, my blood pumping through my legs, the fresh smell of the cold dirt.

I stop at the little grocery store and grab some wine for me and some hot chocolate for Ruby.

While I'm waiting in the check-out aisle, I open the dating app I downloaded last week. One missed message.

Chloe, what a beautiful name. It means blooming like the rosy glow of your...

Delete.

The last thing I need in my life is someone mansplaining my own name to me. I know what my name means. It's Greek, just like my father, who was the first of his family born in the States. I have his sharp nose and dark hair. But I have my mother's blue eyes. I'm not sure where my mother's side was from, I mean, besides here. I should ask Kyle. He doesn't mind talking about her.

I shove my purchases in my bike basket and ride through the chilly night once again. I'm glad I came out. I almost said no the first time she invited me. I didn't want to feel like a pity invite from my brother's fiancée. But it sounded fun, and since all my friends have moved to Seattle or Portland, I have absolutely nothing else to do.

Ruby's red truck is in the driveway as I slowly roll to a stop and hop off my bike. I climb the stairs and punch in the code for the door, heading in. Ruby's setting a bowl of chips on the coffee table, trying to maneuver it over her massive baby bump.

"Are you *still* pregnant?" I laugh. I've been saying it since Thanksgiving. It's our little joke.

"Of course not. This is just too much pizza." She giggles. "Ooh, we should order pizza."

"Sounds good? Where's Kyle?" I ask, shifting in my seat.

"Work. But Heather should be here any minute, though. Oh my God, you look so cute. Should I change out of my pajamas?"

Ruby is in a soft pink onesie with a hood with teddy bear ears. She's adorable, as always. And it's not like I'm wearing anything fancy, in my jeans with holes in the knees and a faded Ramones T-shirt.

"You look amazing. You're glowing."

I put my stuff in the kitchen, open the wine, and put on the kettle for Ruby's hot chocolate. Ruby comes in just as I'm pouring the hot water over the powder in a mug that says *I Bake Better Than Your Mom*.

I bring our drinks into the living room and set them on the table. I have a seat on the soft sofa and snuggle into one of the soft blankets. Despite the fire in the hearth giving the room a soft amber glow, the house is freezing.

Ruby walks in from the hall, holding up her phone, and plops down on the couch. "We should start the movie. Heather is not coming."

A couple of hours later, we're on our second movie, *French Kiss*, and I'm on my third glass of Cabernet. Ruby and I are cozied up on the couch with a large throw blanket over our laps.

Meg is on a plane trying to envision her happy place. Ruby points to the screen. "That's what Heather needs."

I squint. "A happy place?"

"No. A trip. A change of scenery."

"Her and me both." I hold up my wine.

Ruby's eyes are lit up like a kid's on Christmas. She sends the blanket tumbling to the floor and nearly spills her cocoa. She runs to her bag by the door and comes back with her phone lit up. "You're going to Barbados."

I pour more wine into my glass. "What are you talking about? I'm not going anywhere."

"My mom booked me and Kyle tickets on her cruise to the Caribbean before we knew about..." She rubs a hand over her belly. "I can't go. But you can. You and Heather can go together. It'll be perfect. I'm texting Heather now."

Me?

No, I can't go. But even as I'm thinking that, excitement bubbles in my chest. I've never been to the Caribbean. I've never been east of Montana. My dad has always wanted to take us to Greece. But with mom getting sick and all the medical bills, and then just one salary and three kids, it was never possible. Then my ex and I planned a trip to Amsterdam. We got our passports, planned all the stops, and right before we bought the tickets, we broke up. Or rather, he dumped me. I should've left him for all that credit card bullshit, but that's another story.

I take a hearty sip of wine. No need to stroll down that memory dark alley.

Ruby taps on her phone. "The cruise leaves April 4…"

I sit up, crossing my legs. "That's in a little over a month. And you guys need me at the bar. What if the baby comes?"

Kyle walks through the door in dark jeans, a white shirt, and his jean jacket with a sherpa lining. I give a small wave, but his eyes are firmly fixed on Ruby. Don't get me wrong, I'm so happy they found each other, it's just their ooey gooey eyes for each other is too much. I'd love to find something like what they have together, but if my time on the apps is any indication, it might not be in the cards for me.

Ruby winks at Kyle but keeps talking to me. "It's plenty of time, even for you." Ruby smiles, all the while tapping on her phone. "And the baby's not due until the end of April."

"Right, and they never come early." To Kyle, I say, "Talk some sense into your wife."

"What plan does she have now?" he asks with a chuckle that is so quintessentially Kyle it makes my heart squeeze. It really is good to be home.

I gesture to Ruby. "She wants to ship me off to the Caribbean."

Kyle's mouth opens wide. "Oh, right. The cruise." Then his brows furrow. "But isn't it a c—"

Ruby shushes him.

I set my wine down. "Isn't it a what?"

"Isn't it a free Caribbean cruise?" she says with a smile. "Yes. It absolutely is. What do you say?"

I think of my dad's house and my tangled mess of yarn. My stupid dating app with mansplainers. A change of scenery is exactly what I need.

"I'd love to go." And it's true, I would. "But where does the boat leave from? How much are plane tickets?"

I'm also worried about my back. Over the last couple years, my hip seizes and my back goes out. Will I be able to handle a long plane ride? Lugging a suitcase. That's not a question Ruby can answer, though.

Ruby makes a few more taps on her phone, her smile growing wider and wider with each tap. "What's your email?"

I point to myself while I auto-ramble off my Gmail address.

"Perfect. Done. You and Heather have tickets on a flight to San Juan, Puerto Rico, Friday April 3."

I'm stunned. "Did you really just buy us plane tickets?"

Kyle laughs. "She probably also bought you a dress to pack on the trip. In fact, she probably packed it for you." He heads into the kitchen.

Ruby laughs, still focused on her phone. "I did get plane tickets, but I didn't pay. I used my mom's miles. She has a ton, and she never gets to use them because she's always working. So you just have to get yourself to PDX at 6 p.m. I emailed you all the details, and I did find a cute bikini." She shows the phone to me. "This would look amazing on you! I'm texting it to you now."

Ruby jumps off the couch and does a little hop, her face beaming. My phone vibrates in my pocket, and I take it out and click on the link to a white swimsuit. It's a cute suit, what little of it there was, a classic triangle top string bikini. I scroll over to my email and, right there at the top, are the plane tickets. Holy shit. She really booked flights.

I stare down at my phone. "Ruby!"

Ruby dramatically stretches her arms. "Oh man, look at the time. I've got to get to bed."

I stand. "You can't plan this trip in the span of ten minutes, then go to bed."

Ruby rubs her belly. "Honey, you'll thank me. Trust me, this will be good. I'll let you know where to meet Heather."

And with that, she waddles down the hall.

Kyle comes out of the kitchen holding a beer. "Ruby's used to running the show. I'm sure she'll understand if you don't want to go on the trip."

"I want to go." And really, I do. It sounds fun. I need a little fun. "You sure the bar can spare me?"

Kyle nods, swallowing his sip of beer. "We'll be good. If it gets super slammed, I'll just make Dad help out."

"Once you start that, you know he'll never get out from behind that bar. You know he makes the—"

We say this last part together, rehearsed over years of my dad saying it every Christmas, which is really the only time he makes it.

"Best old fashioned in the Pacific Northwest."

Once our laughter dies down, Kyle says, "Honestly, though, if you don't want to go—"

"I do want to. I need…" I don't know how to finish that statement. I don't know what I need, but something doesn't feel right. I want to have passion in my life, and for the past, well, forever, I've just been trying to get through. Make it to my next paycheck, to my next job, to my next date, hoping that something will feel right. Hoping something will light me up. Hoping something will stick and I'll finally stop feeling like a round peg in a square hole.

Kyle reaches out and pats my leg, like he can read my thoughts. "You need a vacation."

I nod, leaning back, watching the fire lick the wood in the hearth. It's all set. I'm going on a Caribbean cruise.

CHAPTER 2
CHLOE

I've double-checked twice that I packed everything. The bus is nearly to PDX, where I'm going to meet up with Heather, and we'll board our flight to Puerto Rico.

Heather is meeting me because she had a late meeting at school, and the thought of getting to the airport late sends white-hot panic coursing through my veins. I can't. I can't stand in the security line knowing my plane might leave without me. I'm fine with taking the bus. And we'll have plenty of time to hang out on the ship. Heather didn't seem to mind when we talked about it. She seemed, honestly, a little out of it.

People mill about the airport like they have nowhere else to be, and it's the one place where that isn't true. I wheel my suitcase to the check-in kiosk, turning my earbuds up to tune out the noise. Security is a breeze, and I grab an iced latte on my way to my gate. The group about to board the flight before mine crowds the gate and fills the seats. I'm two hours early. Just like I like it. I sit back, get out my Kindle, and switch from Taylor Swift to classical music because I love reading with music on, but only music with no lyrics. I prop my feet up on my suitcase and sit back, diving into the romance I picked up for the trip.

I'm officially on vacation.

The group waiting slowly boards, and the waiting area gets a lot quieter. I sit and read in the pleasant silence.

Eventually, people trickle in for my flight. Someone in the seats behind me jostles me. I shift in my seat, sitting up a bit more but not taking my eyes off my book. The love interest has entered the scene, and the meet-cute is about to happen.

The person behind me leans closer. I know who it is by smell alone. I could pick that smell out of a lineup blindfolded. It's spicy and sweet. Like ginger and toffee, but with something a little dangerous mixed in, like a boozy smell even before any of us could ever drink. A familiar voice whispers in my ear, "What do you say we flash mob this place?"

I look up, and our eyes lock on each other like magnets snapping together. His tawny brown hair brushes into his eyes, the dimple on his left side pops, and his blue eyes smolder. My brain stumbles, trying to catch up. What the hell is my brother's best friend—my longtime *what-if* crush—doing at my gate?

In an attempt not to say all of that, I say, "There are only two of us."

He hops over the seat, using his arm as leverage, his forearm flexing in the most distracting manner. He's sitting next to me now instead of behind, and he places an arm around the back of my chair. "Yes, but what we lack in numbers we'll make up for in gusto."

I laugh; it's impossible not to. Holden has always, always made me laugh. "Okay, first of all, what year do you think it is? People don't flash mob anymore."

Holden shakes his head. "I don't think you're right there. I just saw one on TikTok."

"I just saw an interview with Heath Ledger on TikTok. The videos are not always current."

"Heath, huh? He's your type?" Holden's smile is gone now, his face so serious it makes me laugh again.

"Heath is everyone's type. Heath is even your type."

He shakes his head. "I prefer dark-haired women with—"

My cheeks are on fire. I stop him before he can go any further, because this is always our game. He flirts with me, but then makes it clear it's just friendly banter. We would never, could never, be anything more. Today, though, I'm not in the mood to play. "Holden, what are you doing here?"

He pulls out his phone. "I'm waiting to board flight 8732 to San Juan, Puerto Rico."

My mouth falls open. While this was the logical explanation, it still doesn't make any sense. "You're going to Puerto Rico?"

"Mmm hmm." He places his phone back in his pocket.

"You are?"

"Yep."

I take a sip of my coffee, hoping the caffeine will help the situation make sense. "Why?"

"That's where the ship leaves from, apparently."

My coffee slips through my hands, dropping to the floor.

Holden quickly picks it up. The lid stayed on, thankfully, and all that was left was ice. "I'm going to toss this."

He walks to the nearby trash can, his strong, long legs taking him there in about two strides. His light-gray shirt hangs loosely around his torso but snug around his muscled shoulders and arms. He catches me staring and flashes me a smile that sends flutters deep in my belly. I look away.

When he sits back down, I turn in my seat toward him. "You're coming on the cruise? With Heather and me?"

He frowns. "No."

Ahh. See. Somehow, I misunderstood.

But then Holden goes on. "Heather can't come. I'm her replacement."

I don't smile. I don't frown. I don't react at all, in fact, because my face is numb. What the actual fuck?

"Huh?" I manage to croak.

"Heather's mom broke her leg. She has to stay…"

Holden is still talking, but I'm walking away, already dialing my phone.

Ruby picks up on the second ring. "Hey. Are you on the plane yet?"

"Why is Holden sitting here talking to me about flash mobs?"

"Because he knows you love them?"

She's right. I do. Whenever I'm having a bad day, which lately has been a lot, I always look up dance videos or throw on *Dirty Dancing* or, more recently, *La La Land* (and turn it off before the disaster of an ending, obviously).

"Where's Heather?"

"She called me last night. She had to go to Arizona to help her mom. She broke her leg. So I called up Holden. He needs a vacation, too. You guys are going to have the best time."

An announcement to begin boarding comes over the loudspeaker.

"Ruby…"

"I have to run. Love you, sweets. Call me when you land."

And just like that, the call is dead.

I head back to my suitcase, pulling my phone up on my ticket. What am I going to do stuck for a week with Holden Hartman?

They call Section C, and I grab my shoulder bag and suitcase. Both Holden and I move forward.

He smiles at me, warm and genuine, as he reaches for my suitcase. "Let me get that for you."

I tug it away. "It's all right."

We get in line and head down the hall toward the plane. White-hot fear replaces my nerves over spending the entire week with my longtime-never-going-to-happen crush. I've never flown before. I try to smile at each flight attendant as I pass, but my ears are buzzing. How does this metal bus travel through the air?

I find my assigned spot. Holden is helping an older woman with her luggage a few rows ahead. She is beaming at him. Her small, wrinkled hand on his arm.

Looks like he has a new fan.

I open the overhead compartment and freeze. How am I going to get this up there without hurting my back? I should've accepted Holden's help when he offered. It's too late now. I square my hips, engage my core, and am about to hoist my suitcase up into the tiny tubes above the seat when it lifts above my head.

Holden smiles. "I got it."

Relief washes over me. I wasn't sure how I was going to throw my bag up there. I scoot into my seat. The window seat. I click my seat belt and pull it closed. Then I pull again. Holden takes a seat. His forearm rests on the thin shard of plastic and metal between us. Is this entire plane this flimsy? Shouldn't it feel more tank-like?

I tug again at my seat belt, and I swear the fabric frays under the strain. I can feel Holden's eyes on me.

"Everything okay?"

"No."

"What's wrong?" Holden turns more of his body toward me.

"How high does the plane go?"

Holden shrugs, his shirt shifting with the movement. "30,000 feet probably."

A shudder passes through my body. "This seat belt is too thin. And this seat feels like I will break it if I shift too hard. The window is a tiny piece of plastic. I don't think I can do this."

His eyes crinkle at the corners, but he quickly wipes any hint of a smile off his face. "Chloe, it's going to be fine. People fly on these planes every day. It's fine."

I shake my head. He reaches over and puts a finger under my belt. My whole body erupts in goosebumps, and I swear to God, time slows. His scent is intoxicating, wafting toward me as he leans closer. He gives a small tug, and the pressure of the belt on my hips, combined with his finger at my stomach, silences all thoughts of plummeting to my death.

Apparently, my body can't lust after Holden and spiral about this tin can death trap at the same time.

Holden moves his hand. "Seems secure."

I nod, looking out the window at all the people rushing around with small vehicles heaped with luggage, bright-orange vests, plastic batons. This does not look organized at all. This looks like chaos. Does anyone out there actually know what they're doing?

Holden nudges me with his shoulder. "Why don't you tell me about what's been going on with you? It'll distract you. Plus, we haven't had the chance to catch up since you got back. What's been going on? What brought you back to Fortune Falls?"

I nod. Distraction. Yes. That's what I need. "Let's see…What's been going on with me? I moved to Leavenworth for a guy, and then the guy turned out to be terrible, and instead of admitting to myself that's why I moved there, I stayed at an awful job at a dive bar, not the fun kind, where all the customers were handsy. One day, I'd had enough, I threw a beer in a man's face who grabbed my ass, and I got fired. Now I'm back. Living at home. With my dad."

Holden is making a tight fist next to me, his forearm so flexed it's about to pop. "Do you know the customer's full name and address by chance?"

"No." I laugh. "This is not distracting me. Tell me about your life. What's going on with you? How can you take time off from the brewery?"

His fist relaxes a bit, but his muscles are still tense. "I don't really feel like I can, but when Ruby came storming into the brewery, my team pointed out that I have not taken a vacation in the entire six years the brewery's been up and running, so they strongly suggested that I do it."

"You're a workaholic."

"I don't know if I'd say workaholic. I'd say passionate. I'm a very passionate person. It doesn't feel like work. I love the brewery."

My cheeks flame at his use of the word passionate. I smile through it. "You're a workaholic."

He laughs. "Okay, sure, I work too much. It's true. I work too much. I love the brewery, and it's going well, so why wouldn't I work? It's not like I have anybody waiting for me at home."

There's a long silence that stretches out between us as that last sentence hangs in the air like something you could see and touch and hold and give a huge hug to. The flight attendant comes over the speaker and starts giving the safety talk. I sit up and pay very close attention because I want to know all the ways not to die on this metal heap that looks about as fancy as Dad's old truck. Before I know it, she's walking away. The talk is over, and the plane is moving.

Fuck. Nope. I don't think I can do this. I undo the buckle with a light flick of my fingers—there's no way that would hold if we plummeted from the sky—and stand.

"What are you doing?" Holden asks.

"I'm leaving."

CHAPTER 3
CHLOE

I hesitate, wondering if I should face him as I climb over him or give him an up-close and personal view of my ass. But before I can decide, his strong hands are on my hips, tugging me back down in the seat.

A flight attendant comes by. Leaning over, she whispers, "Is everything all right?"

Holden nods. "I know it's not time for beverage service yet, but we have some first-flight jitters. Could we possibly get two whiskeys?" He makes prayer hands.

"Sure thing." The woman smiles, batting her eyelashes. "Just don't tell your neighbors. And put it away during takeoff."

"Yes, ma'am."

She leaves with a smile plastered to her face.

"I'd love a whiskey," I say. "At The Vern, on land. Come on, let's both go." I move to stand, but Holden's hands fly to my hips again.

He looks at me with his light-blue eyes. "Chloe, it's going to be okay. I swear we're not going to crash."

I'm lost in his steady gaze, in the pressure of his hands. He moves them and clicks my seat belt closed. I swallow hard. "Okay."

The stewardess returns with definitely more than two little whiskey bottles. She hands them to Holden with two plastic cups.

"Thank you!" He puts most of the bottles in the pocket of the seat in front of him and pours two, handing me one. "Bottoms up."

He clunks his glass against mine, and I nod. The plane is still moving, this time faster. I lift my glass to my lips and down the shot in one go, the burn a pleasant distraction to how fucking fast the plane is going now.

Holden takes my cup and puts them both by his backpack under the seat in front of him. How does he know how to do all this? I didn't realize he'd traveled so much. Whenever I'm back in Fortune Falls, so is he. I'm about to ask when the force of the plane thrusting into the air slams me back in my seat. I grip the armrests, and Holden puts his hand on mine. Instinctively, I grab it and squeeze for dear life.

"It's okay. This is the worst part, then it's smooth sailing."

I squeeze his hand tighter. He winces the tiniest bit, but I'm not sorry. If it weren't for him, I wouldn't still be sitting here.

"What have you been doing since you've been back?"

"Nothing," I say, which is a pretty accurate sum up of my last couple of months.

"Come on. You have to do something to fill your time. Do you still dance?"

"No," I say quickly and hopefully sternly enough to shut down that line of inquiry. I sigh, and the release of air leaving my body actually feels really nice. "I've been working at the Vern every now and then. They don't need me a ton, I think they actually give me more shifts than they need covering. It's a pity job, really. I've been half-heartedly trying to date, but the apps are terrible, and if I decided to go out with one of those guys, what would I say? Nothing. I've got nothing. I've been trying to relearn how to knit, but so far I can't even untangle the yarn and start the first row, so it's been a disaster, which is actually an appropriate metaphor for my life. Just one big, tangled mess with absolutely no direction. In fact…" I ease the grip on Holden's hand, letting it go. "I don't know what I'm so afraid of. My life is a mess; maybe a plane crash would be a step in the right direction."

The plane jostles as if proving a point.

I grip Holden's hand again. "No. I take it back. It wouldn't. I really don't want to die. Not before I've bloomed."

"Bloomed?" Holden asks, running his thumb over my knuckles.

"The last flower to bloom is the strongest." I nod. "My mom always used to say that to me. I was always the youngest in class."

"August birthday." Holden nods, and my heart lights up. He remembers.

"Yeah. I was always the last for stuff. Losing teeth, needing a bra, getting my driver's license, even with the other summer babies, I always felt behind. My mom used to say I was a late bloomer. I worried for a long time that I wouldn't ever bloom. I was the shortest one in my class until eleventh grade, when I grew two inches."

"You're still pretty—"

"I know I'm a shortie, but I wasn't the shortest. I didn't get my period until I was sixteen."

Oh my God. What am I even saying?

"And that's late?" Holden asks with an adorable hesitation in his voice.

I scoff. "Yeah. I was practically the last one in my class."

The plane evens out, my ears pop, and instead of the incline before the fall on a roller coaster, it feels like we're gracefully gliding through the air. I let go of Holden's hand. He grabs the glasses and raises his eyebrows at me.

I nod. "Yes, please."

He pours us each more whiskey and hands me my glass. "So your period was late."

I laugh. "When you say it like that, it sounds like I'm pregnant."

His cheeks turn rosy pink. "I caught that, but it was already out of my mouth. But what about your dancing? I saw you in *The Nutcracker*. That, to me, looked like a fully bloomed dance."

My eyes shoot daggers. He actually backs up in his seat a bit.

"That was before the accident," I say in almost a whisper.

He nods, his eyes soft, and leans back in. "Okay. You're a late bloomer."

"Yes, but"—I hold up a finger—"I do bloom. I mean, I did eventually get my period, and grew and got tits, although that was quite late too."

Holden's eyes flick to my chest, and he mutters under his breath. "Worth the wait."

I swat him on the arm, but I feel my nipples harden at the praise. "Don't start with that."

"With what?"

I shake my head. "Ever since I turned twenty, you flirt with me like there's no tomorrow. But we both know it's all a lot of hooey."

Holden's eyebrows draw down. "Hooey?"

I lean in closer to him. "H-o-o-e-y." I put a hand on his leg, and he shifts under my palm. "If I said, you and me, right now in that little death trap bathroom, what would you say?"

Holden swallows hard, his Adam's apple bobbing. "Chloe… I…"

I move my hand and take another sip of whiskey, although clearly I don't need one if I'm talking nonsense about my period and propositioning my brother's best friend. "See. You're all talk. Anyway, I just need to figure out what I want to do with my life, and then I'll bloom. Right?"

Holden shifts in his chair and nods. "Yeah."

I turn toward him, his sharp jaw covered in a light dusting of stubble. He's always been so steady. He started brewing beer before he was even old enough to legally drink it. He always knew what he wanted to do. "How did you know you wanted to brew beer?"

Holden blows out a long, whiskey-laced breath. "My

granddad taught me. He used to brew small batches out in the woodshed behind their house."

My mouth falls open. It occurs to me, even though I've known Holden for literal decades, I don't actually know much about him, besides that he's been my brother's closest friend since they were in high school, he's an insufferable flirt, and he's always calm. "That's why you called it Woodshed Brewing? How have I never heard this?"

He smiles, his long lashes moving down briefly. "You never asked. Granddad showed me the ropes before he even let me taste the product. He used all seasonal ingredients. Grandma would tease that it was all we could afford, but he insisted it was his way of celebrating the passing of time. I wanted to carry that on, I guess."

I nod. "That's beautiful." I wrack my brain for any family tradition I could carry on. "My mom made sand castles, but there's no real money in that. She passed away when I was nine. Well, I'm sure Kyle told you."

He nods.

"I remember her, but over the years it's faded a bit. The tighter I try to hold on to what I do remember, the more it slips away. Sometimes I feel like I only know the pieces of her that my brother and sister share. Dad doesn't talk about her much."

Holden is looking at me with warm eyes, but he doesn't interject.

"I don't know what to do." I sigh and drain the last of my whiskey.

"Why do you need to figure it out now?"

I shrug. "If not now, when?"

Holden takes my empty glass and puts them both on the floor. Then he pulls out a tablet. "Well, unless you want to be a pilot, there's not much you can do about career planning right this second."

He hands me an earbud and holds the screen between us. It's *Dirty Dancing*.

I look at him, and shock must be written all over my face because Holden laughs and says, "What?"

"You like this movie?"

He purses his lips. "Honestly, I've never seen it. You like it, though, right?"

"It's one of my favorites," I say, even though somehow I think he already knows that.

He nods and turns the volume up. I sit back, my muscles more relaxed, my tummy warm from the whiskey. This flying stuff isn't so bad, really.

CHAPTER 4
HOLDEN

The plane vibrates, so constant it slips under my skin after a while and settles there. Outside, the night is dark. No stars, no lights, just clouds and a purplish tint to the sky. My elbow rests on the armrest, my thumb tracing a worn-out spot on my jeans as I ignore the almost overpowering urge to place my hand on her leg. It's distracting. So distracting, I've been reading the same paragraph in my book over and over again.

She fell asleep halfway through the movie. Her head resting lightly on my shoulder. Her hair falling across my arm lightly. I lean over, despite all the rational thoughts in my brain screaming at me not to, and take a nice, long whiff. Honey and something distinctly floral. God, I love that smell. And Chloe has smelled like it for as long as I can remember. Since Kyle and I became friends in wood shop class in high school.

My best friend's little sister. Not so little anymore.

There's a small line between her brows. Like she's dreaming about something mildly concerning.

I should move. I should lightly move her so she's leaning against the window. But I don't.

I'm a patient person. I wasn't always. I used to be the opposite until I went and lived with my grandparents, and my grandpa taught me how to brew. He taught me the value of taking time and letting the natural process take its time. You can't rush a good thing.

So I'll sit here and let whatever is between us take its time. The cabin is dark except for the glow of tablets highlighting a few faces and the amber gleam of the galley. There's a guy two rows up snoring and a baby deciding if its small snuffles are going to turn into a full-on cry or not. I hope not.

When Ruby came storming in—more like fast waddling—into the brewery, I should've said I'm too busy. It's true. I am. We're in the middle of batch five of a Helles. I'm worried it's still not quite right. Brewing beer well is a matter of knowing the style, knowing what you want the beer to be, repetition, and process improvement. I don't think you can assign a label of "hardest beer to brew well" to any *one* style, but if I were going to, it'd be Helles. It's a deceptively simple brew, with just one malt (pilsner) and one hop (preferably noble), but the beer is a delicate balancing act between the two. It's been a bitch to get right.

I glance down. Chloe's hand is resting between us. The plane jostles, and her pinky brushes mine. The smallest contact. But it's enough to make my veins crackle.

If I'm being honest, which in every other aspect of my life I am. Just not about this. Not even with myself. But in this weird time outside of time on this dark plane, I will admit I have been in love with Chloe for years. Since she was seventeen and I was twenty. But even then, I knew I could never act on it. Not only was she too young for me then, Kyle is my best friend. More than that. He's like family. When my parents split, his family took me in for a month, until my grandparents found out and made a room for me at their place. I never would've made it through high school without him.

I can't ever act on my feelings for Chloe.

I look out the window. It's so dark, but a few stars twinkle on the horizon. My granddad's words come back to me, *Good things take their own time, bug. Don't force 'em.*

Maybe that's what this is. What this could be. Something good. Something that needs its own time.

Her head shifts slightly, her hair tickling my arm. I can feel the smile on my face.

This is bad. It's not something good that can take time. It can't happen.

Full stop.

I go back to my book. The words swim on the page. My eyes see them, but they mean nothing. My brain is too busy trying to decipher all the subtle notes of her smell. It's lavender, I think, the floral smell. That might make an interesting beer. Honey and lavender ale. Something light and bright. A spring beer, perfect after all those heavy holiday ales. I could call it Chloe.

Or maybe something not quite so obvious that I'm head over heels for my best friend's sister.

I let the words on the page float, listening to the rhythm of her breathing, and put away all thoughts of that beer, of her scent.

THE SKY IS light when the seat belt sign dings. The plane begins its descent. My eyes are raw. I didn't shut them all night. I should've slept. I know I should've at least tried. But I couldn't. Not with her so close.

She stirs, sitting up, moving off my shoulder. I straighten a little. Her hand grazes my forearm as she wakes. Her touch is bumblebee-on-a-flower soft.

She blinks a few times.

"Hey," I say.

She blinks again, eyes stunningly beautiful. They widen when she realizes. "Oh no," she says. "Did I use you as a pillow?"

"Yeah," I say, biting back my smile, "it's all good."

A flush blooms across her cheeks, pink like the roses in my garden. "Sorry, I didn't mean to."

"I didn't mind." I shrug, and I didn't. At all. "You were tired."

She looks down at the seat pocket, her feet moving on the small patch of carpet in front of her seat. She fiddles with the sleeve of her sweater. "Did I snore?"

I laugh. "No."

"Did I drool?"

I make an exaggerated examination of my shirt. "Actually…"

"Really?" She looks at my shoulder closely.

"I'm kidding. It was fine. Really." It was more than fine, but I keep that to myself.

There's a heavy beat of silence. It feels thick. Like a rich porter. It hums beneath my skin like the vibration of the plane. Unless I'm imagining it.

I probably am.

Out the window, pink streaks light up the horizon. The light catches her profile, the swoop of her long lashes, the soft curve of her cheek. She's gorgeous.

Chloe catches me looking. "What?" she asks, smiling a little.

I shake my head. "Nothing. The sunrise looks different up here."

She turns her head toward it again. "Yeah," she says. "It does."

The plane jostles with a little turbulence. Chloe tucks her hair behind her ear. How many times have I watched her do that and longed to follow it with my own hand?

We both look out the window. The sky is brighter. The clouds below them are so thick that it almost looks like a solid land mass. Like a mountain in the sky.

The captain's voice crackles over the speaker, calm but distant. "Folks, we're expecting a bit of turbulence on approach. Should just be a bumpy few minutes."

I glance at Chloe, her face has gone a shade paler. Her knuckles are white from squeezing the sleeve of her sweater.

I take her hand and hold it tightly in mine. "We're going to be fine."

She nods.

Outside, as the plane moves down, the clouds turn gray. Rain streaks across the window. The engines change the pitch, getting louder.

Chloe grips my hand tighter. I don't move. Just let her hold on as tight as she needs, for as long as she wants.

"It's okay," I whisper. "They've got it."

Chloe's jaw is tight. Another drop. The plane jerks hard enough that someone yelps a few rows up. I feel the thump of my own heartbeat mixing with hers as she squeezes my fingers.

Wheels hit tarmac. A hard, jarring thud that makes the suitcases in the overhead bins thunk. The whole plane lurches, then steadies.

Chloe's eyes are squeezed shut.

When it's finally over, the plane stops, and she exhales and opens them again. Her blue eyes are so stunning, I inhale sharply.

"Sorry," she says.

"For what?" For being too goddamn gorgeous?

Chloe lets go of my hand. "For nearly breaking your hand."

"Anytime," I say. And I mean it. I haven't felt this alive in months. Don't get me wrong, I love brewing, I love my work, and my team. But this feels different. It may be the near-death-ish experience of the rough landing.

Nah, I know it's her.

The plane turns toward the gate, morning light reflecting on the wet asphalt. Passengers start reaching for phones, shoving tablets into tote bags. All ready for vacation.

Chloe grabs her bag from under the seat. "I'm not built for turbulence."

I unbuckle my seat belt. "No one is. You just find something steady and hold on."

Chloe looks at me, her eyes filled with amusement. I realize what I said. I meant the seat. Or did I?

The engines shut off, and the plane gets louder with voices and bodies shuffling to stand in the aisle. Normally, I let the pushy people go first and sit until the plane is nearly empty, but today we're on a tight schedule.

"Welcome to San Juan," the captain says over the intercom, voice crackling. "Local time is 7:42 a.m., and the weather is a perfect eighty-one degrees."

Perfect. Of course it is. Hot as balls and probably humid too. I was born and raised in the Pacific Northwest. When I was a kid, you couldn't get me out of shorts even in the dead of winter. My blood runs warm, and my ideal day is fifty-five degrees and cloudy.

How did I let Ruby talk me into this?

Chloe leans forward to peer out the window. "It's so bright," she says.

Ah yes.

That's why.

"Haven't seen the sun in a few months."

She squints, looking outside. "The light is different too. Vivid. Like when Dorthy gets to Oz."

She's right. I didn't think it was possible, but she looks even more beautiful in it.

She turns her attention back on me. "You okay?"

I shift out of my seat to stand in the line with everyone. "A little tired."

"Did you sleep at all?"

I shrug. Of course I didn't. How could I with you sitting right next to me, your head on my shoulder, smelling like that?

We file off the plane and step into the San Juan terminal. The air wraps around me like thick smoke. Coffee. I need coffee.

Chloe pulls her hair up into a messy knot on top of her head, a few strands clinging to her neck.

"This humidity is no joke," she says with a smile.

"It is." I can already feel my shirt clinging to my back.

We make it through the terminal and then back outside, the air thicker if that's even possible. I wish I had opted for shorts instead of these blue jeans. But there was frost on the ground when we left Portland.

Palm trees line the curb, not swaying, no breeze for that. Just hanging there, looking just as hot as I feel.

I point to the taxi stand. "We should grab a cab."

"Right," she says as she gets her bag, and we cross the street. "Do you know much about this cruise?"

I shake my head. "I know where to go. And I have a confirmation code. That's about it."

"Me too."

We find a taxi outside, a yellow cab with so many scratches and dents it almost looks like a pattern. The driver's got aviators, a floral shirt, and music playing low on the radio.

"¿A dónde?" he asks.

I ask him in Spanish to take us to the port where the cruise leaves from. Showing him my phone in case I'm butchering the Spanish I've spent the last three years trying to learn. He nods, pulling into traffic like he's on a timed obstacle course.

Chloe blinks at me. "I didn't know you spoke Spanish."

I smirk, because not a lot of people know, besides some of the Spanish-speaking guys on my crew, who give me endless shit for my terrible pronunciation. "We've already established you don't know a lot about me anymore."

CHAPTER 5
CHLOE

I cross my arms and look out the window. Old San Juan flashes by in bursts of colors. Pink, blue, and yellow buildings whizz by as we bump along cobblestone streets. Holden's right. I don't know him. He was always Kyle's friend. When they first started hanging out, I had a massive crush on him. Any time he came over, I'd get all tongue-tied and usually hide in my room. Then, as I got older, we'd talk more and more, but about nothing important. The weather, school, *Stranger Things*.

If I'm being honest, those butterflies that flutter through my chest and settle in the pit of my stomach still appear whenever I see him. Maybe it's a trained reaction now—Pavlov's butterflies—and he's not all that attractive.

My eyes slide over to Holden in the seat next to me. His short-sleeve shirt, rumpled from the flight, clings to his bicep like sap on a tree. He's looking out the window on his side, his neck stretched, his sharp jaw covered in stubble.

He catches me looking and flashes me a wide, slightly sleepy smile. Holden is, without a doubt, trained butterflies aside, hot.

The car stops, and the man driving says, "Here you are."

We get out, and Holden helps the man grab our bags out of the back. There's one large ship at the dock. It's light pink and covered with hot-pink hearts of varying sizes. It's so bright in the morning sun, I dig my sunglasses out of my purse and shove them on.

Holden comes to stand next to me.

"That can't be it," I say.

Holden looks at his phone. "It says Old San Juan port." He looks left and right. "There's no other ship. This has gotta be it. Let's check in. I bet there's coffee onboard."

Coffee. Yes. I wonder if all flights make you feel this discombobulated or if it's just red-eyes.

We fall into line behind a cute older couple with their arms around each other's waists. The people ahead of them are another cute couple, middle-aged, with smart haircuts, holding hands. Behind us, a young couple approaches and gets in line with a heavy sigh, laughing about almost missing the boat.

My eyes scan the line stretching in front of us, and something is not right. I tug on Holden's elbow.

"What?" he asks, putting his phone back in his pocket.

"Do you notice something odd about this line?"

He looks forward and then behind. "It's long."

"Not that."

"Chloe, I haven't had coffee yet. Can you just spell it out for me? Please."

I lean in and whisper, "It's all couples."

He bites his lip, his brow furrowing as he looks the line up and down again. He nods.

"There's not even any kids. Just all lovey dovey"—I make eyes at the couple three spots ahead that are making out pretty heavily for seven thirty in the morning—"very handsy couples."

Holden lets out a long breath. "Yep."

"What kind of cruise is this?" I ask, rolling my suitcase up with the movement of the line.

"That would be a better question for Ruby. I honestly have no idea."

We are at the front of the line. A woman with shiny black hair pulled back in a ponytail, dressed in a nearly blinding pink uniform that consists of sparkly hot pants and a vest, says, "Hello and welcome to The Shipped Ship."

My FINGERS ARE SLIGHTLY numb as the woman shoves a brochure at me, then gives one to Holden.

"Confirmation code, please."

The woman scrolls through her tablet until her face lights up. "Oh yes, there you are. You two are on the Budding Romance level."

My heart stops. "Excuse me, budding romance?"

She gives me a quick nod, her sleek ponytail bobbing. "It looks like you have an Ocean view room."

I sidestep closer to Holden and hiss whisper, "What is going on?"

"I don't know," he whispers back.

I smile at the woman. "We need just a minute."

Her eyes flick to the large line behind us. "I'll need to check in the next person. We're on a strict deadline. The ship is about to depart."

"We'll get back in line. Don't worry, we won't hold you up. Thanks."

We step out of line and away from the crowd for a moment. The waves are lapping against the ship in a rhythm that's almost soothing. Holden is rubbing his eyes like he could go back to sleep right now.

I read the brochure aloud. "Set sail on a voyage through love's many tides. Whether it be fresh and fun, worn in, or worn out, The Shipped Ship has something for every stage of your relationship journey."

Holden holds up a hand. "Wait, wait, wait. You're saying this is a couples cruise?"

Finally, he's caught up. I look him dead in the face. "I am saying this is a couple's cruise."

He shakes his head, gets out his phone, and starts to dial. Yes. That's a good plan. We need an explanation. I get out my phone and dial the only person I can think of that would know what the hell is going on. The phone rings and rings. A slight breeze blows my hair away from my face. The ocean air is salty and a little bit sweet. I'm used to the ocean. To the crisp salty air, penned in by pine trees. But this is not the ocean I know. Holden is looking at me, so I give him a small smile.

My call goes to voicemail. Holden, on the other hand, gets somebody on the line. I can hear it through the phone, "Vern."

"Kyle." Holden's voice is stern.

I lean in closer and say, "Put it on speaker phone."

He gives me a little nod, touching his phone screen and holding it out between us.

Kyle's voice is much louder as he says, "Hey, dude, are you on the ship already? How's it going?"

Holden starts to pace. "No, no, we're not on the ship already because the ship is a couples cruise. *We* are not a couple."

Should I be offended by how much emphasis he put on *we*?

"Is Ruby there?"

"Dude, she is here, but you better talk to her in a nicer tone than you are talking to me right now. She gave you a free cruise."

Holden softens his tone. "I'd never be mean to Ruby."

"Promise me. Promise me you're gonna be nice."

"I promise."

"Say the whole thing. *I promise I will be nice to Ruby.*"

Holden rolls his eyes to the turquoise blue sky. "I promise I will be nice to Ruby when I ask her about the very generous cruise that she provided for Chloe and me."

"Hey." Ruby's sing-song voice comes over the phone.

On instinct, I grab it out of Holden's hand, taking it off speaker. "Is it possible that you forgot to mention that this is a couple's cruise?"

"Chloe," she says brightly, but there's something anxious underneath it. "Oh yeah. That's right, it might be."

"Why didn't you tell me this is what this was? What were Heather and I supposed to do?"

"Oh, please." Ruby laughs. "There are all sorts of couples on the ships. Lesbians, gay couples, and they even embrace throuples. Just pretend."

"What?"

"Pretend you are a couple so you can get the super sweet seven-night cruise. What does it matter if it's a couple's cruise or not? It's a cruise. You're in the Caribbean. Get a tropical drink. Enjoy it."

"Ruby, Holden, and I are going to have to share a room."

"Honey. Just build a pillow wall. You're in the Caribbean. It's a free cruise. I have to go. We have to do prep for the bar. It's going to be slammed today. Game day. Love you, have so much fun. Drink a mai tai for me."

The line goes dead.

"Ruby, are you there?" I stare at the phone in disbelief. "She hung up. She booked us on a couples cruise, and she hung up." I hand the phone back to Holden.

His shoulders are hunched, and he looks dead on his feet. He taps at the screen of his phone. "So, what do you want to do? We could just go get some coffee. I saw a café on the way. We could probably switch our plane tickets for a flight out today. Just head back home. My team's having some troubles with the batch they're brewing. I should probably pitch in. Not that they need my help, but..."

Holden looks stressed. His eyes are fixed on his screen as he scrolls through what looks like emails. He needs this vacation. I read the brochure a little closer. There are all sorts of classes to sign up for. Yoga and HITT, but there's also how to plot a mystery novel and gardening for beginners. "No, we need this."

Holden looks up from his phone, his eyes sparking when they meet mine. "*We* do?" he says with a smirk.

"This will be good for us."

His eyebrows rise.

"I mean, not the couple part, obviously, but the rest of it. You need a vacation. I need to find out what I wanna do with my life." I show him the brochure. "Look at all these classes. We can try candle-making, or we can do sunrise yoga on the deck. We can take a cooking class. Maybe I'm supposed to be a chef."

"Chloe, you're a terrible cook." He crosses his arms.

"How do you know?"

"You burn Bagel Bites."

"That was when I was in like tenth grade. Do you ever let anything go?"

He looks at me, his eyes intense. "I remember everything."

My stomach does a swoop like one of the butterflies went for a nose dive. I shake it off. "Maybe I'm not a chef because I never learned. If I take this cooking class, then it might be my calling."

Holden steps closer to me and puts a hand gently on my shoulder. "Chloe, I would love to get on that boat, get a coffee the size of my head, and sit by a pool. So, if you want to go on this cruise and pretend that we are a couple, I am willing to do that to get all those things."

"Perfect." I smile, but nerves crackle through my system.

"Great." Holden grabs our bags. "We're a couple. Let's get back in line."

As we head to the end of the line, I read the brochure again. There are three tiers of couples on the cruise, each with its own set of activities and amenities. I look at the couples again, sizing them up. The people in front of us have their hands in each other's back pockets.

There is a couple further ahead of them that are standing close to each other, but not too close. They definitely seem a little bit frosty, arms tucked neatly at their sides, not touching at all.

I pull Holden toward me so he can hear me whisper, "I think we should be Wilting."

He looks at me like I have lost my mind, and it's possible that I have. "It's still early, and it's already hot as balls. I think we will be wilting soon."

"No. Did you read your brochure?" I ask.

"With what time, Chloe? We just got here, she just handed it to me. You pulled me out of line. Shoved me back in line. You're shoving me everywhere. I just want some coffee."

My heart squeezes. He's right. I've been doing a lot of shoving and bossing. I'm not usually this bossy with other people. Usually, I just go with the flow, but Holden brings it out in me, I guess.

"That's fair," I say softly. "Look, there are three tiers of couples on this cruise. One, budding relationship." I point to the couple with their hands on each other's asses. Now one of them has moved their hand underneath the jeans. "They are a Budding relationship. That is where we are currently booked."

Holden raises his eyebrows, his smile wide as he turns to me and says, "We could do that?"

I blow a raspberry at him. "We've already established, you're all talk. We are not doing that."

I find the middle-aged couple with the smart haircuts, holding hands and looking very comfortable—like they've been in love for their entire life. "They are a Blooming relationship. We can't do that. We can't look that comfortable holding hands."

Holden reaches a hand out to me. "We could try."

I look at it for a beat. His hand is large. I grab it with mine. It's strong and rough. Tingles move up my arm from our point of contact. God. It's just a hand, but it makes me feel all warm and melty. I can feel the heat moving to my cheeks, and I drop his hand. "Nope. People will see right through us. We need to tell them there was a mistake and we are really…" I point to the couple that is standing frostily next to each other. "Wilting. We can do that. We can wilt."

Holden bites his lip. "Okay. Let me get this straight, not only do you want to pretend to be a couple, you want to pretend to be a couple fighting, on the rocks, in trouble."

I stomp my foot and, despite myself, raise my voice. "No. I

don't want any of this. I just wanted to go on a cruise." Tears are welling up behind my eyes. "A normal cruise. Not a couples cruise. I didn't want to pretend to do anything. But this is where we are at."

The couples around us are all not so discreetly looking at me. At us. It even caught the attention of the shiny ponytail with the tablet, since we are only about five couples away.

I lower my voice. "It looks like we're going to have to be Wilting anyway. Everyone thinks we're fighting now."

Holden's eyes are warm and full of concern. "Are we?"

I shake my head.

"I didn't mean you wanted any of this. If you want…"

I can feel my blood pressure rise at his phrasing.

He must sense it because he stops and tries again. "If you think the best way forward is to wilt, then we wilt."

I smile. "Thank you." I turn my attention back to the brochure. "Anyway, it looks like they have the nicest rooms."

Holden chuckles. "Makes sense. Their relationship is in the toilet; they might as well get a nice view."

CHAPTER 6
CHLOE

Once we get to the front of the line, the switch is not hard to make, especially after my outburst. We have a sunset room with a private balcony. A woman with wiry blonde hair with some gray here and there, who is absolutely rocking the bright-pink hot pants, introduces herself, though with the resemblance she hardly has to.

"I'm Lillian." Then, in a whisper, "Ruby's mom. I'll show you to your room."

I smile. "Thank you. And thank you so much—"

She cuts me off with a stern "Shh." Then says near my ear, "We'll talk about it in the room."

I nod, but suddenly feel like I'm being called into the principal's office.

She smiles brightly, all seriousness from a moment ago washed away. "Anything that you need, come to me first. You can leave your bags. Our attendants will get everything there."

Holden blinks so slowly you can almost hear it. "Coffee?"

"Oh, honey. Did you two take a redeye? Those are rough on the system. There will be coffee and champagne on the deck as soon as we disembark, but for now, let me show you to your room."

We follow Lillian across the deck filled with couples, through one of the doors into an enormous room with a kidney-shaped balcony that goes up for what looks like a mile, all lit up neon pink underneath each level. There's a pale-pink carpet, white furry chairs, and in the middle is a grand piano and a dance floor. Holden leans in. "We could still flash mob."

I laugh and shake my head.

We head to a glass elevator. Once inside, Lillain hits the button. The doors slowly close with just the three of us inside, and Lillian turns to us. "Level with me, are you two *actually* a couple?"

"No." The question is not funny. Her tone and the you-might-be-in-big-trouble-look in her eye is absolutely not funny. But I laugh. It must be the lack of sleep. I cover my mouth.

Lillian's eyes are fire. "You think this is funny?"

I shake my head. "No, ma'am."

Holden jumps in. "We're not a couple, but we can fake it."

He grabs my hand as if to prove a point; his palm is calloused, but his skin is warm. He feels solid. I tighten my grip without even thinking about it.

The elevator doors open. Lillian turns on her heel. She leads us without a word through a narrow hall with light-pink walls, around a corner through another identical hall, and around another corner. Finally, she claps her hands, a fake smile plastered on her face, probably for the other people milling about the halls. "Here we are." She swipes a key card across the door and opens it, entering the room.

Butter-yellow light fills the room, illuminating the absolutely massive bed. It's covered in a pristine white comforter and takes up about half the space. Maybe even over half. Lillain flits about, talking about this amenity and that at a million miles a minute, but I can't follow what she's saying. I can't tear my eyes away from *the bed*.

Once the door clicks shut, she sags onto the couch. Putting her head in her hands, letting out such a massive sigh, it's like my one little "no" in the elevator was a pin prick that popped her like a balloon. "Why aren't you a couple? This would all be so much easier."

I sit in a chair in the sitting room and place a tentative hand on her shoulder. "We didn't know it was a couples cruise."

With this, Lillian starts to laugh. She shakes her head and leans back on the couch. "Ruby."

Holden comes and perches on the dresser-TV-stand thing.

She takes us both in, her eyes softer now. "What did you tell them? The check-in people?"

"Wilting," Holden says, his voice thick. Maybe from sleepiness or frustration at this ridiculous situation we find ourselves in.

Lillian tucks her legs up, sitting crisscross on the couch. "Good call. Out of the three, probably the easiest to fake. You can't tell anyone you're not a *real* couple."

She places a hand on my knee, catching me in her intense eye contact. "I mean it." Then she directs the same intense gaze at Holden. "They take the relationship thing very seriously. Last month, we had some YouTubers pretending to be a couple so they could film for their channel, and they kicked them off the boat mid-cruise."

My mouth falls open. "Mid cruise?"

She removes her hand, slicing it through the air. "Yep. Mid cruise. So unless you want to fly back home from Saint Thomas…"

It wouldn't be the end of the world. I have some savings. I could afford the ticket. But then I'd miss all the classes. What if my purpose in life is hiding somewhere on this ship?

"…you and Holden need to stick to your story. It has to look *real*." She looks back and forth from me to Holden, like she's sizing us up.

I swallow hard. "What exactly does *real* mean? We're Wilting, so it could be a lot of different things, right?"

She purses her lips to the side. "Yeah, it can. But some things are non-negotiable. Some things are universal. You don't hesitate when they ask how you met. You know each other's medical stuff, allergies, keto, gluten-whatever. And you touch each other without thinking about it."

I stare into my hands like they might give me instructions. I can practically feel Holden's hand in mine, his thigh brushing mine in the plane, his fingers as they skimmed my stomach tugging on my seat belt. It all felt good. "We can do that."

Lillian tilts her head to the side, looking at Holden. "Can you?"

"Yes," he says almost too quickly. Then, a little more controlled, he says, "Of course, we can."

And of course we can. I've been pretending to *not* be in love with him for years. What's one week pretending the opposite?

Lillian studies me and Holden for a long beat, the way people do when they're deciding whether to believe you or not. Finally, she nods. "Okay. Good. Because here's the other thing. I don't want to scare you." She pauses, almost like she's considering not saying it, but moves ahead anyway. "But last year we had a water aerobics instructor bring her friends on the ship, and they pretended to be a couple for the free cruise. The director found out. The couple was kicked out, but the instructor was also fired. So, if they find out you're not a couple, you'll get kicked out for sure. But I also might lose my job."

My palms are sweating. I rub them on the seat, wondering if we should just leave now. We could just call it a day. Leave before anything gets out of hand.

Holden looks so tired, clutching his phone like a life raft. I think of all the classes we can take.

We both need this. And what's a little light PDA? We can do this.

I smile, my brightest, fakest smile. "Don't worry. No one will ever know. Holden and I will be the perfect couple."

"The perfect couple about to break up," Lillian corrects.

"Right," I say, my smile faltering.

LILLIAN STANDS, slapping her hands on her legs. "Right. Okay then." She gestures to the bed. "If you'd rather, the bed can be divided into two twin beds. Lots of Wilters do it."

"Yes," I blurt out. "Yes, please."

Holden arches an eyebrow at me, and I give him a small smile. It's going to be cozy enough sharing the room, we don't need to share the bed as well.

"Wonderful, when you're at the sail-away party, I'll get that all sorted. Let me give you the real tour. The television is equipped with any streaming service you might want or need. Netflix and chill is often a fun way to spend a day at sea. Here is your private balcony."

She opens the sliding glass door, and a tropical, sweet, salty air whooshes into the room. It's delicious. I step out. There is a small round table, two chairs, a frosted glass portion on either side blocking our view of the neighbors, and a massive expanse of blue. The water is a different shade of blue than the Pacific. It's almost turquoise, or maybe an aquamarine.

Holden joins me, placing his hands on the railing. He looks at me with a wide and a little bit sleepy smile. "Wow."

"Yeah," I say, at a loss for words. It truly is amazing.

Before we can admire it any longer, Lillian is ushering us back out the door.

"It's time for the sail-away party. Let's go, let's go. You can't miss any of the big activities. It would look suspicious. There will be champagne." She smiles brightly at Holden. "And coffee. "

Lillian leaves, wrapping me in a big hug before she does. "I'm really a much warmer person when I'm not so stressed."

I hug her back. "Sorry to put you—"

She pulls back and waves me away. "It's my daughter who has some explaining to do. Have some fun while you're here. Just remember," she lowers her voice—"make it look real."

We head back through the labyrinth hallway. All the while, Lillian's voice rings through my head. Make it look real. We can do this. How many times have I imagined holding Holden's hand, or tucking under his arm? Thousands. And now I can with no real consequences. In fact, not only can I, but I have to.

The elevator takes us up to the top deck, where a live band plays on a small pink stage, and there's an absolutely stunning view of old San Juan and the blue, blue sea.

A server walks around with flutes of bubbly liquid. She holds out the tray to us. "Champagne?"

Holden says, "Coffee."

The woman smiles. "There's a café station right over there."

I grab a flute. "It's vacation, honey."

Holden raises his eyebrows at me and nods as he grabs one too. The server moves on.

"I normally hate champagne," I say. "It gives me a headache, but it does feel festive. It's a celebratory bad choice."

Holden clinks his glass to mine. Our eyes lock, his blue eyes nearly the same shade as the sea behind him and just as sparkly. "To bad decisions."

There is an ear-shattering blare of a bullhorn. On the stage in front of the band is a gorgeous woman with thick black hair. Instead of hot pants, she's wearing an elegant pencil skirt version that's still just as pink and glittery. The band behind her leaves the stage.

The woman on stage taps the microphone, each light click of her nails echoing across the deck. "Hello lovers and *'it's compli-cated'* situationships!

"Welcome aboard *The Shipped Ship*! I'm your Cruise Director, Theresa, and for the next few days, I'll be your guide, your cheerleader, and occasionally your bestie if you buy me the right drink. I'm kidding. Drinks are included."

Nervous giggles scatter through the crowd.

"Now, this isn't just any cruise. On this cruise, what happens at sea, *stays at sea.*"

The laughter after this feels more genuine, and Holden gives me a look that I can't quite read, but even with his sleepiness, it's intense to say the least.

"Let's talk about our three amazing love tiers. Budding Couples, where are you?"

She waits for the hoots, hollers, and applause to die down.

"You're the ones still holding hands, finishing each other's sentences, and pretending you didn't argue about luggage at check-in. Don't worry, you'll get through it. We've got Sunrise Yoga and First Kiss at Sea to help smooth it over."

The young couple next to us makes an awkward attempt at laughter.

Holden holds his champagne flute in front of his mouth as he says, "They were definitely arguing on the way here. Maybe even on the plane."

I nod because, while they cheered as a Budding Couple, their body language is screaming Wilting. His arms are crossed stiffly across his chest. She keeps moving toward him, and whether conscious or unconscious, he keeps side-stepping away. Being in the wrong relationship is such a nightmare. I've been there. Leavenworth felt like that the whole time. And I stuck it out thinking it would get better. That it was just a rough patch. Never again. I'd rather be single than walk on eggshells waiting for the other shoe to drop.

"Blooming Couples, make some noise!" Theresa booms into the microphone, bringing me back to the deck.

There's some applause and a few loud wolf whistles.

"You know who you are. You've been together long enough to share a toothbrush and still argue over what to watch on Netflix. You're gonna love Private Balcony Dinners, our Shipped Spa with an aromatherapy couples massage, and Salsa Under the Stars. Because nothing says love like your partner smashing your toes in public."

I laugh. She's funny. I have another sip of my champagne, the bubbles tickling my nose.

"And finally, my Wilting Couples. It's said with love, I promise!"

The crowd laughs.

"You've seen it all, and you're here to see if the sea can do some magic. We've got Moonlight Conversations, Renewal Ceremonies, and the On the Rocks Bar, where you can sip, sigh, and say, 'You know what, we're actually doing okay.' Wherever you are, budding, blooming, or saying goodbye, this cruise is about connection. You are safe here and free. The ocean doesn't judge. It just sways and sometimes spills your drink."

This gets a snort even from Holden.

"We run our cruises a little differently than others you may have been on. It's a smaller crew for a more intimate feel. That being said, you may see some of our crew wearing multiple hats. We also have more built-in time at sea and fewer ports, so you can really foster your connection and take advantage of some of the amazing classes and experiences we have to offer aboard. According to scientists, and if you're not going to believe scientists, who are you going to believe?" She laughs at her own joke and continues, "Couples who engage in *novel* and *arousing* activities report improved relationship quality and increased passion. And what we have planned is more fun than putting together an Ikea bookcase. So, as we sail away, I want you to grab your partner, wherever you're at in your journey, and raise a glass! Here's to love in all its forms."

The deck erupts into applause and hoots. Even I let out a loud, "Whoo hoo!"

Holden smiles. "Okay."

He puts two fingers in his mouth and lets out a whistle that I'm surprised doesn't shatter my glass.

Theresa says, "Now, DJ, let's crank up the music, let those ropes go, and get this *Shipped Ship* officially underway."

The sound system blares The Black-Eyed Peas' "I Gotta Feeling."

Holden places his empty glass on the tray of a server walking around collecting them. I drink the rest of mine and do the same. He holds out his hand. "Shall we flash mob?"

I look out at the dance floor where couples are doing everything from twerking to waltzing, no one in sync with each other. Half of them aren't even in sync with the music. I have to admit, the beat is catchy, and my hips itch to move. But I feel that familiar twinge of fear.

I used to dance a lot. I took ballet from the time I was three until the accident. When I was seventeen, I had a car accident. Everyone was fine, no fatal injuries. My car just stalled in the middle of the road, and the other car coming couldn't stop in time. The driver's side door—my door—was smashed in, and so was my left hip. I was in the wrong place at the wrong time. It was no one's fault. But it changed my life forever.

I take Holden's offered hand and pull him to the café station. "Come on. Let's get you some coffee."

Once we both have a steaming cup of caffeine, Holden says, "Can we find somewhere quieter?"

He leads us back inside, and we make our way back to the lobby with the fluffy white chairs. I sink into one, my bones heavy, my muscles loose. I sip my coffee, the warm liquid not doing much to wake me up.

Holden sighs, his long arms stretched out on either side of the chair, his muscular thighs spread wide, taking up his whole space. "I could fall asleep right now."

"Same."

He sits up a bit and looks at me. "Why don't you ever dance anymore?"

My go-to answers are perched on my tongue. *I found other interests.* Or sometimes I say, *maybe I'll try again soon.* But for some reason, that's not what comes out of my mouth.

"I can't," I say instead of all my go-tos. I don't know what it is about Holden that makes me open up. Maybe I've just hit a new level of exhaustion.

He shakes his head, his brown hair moving into his eyes with the motion. "What do you mean? Like literally can't? Physically."

I sit back, setting my coffee down and crossing my legs. "Honestly, I don't know. Maybe."

His brow furrows. "You haven't tried?"

"When I broke my hip…" Tears are prickling the back of my eyes. I close them for a moment. I'm not going to cry about this. I've shed too many tears over it. Once I'm more composed, I say, "There was no way I could dance professionally. So what's the point in dancing at all?"

That dream was shattered like the windshield that rained down on me as the car spun.

Holden puts a soft hand on my leg. "Because you love it. It's part of who you are?"

I swallow hard and shift, moving out of his touch. "Not anymore. I'm going to see if the room is ready. I need a nap."

I leave Holden with his paper cup of coffee and well-meaning advice. I don't need him telling me who I am. Just because I don't know who I am doesn't mean he does. As I get to the elevator and look at him in the lobby, I see his eyes are still on me.

***

WHEN I GET BACK to the room, the bed has been transformed from a massive king to two reasonably-sized twin beds. Thank God for small miracles.

I kick off my shoes and flop onto one of them, snuggling my head into the pillows. I close my eyes, but my thoughts are swirling too fast to let me drift off. After about ten minutes, I give up.

Instead, I grab the binder from the desk by the television. Then the pad of paper and a pen. A plan. A plan will make me feel better.

I start reading the classes offered and circle the first one I want to take.

Cooking with Love. Location: Chef's Studio. Duration: 2 hours. Indulge in a culinary class designed for two. Discover scrumptious ingredients that all have an aphrodisiac quality. Work on your team-

work in the kitchen. Then taste the fruits of your labor together. Each session comes with champagne.

Perfect. We can learn to cook. Although after I just stormed off back there, I'm not sure Holden will want to cook with me. I let out a heavy breath and keep skimming through the offered classes, circling some and writing down a rough plan. I check the ship's schedule. The rest of today and all of tomorrow are both days at sea, then we dock at St. Thomas.

By the time the keypad beeps outside the door, I have the first three days of the trip planned, packed with classes, one of which has to be my calling.

CHAPTER 7
HOLDEN

I tried to find a lounge chair near the pool to close my eyes for a bit. But the party was still going, and despite it still being before lunch, people were getting hammered. I head back to the room, hoping that the bed, the massive bed that took up the entire room and practically screamed at me, *Just think of all the ways you could touch Chloe on me,* is split in two. I need to lie down and close my eyes. Just for a bit.

I open the door slowly, not wanting to wake Chloe if she's napping, but she definitely is not. She's changed into shorts, so short that there's hardly any fabric at all to them. Her long, silky, smooth legs are propped up on the coffee table, and she's surrounded by little scraps of paper. They're everywhere, strewn about like leaves from a tree after a windstorm, all over the loveseat, the coffee table, the floor. Whatever she's doing, she's very focused.

"I thought you might be napping."

"I couldn't sleep." She gathers up the loose papers while I gather my courage.

"Chloe, I'm sorry I overstepped—"

She freezes. "I should be the one apologizing. I stormed off like a child."

I hold up a hand. "No, you don't need to apologize. I shouldn't have pried. It's just when you danced, I've never seen someone so passionate about anything. It's inspired me my whole life. When I get tired or feel beat down about the brewery, I just think of you gliding across that stage, or always heading to practice, or tearing apart your pink shoes—"

"Slippers," she corrects with a small smile.

"Right. Anyway." I run my hand over the back of his neck. "I overstepped. And I'm sorry."

"Forgiven. Let's drop it."

I smile. "For two people supposed to be pretending to be a couple on the rocks, we sure do a fair amount of actual fighting."

She holds up some of the paper. "Let's make up with a sensual cooking class."

THE CLASS DOESN'T START for a couple of hours, so I lie down, and Chloe scrolls through Netflix. The bed is split in two, but the twins are so close to each other that I could reach out and tug Chloe to me without even much of a stretch. I turn my back toward her.

It's no use, I can still smell her. I get up and take a shower instead. Sleep is a lost cause today.

When I come out of the shower, Chloe is standing waiting, bouncing all the balls of her feet, each motion making her thigh muscles flex and relax. I look away.

I have to stop staring at her legs. She is completely off-limits. I met Kyle when my mom and I moved to Fortune Falls after my dad left. She wanted to be closer to my grandparents, so they could pitch in. Mom was always working, so I was either at Kyle's or he was with me at my grandparents'. He had lost his mom, and though it absolutely wasn't the same way I lost my dad—he was still alive and well, just a dick—it felt like we understood each other in a way the other kids at school didn't. And even though he was a grade above me, we spent all our time together. He's the closest thing I have to a brother. And there's absolutely no way I can risk losing that.

"Ready?" Chloe says with an excited smile.

We head to the class. Chloe keeps wiggling her fingers and shaking out her arms.

I give her a concerned look. "You okay there, Wiggles?"

She barks out a laugh, and pride fills my chest. "Fine. I'm fine. Just nervous."

"Why? It's a cooking class."

"But what if it's not just cooking? What if it's my calling?"

She shakes her hand again, and I take it in mine.

"If it is, it is. If it's not, it's not. I used to be a really anxious kid. Like, I didn't want to go to school most days in second grade because I didn't know what would happen. There wasn't anything specific I was afraid of, just the unknown. You know."

Chloe nods. "What did you do?"

I shrug, rubbing my thumb on the smooth skin of her hand. "My mom made me go anyway, and she told me something that stuck. Worry won't make a difference one way or another. Some things are inevitable."

She gives me a thoughtful look and says, "Huh."

"It made me feel better. Like a weight was lifted. I couldn't possibly control everything. Even though sometimes I still try." It's hard when you own your own business to let some things go.

She squeezes my hand as if to say she's aware but gives me a warm smile.

We walk into the Chef's Studio hand in hand, and I nearly stagger backward, knocked off my feet by how amazing it smells. Rosemary and butter. My mouth is watering. The space is sleek. While I'm not in love with the business model of cashing in on love or its demise, I have to say every space I've seen on the ship has looked *expensive*. This room is filled with light and overlooks the sea. Copper pans gleam from overhead racks.

"Ahh, some more lovebirds are here to join us," a man with a thick mustache and an even thicker French accent says as he glides over to the door and hands us bright-pink aprons. He lowers his voice, looking pointedly at our clasped hands. "Let me guess, budding?"

Chloe drops my hand like it's on fire. "Wilting, actually," she says while trying to turn her entire face into a frown.

I try, unsuccessfully, to hide my smile. She nudges me with her foot, and I wipe the smile off my face. "Yep. Wilting."

The chef runs a hand over my arm. "Ah, so hard. Well, come join us. You can have station six. We are just about to get started."

He sashays away. We take our spot at station six, in between an older couple and a very young couple, possibly about to have full-on sex on the counter.

"Looks like they have the sensual part down," Chloe mutters to me.

I chuckle, but damn, they're really going for it. The dude is about to put his hand all the way up the woman's shirt when the chef clears his throat.

"Bienvenue, mes amis! Welcome to Sensual Cuisine or Cooking with Love. I am Chef Paul. Today, we do not just cook. We seduce with flavor."

He spreads his arms dramatically as the sea shimmers through the tall windows behind him.

"Love is like cuisine in many ways. They both require passion and attention. Who here has ever gotten hot and heavy in the kitchen? With cooking, of course."

The make-out couple next to us laughs, while a few hands raise.

Chef Paul grins. "Wonderful! We are going to start with a simple exercise."

He pulls a bowl of cut-up strawberries forward.

"You should all have some strawberries at your station."

Chloe grabs ours, sliding it toward us. I feel like if she could, she'd be taking notes.

"These are marinated in balsamic and vanilla. Feed one to your partner. Slowly."

Chloe grabs a berry from the bowl, wrinkling her nose a bit. "It's a little slimy." She brings it toward my face, and I instinctively back up.

"Holden. Open up," she hiss-whispers.

"You made it sound so appetizing."

"It's slimy in a good way." She smiles.

I laugh, and as I do, she shoves the strawberry in my mouth.

Chef Paul's voice projects as he strolls around the space. "Notice how the sweetness lingers, offsetting the tang of the vinegar. That, my friends, is foreplay."

It is sweet and tangy. It might make a fun beer. A balsamic and vanilla porter, maybe.

Soft laughter fills the room. The couple next to us is at it again.

Chloe's eyes dart toward them, and she bites back a grin. The couple—in matching light-blue shirts—are practically reenacting *Lady and the Tramp* with a strawberry instead of spaghetti.

"They have the foreplay down, too," I murmur.

Chloe bites back a smile. "They're committed to the exercise."

"Committed to public displays of affection, maybe."

She giggles, and the sound is way too satisfying. I'm highly aware that making her laugh gives me too much pleasure.

Chef Paul claps his hands. "Now switch! Food should feel like a conversation. Sometimes one whispered between the sheets."

Chloe's cheeks turn almost as red as the fruit.

I pick up a strawberry, and it shines under the lights. "Ready? It's the good kind of slimy, right?"

Her chin lifts. "I can handle slimy."

That shouldn't sound flirtatious.

It does.

I bring the berry up, hovering just an inch from her lips. The rest of the room fades to a hum of laughter and clinking utensils. For a second, she stops breathing. I do too.

When she finally takes a bite, her lips brush my fingers—

barely, accidentally—and I feel the contact like an electric shock straight to my dick.

She chews, eyes fluttering, and the moan that escapes her isn't decent. "Oh my God," she says softly. "That's *really* good."

Chef Paul passes behind us. "Ah! I see passion blooming here," he declares, gesturing dramatically toward us.

I shift uncomfortably, feeling like my attraction to Chloe is obvious to everyone in the room. And I can't be attracted to Chloe. Not when we have to share a room for...*fuck me*...seven nights. I fiddle with some of the other ingredients at our station. "Just culinary appreciation."

Chloe is frowning but nodding.

Chef Paul has made his way to the front of the class. "We are going to start by learning something deceptively simple, but in truth, it takes patience, care, and attention, which is also a lot like love."

There are nods around the class, and Chloe is back into perfect-student mode, standing at attention, her posture ballerina straight.

"First, you're going to crack your eggs into the bowl and beat them until they are all the same golden yellow color."

Chloe cracks the eggs and starts to whisk like there's going to be a test later. Iron grip, tense muscles, lips set in a tight line.

I place a hand on her shoulder. "Easy. You're whisking like you're trying to kill it."

She lightens up, but only a tad. "I want to do it right."

Chef Paul says, "Next, we are going to add a little water. This is going to add the steam."

The couple to the right of us isn't even pretending to participate anymore, their tongues firmly in each other's mouths. I nod toward them and whisper, "Looks like they have enough steam already."

Chloe snorts, and some of the tension leaves the delicate tendons of her neck. I have an overwhelming need to run my fingers along them, to soften them further, to bring my hand to the back of her neck and pull her closer. The impulse is so strong that I reach my hand out, but stop myself and instead tuck a stray hair behind her ear.

She smiles at me and blows another one out of her face.

Chef Paul continues, "Now we add the salt, and then…and this is the hard part for some…we wait." He pauses for dramatic effect, which would've been more dramatic if it wasn't broken up by a titter of laughter and a very loud sucking noise from the make-out couple. "You must wait for the salt to work its magic. While you're waiting, there is a series of questions at your station. Find one that speaks to you and try to connect."

Chloe, good student that she is, picks up the paper and starts to scan. Her eyes go wide, and her cheeks go pink.

"What?" I ask, and try to peer over her shoulder at the paper.

She presses it to her chest and shakes her head.

"Come on," I say, smiling. "What are the questions?"

"They're all about"—she lowers her voice to a hushed whisper —"sex."

A loud laugh escapes me, startling even the make-out couple. "They can't be that bad."

She scans the list again. "I assure you, they are."

Chef Paul is making his way around, and Chloe scans the list again. "Okay, here's one that's not too terrible—"

"Chloe, we don't have to do it if you don't want to."

"It's part of the instructions," she says, looking at me like I'm the one who's nuts.

I hold up my hands. "I'm just saying, you wanted to learn to cook. Not sure this has anything to do with it."

She steps a little closer, her eyes locking on mine. "Are you afraid of the questions?"

"No." I scoff, but in truth, I am. I'm desperately trying to hold it together. Not to make a move on my best friend's sister. Not sure talking about sex is going to help.

Her eyes flick to my mouth and back up. "Good. What are your top three turn-ons?"

You. You in those shorts. You bent over this counter with your hair in my face and my cock in—

"Holden?" Chloe says.

I let out a breath and take a step back. "Um, well, I like legs. I find legs to be very sexy."

Chloe shifts, and I might be imagining it, but she arranges herself in almost a pose that makes her legs look amazing.

"And scents turn me on," I say, tearing my gaze away from Chloe's amazing and now clearly flexed calves.

"Scents?" she asks.

"Yeah. Nice scents." Like the honey and lavender of your hair.

"Nice scents?"

"Yes, Chloe. I like it when a woman smells nice."

"Okay, but what's nice?"

"It's a chemistry thing, I can't explain it," I say honestly, not knowing how to clarify what I'm talking about without outright saying *I like the way you smell.* "It's your turn."

She shakes her head. "Uh uh. You have one more."

"Come back to me." I cross my arms. "Your turn."

CHAPTER 8
CHLOE

Shit. Shitty shit shit. It's my turn. Why did I even pick this stupid question to begin with?

"Chloe?" Holden says with an adorable smirk that I want to kiss off his face. Fuck.

A leg man, huh? I'll give you some legs to look at. I don't dance anymore, but I love to ride my bike, and I never miss a barre class at the local studio downtown. I use my arms and push up to sit on the counter, crossing my legs. Holden watches me with a hungry look. Mission accomplished. If I knew exactly what my mission is. Do I really want to hook up with Holden Hartman?

His arms are crossed, the tattoo on his bicep stretching, and the muscles in his shoulders flexing. I really do. But I can't. I couldn't do that to Kyle. If something were to go wrong, or one of us (me) caught feelings for the other (him), then how could I ever look at him again at the Vern knowing he'd seen me naked and didn't want something real.

"Chlo, you're stalling."

"Right, okay. My top three turn-ons are kindness, especially when it's not expected."

Holden steps a hair closer to me. "You know…I once saved a kitten."

I roll my eyes, but a tiny smile plays at the corner of my lip. "Remembering things, important details about me. Actually, remembering unimportant details gets me more."

"Unimportant like what?" He takes another step closer, placing his hand on the counter, his fingers inches from my thigh.

Like my secret comfort movie that I thought no one knew about except my family, I think but don't say. "Like how I take my coffee or what my favorite ice cream flavor is."

"A little almond milk, no sugar and…" His eyes search the ceiling, then land back on mine. "Chocolate with Oreos crumbled on top."

Heat pulses straight to my core like he just ran his tongue up the side of my neck.

I smile, and he moves his hand even closer, his pinky grazing my thigh. My skin is on fire.

"What's the third thing?" he asks, his voice husky.

Chef Paul claps. "Now it's time to sizzle. Turn your heat to high and place the butter in the pan."

I hop off the counter and get to work, trying to ignore the goosebumps on my leg from Holden's light touch. It was a pinky, for Pete's sake. *Get it together.*

Pouring the eggs in the pan, I try following Chef Paul's instructions, scraping the curds and arranging them in the pan, turning the heat down, but I'm distracted by Holden standing so close to me.

It feels like it's not really cooking. Without thinking, I turn the heat back up and keep stirring the curds.

"Chlo, I think you have to let it settle."

I shake my head. "This is what he said to do."

The couple next to us is about to fornicate, and it's almost as distracting as Holden standing behind me. I keep stirring the pan, the eggs pulling up from the metal.

"I think you might be scrambling them." Holden places his large hand on the small of my back, and the electric pulse that shoots to my core is so powerful my hand flies up, knocking the handle of the pan.

It's like watching a slow-motion scene in a movie. The pan flies up into the air, spinning, and eggs fly everywhere. Pieces bounce off the heads of the make-out couple; one large piece hits me in the cheek. Holden's hand moves, and he covers his face as eggs bounce off him. And with the perfect timing that my life always seems to have, Chef Paul walks by just then, and a large glob of barely cooked egg sails through the air and smacks him right in the eye.

I lean back in an awkward way in an attempt to stop it all, and my hip tightens, my low back cinching up.

The pan falls to the stovetop with a clatter, turned over, all the eggs gone. Chef Paul is holding his eye with one hand. I step forward, and even that motion sends a pulse of pain to my hip. Not a ton of pain. A three on the scale, but enough that I'm nervous on top of feeling like a failure. "Oh, my God. I'm so sorry."

Chef Paul steps back, holding a hand up, warding me off like I'm a wild animal.

Holden is shaking behind me. I look, and he's laughing. His hands are still covering his mouth, trying to disguise his chuckles.

My cheeks are burning, my back is pulsing, and Chef Paul is still clutching his eye like he might lose it to this glob of yolk. He'll have to wear a patch the rest of his life, which on a ship would be very fitting.

It's the vision of pirate Chef Paul that tips me over the edge. I break.

Laughter bubbles up from my stomach and erupts out of me as a loud chortle. I cover my mouth, trying to contain it, my shoulders shaking with the effort, but it's no use. It keeps coming.

And now both Holden and I are laughing hysterically.

"Clearly, you two are not taking my class seriously. You can go."

That stops my laughter. "I am, I just…"

"Go. Goodbye." With that, Chef Paul clutches his eye and returns to the front of the class, and I walk out the back. The make-out couple gives me a death glare as the man picks eggs out of the woman's hair.

Holden follows after me. "Hey, he can't kick us out."

"Pretty sure he just did."

I stop, the fire taken out of my step. I have no idea where to go or what to do, not just at this moment on this massive ship that I don't have the foggiest clue where everything is, but also in life.

"Wait up." Holden comes after me.

I don't wait. My face is hot, and my throat is tight. Despite not waiting, Holden catches up easily with his stupid, strong legs.

"Chloe…" He touches my shoulder, and I turn my face to him. He's smiling, but it instantly falls when he sees my face. "Wait, you're crying?"

Tears have welled up in my eyes, but none have fallen through sheer will. "No," I yell at him. I sit down right there on the deck and stretch out my leg, leaning over. At the very least, I can try to help my hip.

Holden sits down, too, nodding slowly, his eyes on fire. "I think it's been a long night and a stressful morning. Why don't you go lie down, and I'll go have a little chat with our chef friend?" He cracks his knuckles.

This makes me smile, some of the tightness in my chest wearing off. The stretching is also helping my hip and my back. "Don't."

He raises his hands and stands. "Don't what? I just want to thank him for the excellent class."

"Holden." I laugh and wipe away a tear. I stand, too, feeling looser and lighter. It's not going to be one of those times where I'm laid up with an ice pack for days. Thank God. "You can't beat up Chef Paul. This isn't high school."

"Beat him up? Who said anything about that? I'm just going to talk to him about his teaching skills. That's all. Just give some honest feedback."

I laugh. But he's actually headed back toward the class. I grab his hand, and the warmth of it startles me. I ignore the electricity, the tingles, the heat slowly traveling down to my belly, and tug him the opposite direction. "Come on. Let's find some food on this boat."

He resists at first, but as soon as I say food, he's falling into step with me, and instead of letting go, he keeps holding my hand.

We walk down the hall toward the elevator. As the doors close, I realize I have no idea what button to push. I look at Holden.

He pushes the button for the main deck, shrugging. "We should be able to find something there, or at the very least look up the map on our phones."

I nod. That seems reasonable.

We get to the main deck, and Holden pulls out his phone, his brow lines getting deeper and deeper like something slowly sinking.

"What?" I ask. "What is it?"

"Does your phone have service? Mine is on SOS."

I pull out my phone. It's the same. I shake my head. "Nothing." But then I get an idea. "The ship must have Wi-Fi."

Holden's face lights up. He taps at his phone, and I find the Wi-Fi section in the settings on mine, but there are no channels. Then one pops up. ShipShipStaff, and it's locked.

"There must be a mistake," Holden says. "There has to be Wi-Fi. I need to check in with my team tomorrow. We have a meeting."

"You have a meeting?" I'm stunned and a little hurt. And I'm not sure why. It's a day at sea. We're not a real couple. We don't need to spend every second on this ship together. In fact, it's probably better if we don't.

"Yeah, a check-in. We have some tricky brews at the moment."

He's staring at his screen with such intensity, it's like he's trying to will Wi-Fi onto it with dirty looks.

He lowers his phone, letting out a huge breath. "I have to figure this out. Is it okay if we catch up later?"

I melt. Just a little, but there is definitely melting there, my limbs feel loose, my heart warm. He's checking with me. Checking if it's okay that he attends to something he *really* needs to do. God, my last boyfriend didn't even check with me before backpacking in Mexico for two weeks. Just told me the night before. Asked me to water his Monstera. He even put it all on our joint credit card without me even knowing. And we were *actually* a couple.

"Of course," I say. "I'll see you later."

He smiles at me, but it's tired. Heavy. I should tell him to take care of it after a slice of pizza or something, but it's not my place. Then he's off, headed toward the first sparkly pink uniformed person he sees on the deck.

The sun is so bright, and the heat is overpowering. I can't even count the number of couples casually touching on one hand. There are far too many. I'm so tired. I see a sign pointing toward On the Rocks, the Wilting couples bar. Perfect. They'll probably have food.

ON THE ROCKS does not disappoint. It's tucked away in another labyrinth of hallways. I wouldn't have been surprised if David Bowie popped out in gold pants singing about the babe. What babe? The babe with the power.

Oh man, I need sleep.

The bar is dark, thank goodness, and empty. No window to the ocean here. The black and white tiled floor gives it almost an *Alice in Wonderland* feel. Or that could just be my exhaustion rearing its head again. Dark-red velvet booths with walnut tables each have little lamps. A long, shiny wooden bar. The shelves of liquor lit up behind it are the brightest thing in the whole place.

I sit at the bar. After a minute, I wonder if maybe they're not open yet. I pull out my phone, but with no service, there's not a lot to do on it. I should've grabbed my Kindle. I'm about to leave when a woman comes out of the back, her pink hair tied up in a high bun on top of her head. She is not wearing the sparkly pink uniform. Instead, she has a ripped-up tank top with a faded picture of John Lennon and Yoko Ono on it and cut-off jean shorts. Both of which show off her flawless, tanned skin and super-toned arms. She's carrying a red bucket and plops it under the counter. Once it's down, she looks up and jumps back, clutching John's face at her chest. "Holy shit. Where did you come from?"

"Uhh, Oregon."

She laughs, and it's so unguarded and loud that it immediately puts me at ease.

"I didn't realize…I just didn't know anyone was here yet. Usually, we don't get people until the second day. I think it's the name. The Honeymoon is usually packed on the first day, even with the Wilters. Anyway, what can I get you, Oregon?"

I smile. "Food."

"We have that. *Ish.* Light menu until four." She hands me a menu. "But we have chips and salsa, or a hummus plate, or—"

I cut her off. "A hummus plate, please."

She smiles. "You got it. Anything to drink? On the house for leaving you sitting here for…How long were you here?"

"Just a couple of minutes."

"Ahh, too long. I got distracted. I think I met someone… special. Maybe. I don't know. They just started, so I'm not sure if work and romance go together." She laughs. "God, I should not be talking about this to a Wilter. You are, right?"

I nod.

She grabs a bottle of wine from the fridge and holds it up. "Sure."

"Right." She pours the wine, and I'm surprised it's red. I

expected white since it was in the fridge. She must see my surprise. "We keep reds in the fridge here. It's a thing. You'll love it."

She hands me the wine, and I take a sip. It's surprisingly refreshing, and so different from what I'm used to. I love it.

"Well, I shouldn't talk to you about it, but I'm going to. Do you mind? If you do, I won't."

"I don't mind."

She gets down a plate and pulls out some vegetables as she talks. "I'm Dee, what's your name, Oregon?"

"Chloe."

"Love it. You look like a Chloe. What's your sign? Oh no wait, let me guess…Pisces?"

"No, I'm…"

"Don't tell me. I'm good at this." She slices some pita bread and pops it in the toaster oven. "Hmm, would you say you're more practical or more of a dreamer?"

I consider this question. I had dreams. But for the past ten years, I've been more practical. Taking jobs that pay the bills. I'd like to pursue my dreams again, though. I just need to find one. I'm not sure how to answer, so I say, "I'm a practical dreamer."

"Hmmm. Leo?"

I laugh. "Yeah. I am. How did you know that?"

"It's a gift."

She sets the hummus plate in front of me, and my mouth waters. The vegetables look crisp, the kalamata olives oily, and the hummus creamy. It's literally perfect.

I smile, picking up a pita square and running it through the hummus. "So, tell me about this someone special."

CHAPTER 9
HOLDEN

This is not happening. My phone feels hot in my hand. Hot and apparently useless. I find a reasonable-looking man in hot-pink pants and a short-sleeve white shirt with *Shipped Ship* printed on it. It's probably just a glitch. The Wi-Fi is probably just temporarily down.

"Hey, man." I realize as I get closer that kid would be more accurate. He looks to be about nineteen. I'm only thirty-three, but after the red-eye, I feel about a hundred years old. "Just wondering what Wi-Fi channel I should be looking for? I see the staff one, but I'm not pulling up any others."

The attendant takes a step back and frowns like he's answered this question a few times today, and it hasn't gone well. "We don't have Wi-Fi on *The Shipped Ship*, sir."

I laugh, an actual laugh, because this day could not get any more ridiculous. First, I'm expected not to pine after my best friend's sister; this is not new. This I'm quite practiced in, but trying to pretend I'm not head over heels for her while at the same time pretending to be a fighting couple is a whole new level of mindfuck. Now, the one thing that keeps me sane, steady, on track —my brewery—I'm expected to go no contact with for seven days. In the middle of a Helles. No. No.

I rub my eyes, like maybe I'm dreaming. That must be it. I fell asleep on the plane, and this is all a dream. "I'm sorry, what?"

The kid's frown deepens, then his eyes light up. He raises an arm in a help me wave. "Oh, Ms. Theresa. This gentleman has questions about Wi-Fi."

I turn, and it's the woman who gave the speech at the party. She saunters over. "Ah, yes. You can go."

The kid walks away at a breakneck pace.

"There is no Wi-Fi available for guests on *The Shipped Ship*. We want to encourage people to put down their phones and make a real connection with their partners." Theresa holds her hand out to me. "I'm Theresa, and you are?"

"Holden Hartman."

She smiles, pulling out a large phone from her back pocket, and starts to scroll. "Holden?" She scrolls her phone, which is obviously connected to Wi-Fi.

Shit. I remember, we're supposed to be Kyle and Ruby. So much pretending, so little coffee. "Yes, I go by my middle name. The registration is under Kyle Papadopoulos."

"Ahh, there you are." A small indent appears between her brows, which I have a feeling would be deeper if not for Botox. She sighs. "Wilting. I'm so sorry to hear that. Do you think your addiction to Wi-Fi may have played a role in the current state of your relationship?"

My mouth falls open. "I...there's no addiction. I just need to check on work."

She nods, her eyes warm and all-knowing. "Hmm, so focused on work. You even need to work on vacation. Do you think this played a role in where you're at with your lover, or is it a coping mechanism since the downfall of the relationship?"

I shake my head.

She clicks a few things and places a hand on my shoulder. "You know what, don't answer that. Here. You can talk all about it in therapy. Your appointment is at 2 p.m." She looks pointedly at her watch. "Ooh, really soon."

She pulls a brochure out of her back pocket and hands it to me.

"My appointment?"

"Yours and Ruby's. There's a map in the pamphlet." She places her hands on my shoulders and squeezes tight. "It's going to be okay."

"The Wi-Fi? Could I get the staff password?"

She drops both hands. "No."

"What if it's an emergency?"

"Is it?" she asks, her tone much cooler than when we began the conversation.

"I wouldn't know," I yell, unable to keep my cool any longer. "No one can reach me."

She tilts her head to the side and crosses her arms. "Except your partner, who you came here with on the precipice of a decision. Stay together or split. It sounds like you may have already made your decision. Do you think she's made hers?" She grabs my arms again. This woman is awfully handsy. "Close your eyes and picture your partner Ruby."

"She goes by Chloe."

"Huh," Theresa says. It's small, but it ripples panic through me.

Is she suspicious? That, huh, sounded suspicious. I can't get Ruby's mom fired. How many ways can I fuck up things for my friends in one short week? Thousands, apparently.

Theresa continues, "Okay, close your eyes and picture Chloe."

My eyelids are so heavy, my eyes so dry and scratchy, that closing them is not hard. The ocean laps, there's a murmur of conversation, distant laughter, splashes from a nearby pool. Then I do as instructed. I picture Chloe. She has surprisingly long legs for her short frame. Her brown hair always gets in her face, and she blows strands with the side of her mouth. She has full lips and a wide smile. Her eyes. Her eyes are a stunning light blue, so striking with her dark hair. Ice blue, but never cold-looking. She is warmth and light, and lavender and honey.

Theresa breaks into my thoughts. "Is there anything in you, anything at all, that might still have feelings for her?"

"Yes." It flies out of my mouth. Because I do. God, as much as I have tried not to, I do have feelings for Chloe. Everything in me longs to touch her, to talk to her and make her laugh, to be there for her. But Kyle would kill me. And if it didn't work out—which none of my relationships ever have before—I can't risk losing her in my life, or losing Kyle. Or having Kyle beat me into a bloody pulp.

Theresa slaps me on the arm and removes her hands. "That's the spirit. Better go find her. Your appointment is in twenty minutes."

She smiles brightly and saunters away.

WE SHOULD JUST SKIP the appointment. What are they going to do? Throw us off the boat? But then I think of that little "huh" Theresa said when I let her know that not only do I, *Kyle*, go by Holden, and my partner, *Ruby*, goes by Chloe. We're skating on thin ice, and I don't want to raise any red flags.

There's one big problem, though. I have no idea where Chloe is. And I can't text her because at the moment, my phone is purely ornamental.

I retrace our steps from the cooking class and spot a sign for On the Rocks bar. Worth a shot. And if she's not there, maybe I'll take a shot. I must be tired. My dad jokes are showing.

The bar is quiet and dark. The colors are rich and warm. It's not the vibe I want when I expand the brewery, though. Right now, the brewery is mostly a warehouse where we make beer. We have a small bar, but the ambiance leaves much to be desired, and there's hardly any place to sit. It's more of a tasting counter than anything. We sell our beers at lots of places up and down the coast. The Vern was our first and remains our best customer, but I would like to expand. I'd like to branch out, sell beer in other states, and—this is the big dream—I'd like to have a big space for customers. Keep the warehouse for the big batches, but find a place where we could brew some small batches and have a large space for customers to hang out, drink, and eat. I want Woodshed Brewing to be a home away from home. A place you want to take your kid in the summer after he won his little league game, and sit on the patio eating wood-fired pizza while the kids play corn hole.

Laughter tinkles from across the room, and I would know it anywhere. I could pick that laugh out of a lineup. Chloe. She's perched on a bar stool, legs for days in her jean shorts, holding a glass of wine in one hand and a carrot stick in the other. The bartender is doubled over, laughing too.

I pull my shirt down, smoothing out the wrinkles, and make my way over. Chloe's face lights up when she sees me, and it sucks the breath out of my lungs.

Can she look at me like that for the rest of our lives? Please.

"Holden! You have to meet Dee!"

Chloe makes friends the way Messi plays soccer, with what looks like very little effort and a whole lot of style. I smile. "It's nice to meet you."

Dee stands up straighter, her light-pink hair falling out of its bun. Her eyes widen, then she hiss-whispers to Chloe, "I see what you mean."

So, they've been talking about me. Great.

Chloe raises her eyebrows at Dee and takes a sip of wine.

I'd love to know what they've been saying, but these two already look like a vault. I catch a whiff of the hummus on Chloe's plate, and my stomach rumbles. I grab a piece of pita and dip it in some hummus. Through a bite, I say, "We need to go."

"No, we don't, pita stealer." She pushes out the stool next to her. "Here, have a seat. Have a beer." She turns back to Dee. "Ooh, did I tell you he brews beer?"

Dee smiles in a way that makes it obvious she has told her that and a lot more. I glance at the taps and am surprised to find some really small East Coast breweries on there. "How do you pick your beers?"

"My boss does, really, but he likes craft beers. He's always looking for new small-batch brews. He says it makes the experience more special."

Mentally, I'm working out the logistics of getting our beer all the way to the Caribbean and what kind of import might be involved in that. "And he stocks the beers for this bar, or all of them on the ship?"

Dee smiles. "Gio orders all the booze for all the *Shipped Ships*."

"There's more than just this cruise?"

She's nodding. "Yeah, there's an Alaskan Cruise, and there's one to Hawaii."

An electric charge is pulsing in my chest. We'd have a much easier time managing either of those. This could be a huge account for us. "Is he here?"

Dee laughs. "Nah."

My heart sinks. Of course, he's not on the ship.

Dee grabs a pint glass. "He's probably just getting up. He'll be in later. He always gets here around 7."

"So, he's on the ship?"

She nods.

"Great. That's great." I check my watch, and shit, we're going to be late. "Chloe, we gotta go."

"Ahh, why? We were just having fun." Chloe finishes off her wine, and Dee is going for the bottle.

I grab Chloe's hand. "We have an appointment. We can come back."

Dee smiles and waves as I pull Chloe out the door.

"Where do we have to go?" Chloe asks.

I blow out a heavy breath. "You'll see."

CHAPTER 10
CHLOE

"Therapy?" I catch the whine in my voice as it comes out of my mouth, but I can't help it. I was having a lovely time. Eating one of my all-time favorite snacks, having a refreshing glass of cold Tempernillio, and trading secrets with my new friend. And Holden comes and drags me away, now we're standing in front of a closed frosted door, with loopy scripted paint on it that says *Dr. Diaz LMFT*. And under that it says, *love expert*. "What the hell, Holden?"

He's staring at the door, too, his shoulders slumped. "Yeah. It all just kind of happened."

He opens the door, and we step inside what would look like a normal physician's office lobby, if everything wasn't pink. The carpet is a soft bubblegum pink, while the chairs are a deeper Barbie pink. There is a woman sitting at a clear desk, and Holden walks up to her. She smiles brightly. "Ahh, you must be the two o'clock?"

"Yes," Holden says.

"Wonderful!" Her enthusiasm makes Holden take a step back, and I step to the side to save my toes. The woman gestures to a pink clipboard. Even the pen is pink. "If you could just fill these out and take a seat. She'll be with you shortly."

We both reach for the clipboard at the same time, and my fingers brush his hand. Even though it's just the back of his hand, his skin is warm. We lock eyes, and my fingers shoot away as I turn and take a seat in one of the absurdly pink chairs. This has been a lot of casual touching for one day. My nervous system is overwhelmed. Holden takes the seat next to me, and the chairs are so small and so close that his jean-clad thigh touches mine.

I close my eyes. This is fine. It's not skin to skin at least. Then my mind runs through all the skin-to-skin possibilities, and my eyes fly open.

Holden is staring at me. "You okay?"

I nod. "Hmm, Mmm."

Holden looks unconvinced but starts to read. "Duration of relationship."

"Six months?"

Holden shakes his head. "No, I think longer. Two years?"

"Sure, but if we've been dating for two years, we should know a ton of stuff about each other."

Holden smiles. "We do."

The lobby smells like vanilla. It was softly pleasant at first, but now it feels like too much.

"No, we don't. I am well aware that this has been the longest day in the history of the universe, but don't you remember we agreed earlier that we don't even know each other anymore? I know you own a brewery. For some reason, you're very comfortable flying. And that you're learning Spanish."

Holden nods. "I'm comfortable flying because when my dad left, he moved to Chicago. Every summer, I'd fly and visit him, until I didn't. I own a brewery, and it's my passion, my proudest accomplishment, and also my burden. And I'm learning Spanish because I don't want to be an asshole."

"Um, what?" I was following along just fine, even in my sleep-deprived wined-up state, but because he doesn't want to be an asshole?

There are hundreds of millions of people in the world who

speak Spanish. It's presumptuous of me to not want to learn. Plus, I'd like to explore one day. And some guys who work at the brewery speak it. I want to know exactly what they're saying when they're giving me shit."

I laugh, and he smiles in return. Before I can respond, a door opens, and a woman in a black cardigan over a pink dress and dark-brown curls piled on top of her head in a loose knot appears.

Oh my goodness, it's the woman who gave the speech at the sailaway party. Only it's like she's in disguise with thick black hipster frames perched on her nose, and I notice a small tattoo on her ankle of a cassette tape that says *for you* on it. She pats a woman who's dabbing her eyes with a tissue and says something quietly to her. The woman is nodding earnestly.

After she leaves, she says, "Holden and Chloe. Or should I say, Kyle and Ruby?"

I look at Holden and he's gone a bit pale.

"I didn't realize you'd be our therapist." He nearly chokes on the word. "This is Theresa, the cruise director..."

Oh no. Lying to a therapist is one beast; lying to the woman who can personally kick us out is something else entirely.

She adjusts her glasses. "All our usual therapists were booked. But I am certified, trained, and happy to help you two find your way back on the road to love. Let's go."

She turns, holding the door open for us.

Holden stands first, and as I do, I tug his arm, whispering, "We can't do this. We don't know any of the logistics. We don't even have a 'how we met' story."

He smiles. "Just keep it simple. We'll be fine."

The office is beige with accents of sage green. There is not a speck of pink anywhere to be seen. On the wall is a framed print that says *Love is a Verb* in what can only be described as aggressive cursive.

"Dr. Garcia graciously let me use her office. Holden and I met on the deck." She holds out her hand to me. "As your partner said, I'm Theresa, the cruise director. But I'm happy to help here. I was a practicing couples therapist for fifteen years before coming here."

I shake her hand, noticing her pink nails are the exact shade of her dress.

She motions to the loveseat with two huge green pillows on it. "Please sit."

We do, but the sofa is so small that it forces us to sit very close together. So close that Holden's thigh is once again brushing against mine. It's fine. This is fine.

Theresa sits in the chair opposite us. She picks up a notebook off the coffee table between us, which also has a box of tissues on it. She smiles. "So, you're Wilting."

Holden nods, his whole face an exaggerated frown. It takes everything in me not to roll my eyes. He's a terrible actor. He always has been. Once, he and Kyle tried to take some girls camping. When they asked my dad if they could go, he asked who was going. Kyle said "just us" at the same time Holden said "Billy and Ted." Kyle kicked him, and my Dad, chuckling the whole time, said, "Billy and Ted? New friends? Sounds like an *excellent adventure*."

We're so screwed.

Theresa continues. "Let's start at the beginning. How did you two meet?"

Reflexively, I hit Holden's arm. I knew it. I knew at the very least we should've got this story straight. Holden gives me a what the fuck look, which is fair, and Theresa is furiously making notes. I rub his arm where I hit it. "Mosquito."

"Thanks, hun," Holden says, still frowning. "We met in high school. I met her brother first; he's my best friend."

I'm stunned that he went for the truth.

Theresa smiles. "Ahh, young love."

Holden shakes his head, scooting forward, his thigh brushing mine. "No. It wasn't like that. When we met, she was too young. She was fourteen, and I was almost seventeen. I didn't see her that way, she was just my best friend's kid sister."

My heart sinks. I knew it. I've always known it. He doesn't see me that way.

Holden says, so quietly that if you breathed too loud, you'd miss it, "I didn't fall for her until a couple of years later."

I'm speechless. Is there truth to any of this?

Theresa is making notes. "So, you were?"

"I was twenty-three, she was twenty, but we didn't start dating until more recently. Two years ago."

"Wow. And how old are you?"

"Thirty-two."

"So, you had feelings for Chloe for years before you made a move. Why wait so long?"

He sits back in his chair, his eyes finding mine. "I didn't want to fuck it up. It'd cost too much."

I know we are acting. I know none of this is true. But his tone, his look. It feels true.

Theresa turns to me. "And you, Chloe, when did you develop feelings for Holden?"

"I've been in love with Holden Hartman since I was fourteen years old." It comes out of my mouth like it's been perched on my tongue for decades. I look away, unable to meet Holden's eyes, but I can feel them tracing my face. Over my warm cheeks that must be pink if not full-on red. Over my lips, suddenly dry after my declaration. I lick them. Not a declaration. Acting.

Theresa leans in, her brown eyes warm and thoughtful, her pen poised on her notebook. "Why?"

The question startles me. Holden shifts beside me, his thigh rubbing on mine.

"What?" I say more to buy myself time than anything.

Theresa smiles. "What made you fall in love with Holden?"

Is it hot in here? I look out the small window behind Theresa, the ocean sparkling in the late afternoon sun, and wish we could crack it open to let in some fresh air. "At first, it was just a crush. I was young, and he was always around. He was so tall and muscles for days."

Holden chuckles next to me. "Swimmer."

Theresa nods. "When did it change into something more?"

Holden and I both look at each other. That's the unspoken question that's hung between us for years. Could we be something more? But neither of us answers.

"It's time to move." Theresa stands. "We're going to do an exercise. I want you both to sit on the floor back-to-back."

Neither of us moves.

Theresa claps. "Come on. I have a cruise ship to run. Chop, chop."

Holden raises his eyebrows at me but moves to the floor. I do the same, and we sit back-to-back, barely touching.

Theresa says, "Scoot closer. And I want you to lean into one another."

We scoot closer, and his back is on mine. The heat of him is powerful. His back is solid, sturdy.

"Now take some deep breaths," Theresa instructs.

I can feel his breath through my back, and mine syncs to it. He breathes in, and so do I. He breathes out, and so do I. Our breaths become a tide. In and out.

"Now I want one of you to lean more."

There is no thought, I start to shift my weight back.

"While the other leans forward."

Holden leans forward, and my body stretches onto him, the muscles in my stomach stretching.

"Now switch."

I sit up with the assistance of Holden's back and walk my hands forward. He leans back, but I can feel he's holding back.

"Holden," I whisper. "You can really lean back. I got you."

"I don't want to crush you," he whispers back.

"Come on, muscle man. I can take it."

I can feel his chuckle through my back. He lets go a little, but I can tell he's still holding back, not completely letting himself go.

"Good," Theresa says. "Come back to a neutral position and take one more deep breath."

We both do. As I let my exhale out, a deep calm washes over me. When's the last time I did yoga? Or anything with my body that wasn't a punishing workout. One more mile, one more hill in spin class. Feel that burn. When's the last time I relished my body with ease, softness, compassion?

Theresa claps. "Wonderful."

Holden scoots away first. I get up off the floor, my hip popping as I do.

"Now for your homework," Theresa says with a mischievous smile, and my heart rate kicks up a notch. Homework? "I want you to give each other one compliment, each day."

Ah, that's not so bad.

"And while you do," Theresa continues. "I want you to look each other in the eyes and touch each other. It can be holding hands, or a light touch on the leg, or something more if you wish. You also can't dispute the compliment. You must just listen with an open heart. And I'll see you…tomorrow. Yes, that should work."

Holden is nodding. "But we probably don't *need* to come back."

Theresa pats him on the shoulder. "Yes, you do. No reusing compliments either. They must all be unique."

I swallow my laugh at the look on his face, but part of me is stung. I actually had a nice time, but clearly he didn't want to be here. Which, of course, he didn't want to be in couples therapy with someone he has never been nor will ever be a couple with. My imagination just ran away with me again.

CHAPTER 11
HOLDEN

Chloe said she's been in love with me since she was fourteen. And my mind won't stop replaying it over and over and over. I could hardly focus on the rest of the session. I just kept thinking, Chloe is in love with me. But she was faking it, of course, for the cruise. She's not in love with me. She never has been.

Even if there were feelings there, for both of us, I could never do that to Kyle.

My back is still tingling from our point of contact as we head out the door, back through the sea of pink and to the hall. "Feel like getting a burrito?"

Chloe shakes her head, crossing her arms tightly over her chest. "No. I'm beat. I'm going to chill out in the room."

I nod. "Do you want me to bring you something back?"

She shakes her head and makes a beeline for the elevator. I stand and wait with her and, without thinking, grab her hand. She looks at me, and I say, "Chloe, you have the hottest legs in any room, on any day."

So much for not flirting. God, I must need to sleep. I laugh, more at myself than anything, and Chloe pulls her hand away.

"Oh right. The compliments. We don't have to. I mean, there's no way she'll know."

I nod. "Yeah. You're right."

The elevator comes, and Chloe steps inside. She looks at me with a small smile, and before the doors completely shut, I put my hand in between to stop it and lean my head in once it opens. "It wasn't just the 'compliment homework,' you really do have the best legs on this whole boat. Probably in the whole country."

She laughs and shakes her head, her cheeks turning a light pink. "Okay, okay."

She playfully shoves me out of the elevator, and as the doors close, she does a little pose with her legs, bending one at the knee and pointing her toe.

I should not flirt with her. But Chloe is so cute. If she wasn't Kyle's sister, I would ask her out in a heartbeat. But she is. So I won't.

After wandering the deck, equally as lost in my thoughts as on the ship, I finally find a place to grab a burrito. I order a carne asada one for me and a chicken one with no jalapeños for Chloe. I know she said she didn't want one, but she'll probably be hungry soon. I take mine to the deck and sit, enjoying the sunshine while I eat. When I'm done, I sit back and close my eyes just for a moment, and think of Chloe.

I wake up to loud laughter behind me. I turn and see a group of couples, dressed to the nines, walking by. The sky has turned a deep shade of blue. Fuck, I must've fallen asleep. I grab the bag with Chloe's burrito and try to remember if the room has a microwave. If not, I'll go find her one.

Back at the room, I swipe my key card and enter. The television is on a true crime documentary. Chloe is curled up on the couch in white sleep shorts with little pink bows all over them and a matching tank top.

They're criminally short. I find my eyes have a hard time moving away from them.

She's fast asleep, surrounded by her plans. The activities

binder open. A pen in her hand, and a notebook that has fallen onto the floor. I pick up the notebook and place it on the coffee table. I take the pen out of her hand and put it next to the notebook. I look in the closet and find a light-blue throw blanket. Gently, so as not to wake her up, I place it over her. I think about turning off the murder show but worry the lack of noise might wake her. Instead, I put her burrito in the mini fridge and head out.

ON THE ROCKS IS PACKED. Couples fill all the booths. Some laughing, some sitting drinking fancy cocktails and deliberately not talking. The kind of not talking that's clearly on purpose.

I take one of the only spots open at the bar. Dee is gone, and instead a man in a tuxedo asks what I'd like. I choose one of the lagers from a brewery I recognize the name of but haven't tried. I try it, and it's pretty good, light crisp and it has a slight biscuit-like sweetness. It's nice, if not a little boring.

The stool next to me swivels in my direction. The man in a black shirt, sunglasses hanging from the collar, and his hair slicked back in a way where it could be from product or he could've just come back from surfing, asks, "How is it?"

I taste again, considering, but yeah, for all intents and purposes it is a fine beer. Which is what I decide to say, "It's fine."

The man lets out a long sigh. "Terrible. Manny, get this guy something else." He looks at me. "What do you want? Do you like IPA? They do a hazy IPA that is much better, less bland. I should've never ordered that one. Who wants to come on a cruise and drink something fine?"

This has to be Gio. I hold out my hand. "I'm Holden Hartman."

He shakes it. "Gio Ramos."

I've never been good at bullshit, so I just jump right in. "I was actually hoping to meet you. I own Woodshed Brewing on the Oregon coast."

Gio sets down his water and calls Manny. "Make that two." He swivels more in my direction. "You won the Oregon Small Brewery of the Year, was it last year?"

"Two years ago." I smile, because even now that moment fills me with joy. Pride. Panic that it's been two years since that award and my expansion plan hasn't gone much of anywhere. We've won awards since. Our Pilsner won at the Oregon Beer awards, and it took one at the Best of Craft Beer awards. Our beer is really fucking good, my brewers work so hard, and they're innovative. I need to be better at my job so more people can taste it. But there's a fine line between success and selling out. I don't want to turn Woodshed into just a beer factory.

I'm getting ahead of myself. The bartender hands us our hazy IPAs. It's smooth, with intense notes of…I sip again…mango. The bitterness is low, just enough so the mouthful isn't too sweet.

Gio is smiling and nodding. "See."

"It's great."

We talk about beer for a long time, through tastes of almost the entire beer menu. Gio would like to try some of Woodshed. He's been looking for some new Northwest beers for the Alaskan cruise. I tell him I'll get him some tastes before the cruise is over, which with no internet I'm not exactly sure how I'll do. But that's a problem for future Holden.

We have full sized drinks now, me with a hazy IPA, Gio with a margarita. He sips and sighs. "Ahh, that's good. So what brings you on *The Shipped Ship*? Don't tell me you came here just to sell me beers?"

I laugh. "Happy coincidence. No, I'm here with my lady. We're Wilting. I'm a Wilter. Just call me Wilty McWilterson."

Maybe the small tastes were larger than I thought.

Gio is laughing, though, then stops. "I'm sorry, it's not funny. But Wilty McWilterson is. I've been there. After enough years, the spark fades."

I shake my head, a little too hard. "Nope. Spark is there. Lots of sparks."

Gio tilts his head. "You're not Wilting then. If the spark is there, the rest can be fixed. All you need to make any relationship work is the spark. The spark is hard to find, but once you do, man, you gotta hold on to that shit."

I watch the bubbles settle as I set my beer down. Is that true? Is that all you need? Could Chloe and I...be something real?

Gio changes the subject. Turns out we both have a love of nineties mafia movies. We finish our beers and make plans to meet up again.

When I get to the room, Chloe's still asleep on the couch, her neck at an odd angle. I kick off my shoes in the closet and, as quietly as I can, tiptoe over to her. As gently as possible, I scoop her up in my arms, trying to keep my eyes off the teeny tiny sleep shorts. I lay her in bed, covering her with the blanket, then go to the bathroom and splash cold water on my face, waiting for my heart rate to slow. Is the hardest part really the spark? And if so, does Chloe feel it too?

CHAPTER 12
CHLOE

The next morning I'm up before it's light out. Maybe it's because I passed out so early last night. After couples therapy yesterday, my whole body was exhausted and I just needed to lie down. Once I did, I fell asleep before dinner even. But I did wake up briefly as Holden was carrying me to the bed. I pretended I didn't. Played along in his strong arms.

I look over at the other twin bed and quickly cover my eyes with my hand. Holden is sleeping on his side, his leg out of the covers and wrapped around the comforter, in nothing but his boxers. I peek through my splayed fingers. There's so much skin, and muscles. He must still swim. Or maybe that's all from moving barrels, but damn, he looks *good*.

I scold myself but let my hand drop away as I do. His hair is sticking up at odd angles like he tossed and turned all night. Maybe he did. Probably worried about work and the Wi-Fi situation. There's a faint line of stubble lining his jaw, and I have the overwhelming urge to trace it with my mouth, to feel the roughness on my lips.

Nope. No. Time for me to get up. I sit up too fast, and the bed creaks. Holden stirs, pulling the comforter closer in, and he makes a soft noise. A delicious noise that goes straight between my thighs.

I jump out of bed and tiptoe to my luggage, grabbing my running clothes as soundlessly as possible. I lace my sneakers and slip out the door, only allowing myself a full breath once the door softly clicks shut.

Why? Out of anyone I could be here with, having to pretend to be a couple with? Why does it have to be the man I have pined for literally for decades?

I head up to the deck and find the running track. The sky is still black as night, stars twinkling but starting to fade. I find a rhythm with my feet and breaths as I pound around the track on a large loop with just a handful of other runners. Sweat trickles down my back as the sky shifts from black to blue. The blue is just shifting to a lighter shade when a pair of feet in bright-orange sneakers falls into step with me.

"Girl, how long have you been running already?" Dee asks, throwing a hand towel at my face.

I laugh as I catch it right before it hits my nose. "A while."

"The room arrangement wasn't good?"

I shrug and wipe the sweat off my brow. I told Dee all about Holden, sort of. I didn't say we were *pretending* to wilt, I just said we were together, now we're breaking up. Because that's the official story, right? But even in my brief time with her at the bar, I felt bad for lying. I quickly change the subject. "What about you? Did he text you back?"

Dee has fallen head over heels for the new scuba instructor on the ship, but she's not sure if he like-likes her back yet. She frowns but says, "Yes. But I don't know what it means."

We fall into step, running and chatting and laughing. I'd forgotten how nice it is to have a friend that isn't my brother's wife.

We dissect her text thread with the scuba instructor, then Dee says, "What about you? How are things with Holden really? Is it awkward?"

Maybe it's the endorphins from the run, or how nice it feels to have a friend, or maybe I'm just a terrible liar. "We're not Wilting," I whisper.

Dee leans in, her brow furrowed. "Does that mean you've made up?"

I stop running. "We never were. It's all a lie."

Dee leads me to the railing, and it all comes tumbling out of me. About Ruby and the free cruise, Heather bailing and Holden showing up. *All* about Holden. How I've known him forever, how he's my brother's ride or die.

It's like the momentum of my feet from the run just keeps going with my mouth, words pouring out faster than I can stop them.

I tell her about feeling lost in life. About my last terrible relationship. About the stupid dating apps. And then I even surprise myself by saying, "It's all the more intense that it's Holden I have to be in fake love with. I've had a crush on him *forever*. Since I was like fourteen."

"Damn," Dee says, leaning on the railing. "And now you have to pretend you're a couple. That's a lot."

I lean on the railing, too. Now that the secret is out, I feel exhausted and shaky. I was not supposed to say any of that. I've never told anyone about my crush on Holden, and the whole not-being-a-couple thing is supposed to be a secret. "I shouldn't have said anything. I don't want to get anyone in trouble."

"You won't. Your secret's safe with me." Dee smiles. "This could be a good thing. You can get it out of your system."

"What?" I ask, not following her logic.

Dee props a foot on one of the low rungs of the railing and stretches out her calf. I do the same, while she says, "It's possible you haven't been able to really be fully invested in your relationships—picking the wrong people, not into anyone on the apps—because you are hung up on this perfect idea of Holden. But if you use this cruise as an opportunity to indulge in your crush, you can see he's real. With normal habits. He's got boogers just like the rest of us. His dick might even be smaller than average. Although for your sake I hope it's not."

I laugh. "Dee."

"What? If you're going to have vacation sex, it might as well be good. I know some people say, *motion of the ocean*…but who are we fooling? Come on."

"I can't sleep with him. He's my brother's best friend."

"Right. So you said. But your brother is not here. We're in international waters."

"Really?" I sit down on the deck, feeling a little light headed.

Dee sits, too, stretching her leg out. "Honestly, I'm not exactly sure. But the sentiment is the same, what happens at sea stays at sea. No one has to know. I mean you're terrible at keeping secrets, clearly."

I swat at her, and we both laugh.

"But I'm sure you could if you tried," Dee says. "Let go a little. Have fun. Get it out of your system. Then you can bloom unencumbered."

"Get it out of my system. Hmmm."

It could be fun. And Dee might be right. Maybe I haven't been able to be fully present in my relationships because I'm comparing them all to this phantom idea of Holden.

We grab some water from the cooler near the edge of the deck. The sky is now brilliant shades of pink and peach and light blue. In the middle of the deck, people are rolling out yoga mats. I point. "We should go."

Dee laughs. "No. I have met my exercise quota for the day. Thank you very much."

The sunrise and the mats look so inviting. I think of how nice those deep breaths felt during couples therapy. It had to be the intentionally breathing that felt so good and not Holden. Right?

Dee catches me looking. "You should go. Have fun. Here, give me your phone."

I hand it over, and she puts her number in.

"Come to the bar later, but if you can't then text me."

"There's no service."

"Ah, that's right. Well, if you don't show, I'll know you couldn't come."

I step forward for a hug, and Dee steps back. "I'm a hugger, but you better buy me a drink before coming at me with all that sweat."

I laugh as we wave goodbye.

Grabbing an open yoga mat near the back, I sit and stretch my legs out in front of me. There are pairs all around me. Fingers brushing, eyes lingering, one ruffling the bed head of their partner, both of them laughing. Fucking couples cruise.

I lie back on the mat, feeling my back completely supported by the wood deck and breathe. A familiar voice comes over the loud speaker. "Rise and shine, my lovelies, and welcome to Couples Sunrise Yoga."

I nearly forgot that absolutely everything on this entire ship is couples. I sit up, and the sea beyond the deck is a pale pink, reflecting off the sky. All of it soft. Relaxing. Lilian stands in front of the group in cute pink yoga leggings with a matching top.

She flashes a warm smile that seems to be just for me and says, "Whether you are here in a pair or flying solo this morning, this is a safe space for you to breathe, stretch, move, and be present."

I inhale deeply. Yes. That's what I would like. To be present in my body. As couples fold toward one another, I fold inward. As they reach for each other for balance, I spread my arms wide until the wobbles subside. See, I'm fine. Absolutely fine. I don't need a man to be complete.

Before savasana, the instructor says if there's any last poses we can feel free to move through them on our way to our final relaxation pose. I move myself through a headstand, thinking how morbid final relaxation pose sounds. As I come down, the couple in front of me are already lying down, their faces toward the clouds, their eyes closed, and their fingers intertwined.

I lie down on my mat, breathing deeply. I may not need someone. I can stand on my own two feet. But I really, really want someone in my life. I miss touching. I'm a very tactile person. Maybe I will have just a fling with Holden. It could be fun.

The instructor tells us to lie for as long as we need. I'm the last one to come out of savasana. Couples are already wandering away toward coffee, classes, maybe a shared shower. I lace my running shoes back up.

Lilian is rolling mats up, and I roll up mine, placing it over in a bin near the front. She smiles at me. "Thanks, hun." Then she lowers her voice. "How's it going?"

I smile, thinking about Dee's idea to get it out of my system, and she might be onto something. "It's going great. Really great."

CHAPTER 13
HOLDEN

"Wakey, wakey." Chloe throws open the drapes, and butter-yellow light floods the room.

I throw the blanket over my head. I did not sleep well. How could I with her just a couple feet away in those little shorts with the tiny bows?

She tugs the blanket off me and shoves a plastic cup of green goop in my hand. "Drink this in the shower. Then we have to go. Chop. Chop."

I sit up, relieved to see at least she's not wearing the little bows anymore. But what she's got on is not much better. A light-blue cotton sundress that makes her waist look teeny tiny and her eyes sparkle.

"You know for someone on vacation, you're not very relaxed." I look at the green sludge, swishing it back and forth. "What is this?"

She rolls her eyes and picks up her matching green sludge in a cup from the desk. "Vegetables are not the enemy." She takes an exaggerated sip, and I realize maybe too late that I'm far too focused on the way her lips wrap around the straw. I quickly look away and adjust the blanket on my lap. She says, "It's delicious. Drink it."

I take a sip and am immediately hit with sweetness. Mango. It reminds me of the hazy IPA from last night. I lie back on the pillow, my head suddenly throbbing. Shit. Did I really agree to get a beer sample sent to the middle of the Caribbean when I have no cell service and no Wi-Fi.

"Holden, are you going back to sleep?" Her voice is small this time.

I immediately sit up. "Nope. I'm up." And the problem is I am in more ways than one. Still half hard from the whole sucking the straw thing. What is it about Chloe that turns me into the horny teenager I used to be. Fuck. "Avert your eyes."

"What?" She laughs and takes another suck of her straw, her cheeks hollowing. Goddamn.

"Hide your eyes. I'd like to get to the shower with some decency."

She makes a big show of covering her eyes with her hand, and I run to the bathroom, cup of green sludge covering the tent of my boxers.

Ten minutes later, I'm showered, dressed, and ready for whatever it is Chloe's in such a hurry to do. She's waiting by the door, bouncing on her heels, the motion flexing her calves. We head out into the hall.

"Where are we headed?"

Chloe smiles. "Painting class."

"Painting?" I ask, surprised that out of all the classes offered, this is what she picked this morning.

She shrugs. "It might be my calling. You never know."

I bite my lip. I want Chloe to find her passion in life, but part of me hopes it isn't painting. I used to be really into painting in middle school, but my dad always said it wasn't a manly pursuit. I don't think that's why I stopped, but it couldn't have helped. If painting is her dream, how will she make a living? But I guess the same could be said for anything artistic. The same could be said for my brewing and it's going really well. So well in fact, I need to figure out how to get beer here.

"Where does the ship dock tomorrow?"

Chloe searches the ceiling for the answer, her blue eyes catching the sun as we head out onto the deck, taking my breath away. "St. Lucia I think."

I nod. It's still early. I could find a way to call Woodshed. After this class, I can call and have them ship a sample overnight to somewhere in St. Lucia. That should work. Hopefully.

At the far end of the deck, umbrellas are set up, and under them are rows of easels, two stools at each, some with couples already seated.

There is a man that looks familiar standing at the front of all the easels, his back turned to us. When he faces the class, his thick mustaches twitching with a smile, I see it's Chef Paul. That fucking guy. He sees us, and his mustache turns down into a frown. He says in his thick accent, "Find a seat at an open easel. Preferably one with some space around it to move, in case paint brushes also go flying. We'll get started in just a minute."

I crack my knuckles. "Are you sure you want to suffer through another class with this dude?"

If he makes her cry again or says one disparaging thing about her painting, I will make him *suffer*.

She places a hand on my arm, and my muscles ease. "Holden, it's fine. New day. New class. New *us*."

There's a hint of mischief in her voice when she says us. I'm not sure what it means, but I don't hate it.

Chloe picks an empty easel near the edge of class where we can see the ocean between the rails. The deep blue water sparkles in the sunshine, and it makes me think of her eyes. I shake the thought out of my head. I need to stop pining after her if I'm ever going to get through this week in one piece. The air smells of salt and sunscreen, and I wonder if Chloe rubbed any on her shoulders.

I pull out a stool for her, and she raises her eyebrows but sits. Without thinking, I lean in and smell her by her collarbone. It's still lavender and honey but with a hint of coconut. She must've sunscreened. She backs up. "Holden?"

"Just making sure you have sunscreen on?"

She laughs and pulls some out of her bag tossing it my way. "You should put some on too. Your nose is a little pink."

I touch it reflexively. "Ahh, yeah. Fell asleep on the deck."

The instructor claps her hands. "Lovebirds. We are painting portraits today of each other."

Fuck. I've been trying *not* to stare at Chloe all day.

"Art is not a monologue. It is a dialogue."

"I thought that was food?" I mutter to Chloe. She snickers.

Chef Paul continues. "This is about seeing your partner, really seeing them."

Chloe opens her eyes wide and lunges her face toward me. I laugh, but cover it quickly with a cough when the instructor shoots daggers at me.

Chef Paul starts handing out palettes and brushes. " We want to see our partner and feel the painting. We want to paint there essence. And there is no judgement and no making fun, even if teasing is part of your love language."

Chef Paul hands me the paint and brush. "You're first. Remember, look only at your partner."

Chloe sits up straighter in her chair, crossing her legs and hiking her skirt up a little as she does. She throws me a wink. "Try not to fall in love."

I smirk, but God, she doesn't know the half of it. "I make no promises."

Her cheeks turn pink. And that's the first color I put on the canvas. I've looked at Chloe's face so much over the years, I could paint this with my eyes closed. I know the exact shade of blue of her irises. I know the swoop of her collarbone. I know the way on her left side she has a small point on her ear like she's a fairy masquerading as a human.

She smiles. "You have a very serious expression."

"Do I?" I say, still drinking her in. This rare moment where I don't have to look away or hide my stare.

She nods, and her hair falls over her shoulder. "Like you're doing your taxes. Or trying to solve one of life's great mysteries."

I smirk. "Maybe I am." Like how can she be so beautiful.

A timer dings, and Chef Paul claps. "Okay, set that to the side. Don't look at it yet. We'll look at the paintings at the end. Now switch spots. It's your partner's turn."

Chloe settles in the stool in front of the canvas. As her eyes move over my face, my heart hammers in my chest. I want to reach for her. Grab her by the waist and pull her onto my stool.

"You look awfully serious too."

She sighs. "I don't think painting is my calling. I'm worried I'm messing it up and you won't like it."

I smile, because of course Chloe made painting into something stressful. "I'll like it."

She shakes her head. "You could not like it."

"If you gave me a unibrow or something. But I know you. You wouldn't ever be intentionally mean."

"No. I wouldn't. But I'm not sure I have the talent to capture… your essence."

I laugh. "My essence? What exactly is my essence?"

She purses her lips to the side. "It's hard to explain. You are a unique mix of laid back while also being passionate, driven and sometimes overprotective. It's confusing, honestly."

"Huh." What she says strikes a chord. I am mostly laid back. I let people be who they are, and I generally enjoy most of them. But she's also right. I am driven. I want to make something of my brewery, not just for me but to show my granddad that all his time with me wasn't wasted. And for all my brewers. They work so hard, they're all so dedicated, and I do demand a lot from my crew. When it comes to small stuff, though, like being a couple minutes late, or having to leave early for something, even coming in hungover, I'm not that concerned.

Overprotective is where I'm not sure exactly what she means.

"Overprotective?"

She smiles her eyes wide. "Yeah. Like when I was nineteen and started dating Todd."

"Fucking Todd." It comes out like it's all one syllable.

"He told me you and Kyle let him know that if he ever cheated on me, or broke my heart in any way, you'd both end him in what sounded like really terrible ways."

I smirk, remembering. But we *knew* Todd. He was an asshole that cheated on every single girl he was ever with.

"See," she says. "You think it's funny."

"No. It's not. But that guy was an asshole. He needed to know that there would be consequences to breaking your heart."

She shakes her head. "See, overprotective."

"It's just the right amount of protective."

"He couldn't have broken my heart. He never had it."

Her eyes are still roaming over my face, her hand flicking the brush onto the canvas, and I'm trying not to read into what she just said.

The instructor claps. "All right. Final touches. Perfection is boring. Connection is everything."

Chloe's neck is tight. "It's not a lot of time for a masterpiece."

I smile. "It doesn't have to be. It could just be fun."

Her blue eyes blaze a trail straight through me. "Right. Just a little fun. No one ever has to see it."

My voice is husky as I say, "No one ever has to know."

I wonder if we both have strayed from talking about the painting.

She smiles and places her brush down. "What happens on the ship, stays on the ship."

CHAPTER 14
CHLOE

A stiff gust of wind takes my hair and blows it back, making my skin tingle. I think Holden Hartman is flirting with me for real. And I like it. A lot.

Chef Paul claps. "Lovebirds. It's time to show each other your paintings. Remember, this is a judgment-free zone. Appreciate what they have done."

Holden grabs his painting from where he leaned it on the railing. I move my painting over so we can prop them both on the easel. He places it up there, and we stare at our paintings side by side.

My breath is stuck in my chest. His painting is gorgeous. It's rough, but given the fact that we each only had about twenty minutes, that makes sense. But even the roughness of it looks on purpose. Large brush strokes with fat dabs of paint make up my lips and cheeks, while my eyes have a softer touch. It is stunning and looks exactly like me.

Mine, on the other hand, is a mass of colors, definitely more abstract. You can sort of see a face if you squint.

"I love it," Holden declares next to me.

I'm still at a loss for words.

I finally manage to tear my eyes away from his painting and

look at mine again. Then back at his. The comparison makes my stomach do a slow, humiliating somersault.

"You don't have to lie. Chef Paul just said it's a judgment-free zone."

He laughs, a soft, low chuckle, and despite myself, I smile.

"I'm not lying," he says while examining my painting. "I think you managed to get my essence."

I shake my head while Chef Paul takes one exaggerated tiptoe toward us and then another. He blocks his eyes. "Should I wear protective eye gear? Is everyone's grip firm?"

Holden's jaw ticks, and I laugh. "We're good. No paint to the face."

Chef Paul lowers his hand. I make a fake lunge with the brush.

He hops back with a high-pitched giggle that cracks Holden's frown.

Once Chef Paul is composed, he says, "Ooh. You two are clearly better painters than cooks. Lovely. Now tell each other what the art makes you feel."

He leaves to dispense instructions to the next couple.

I stare at the painting. And it makes me feel seen, really seen. But looking at it next to mine, it makes me feel something else, too. Inadequate.

Holden says, "Grateful."

I snap my focus to his face. "Grateful?"

He leans toward the canvas then steps back, his shoulder brushing mine. He turns to face me. "It's not every day that I get the opportunity to look at you for so long without feeling like I'm crossing a line."

I take a small step closer. "What line is that?"

He inhales deeply, his shirt moving with the motion. But he doesn't back away. "The your-brother-would-kill-me line."

I shake my head. "He's not here."

Holden swallows hard, his Adam's apple bobbing with the motion. "He's not. What about you? What does it make you feel?"

"Pissed."

He laughs, but I don't. I turn back toward his painting. It's not perfect, but it's so good. He's so good at everything he does, and it feels supremely unfair.

"Oh, you're serious?" he says.

I shrug, and despite myself, tears well up in the corner of my eyes. "It's just, I was really good at one thing. And I loved it. And now, it's not an option for me. I'm not *good* at anything else. But look, you're fucking Michelangelo."

"He primarily wanted to sculpt."

I level him with a death glare.

Holden holds his hands up. "I'm just saying he didn't get exactly what he wanted in life. He had to adjust his dream. I painted as a kid. I practiced a lot. I thought I wanted to be an artist when I grew up, but it was pretty actively discouraged. Either way, my dreams shifted. But my point is, I practiced a lot. I'm sure if you wanted to, you could be a great painter."

I nod, because he's right. I can't expect to pick something up and be the best at it right away. When I danced, I always had an inclination toward it. I was always good, but it took hours, months, and years of practice to be at the level I was at. The thing is, I don't want to practice painting or cooking French omelets. "It's not what I want to do."

Holden peers into my face that's pointed firmly at the deck. He places a finger under my chin and brings my face up. "You really can't dance at all?"

I sniff back a fresh wave of tears. "I…I'm not sure. I haven't tried. After the accident, there was so much pain, and they said… It doesn't matter what they said. It was never going to be like it was."

"Just because it looks different, doesn't mean you have to give it up completely."

His words sink in and strike a chord, then bounce back, bringing heat with them. Until my cheeks burn.

"How would you know? You've never had to give anything

up. You loved brewing, and now that's what you do. You have everything that you want."

"Not everything." He puts a soft hand on my shoulder. It's warm and solid, his skin a little rough. "But you're right. I haven't been through something like that."

He pulls me in and wraps me in a hug. And I sink into him. His warmth, his spicy-sweet scent. Him.

He runs a hand down my hair, his finger brushing my back.

"Maybe you could still dance, just differently. Maybe you could teach. Open a studio for kids or something. So you could still do what you love. Just different."

I've thought about it. About teaching. My hip is still stiff and painful sometimes. There is no way I could ever perform at the level I was at. But I could teach. Maybe. Every time I've tried or thought about trying to dance, panic surrounds me. It won't be the same, and every grand jeté is a harsh reminder of all I lost.

I step back from Holden.

"Leave your paintings to dry. They'll be sent to your room later," Chef Paul says. "And be sure to thank your partner."

I look into Holden's intense blue eyes. "Thank you…for coming here with me. And for the painting. It's the most beautiful thing."

He smiles. "Easy given the subject matter."

I shake my head. "Such a flirt."

He takes my hand, and his eyes search my face. "Thank you for bringing me here. I haven't painted for a long time. And while I'm not as good at it as I was, it felt good to do it."

I breathe out a sigh and take my hand back. "It's different, Holden. You didn't break your hand. You just stopped."

"It's different," he says. "You're right."

"I'm going to…" I motion to the deck, to anywhere but here. I need some space, some air that doesn't smell like Holden. Some topics of conversation that aren't centered around my life's greatest disappointment.

He nods, taking a step back. "Okay. See you at therapy?"

I nearly forgot we have another session. "See you then."

I WALK AROUND THE DECK. My legs are tired from the run this morning and the yoga, but I need to move. I need to get Holden's words out of my head. Since he's said them, though, they've been playing on a loop. I could teach.

I could teach dance.

I could have my own studio.

These are thoughts I have had before. But they're the kind of late-night thoughts that come up, and you Google a bit, but it's not an *actual* possibility. Okay, I may have googled more than a bit. I may have a fully written business plan.

There's one real flaw in my plan. I can't teach dance if I can't dance.

Period.

The end.

There must be something else. Something I haven't tried yet that fills my soul with as much joy as dancing once did. I just have to find it.

I head back to the room, back to my plan. My master find-my-new-passion-in-life-on-this-ridiculous-couples-cruise plan. I get out the itinerary and see what class is next.

Meditation. Find Your Inner Peace.

No. Not happening today. I cross it off and look at what else is available, but accidentally drop the paper. When I pick it up, my back pulls again, this time a little stronger. I straighten immediately. Reaching for the muscles. It's tight but no knot. I stand and move side to side. My hip lets out a loud pop, which actually feels nice.

I breathe a sigh of relief. It's not a full-on spasm. Just tight. I've been doing a lot, maybe too much with the run and yoga, especially after all that travel. I'll have to be more careful.

Turning my attention back to the classes available, I find a couple's massage.

That would be nice. It could loosen up my back before one of these winches turns into something more.

I wonder if I could do it without the couple part. A nice, relaxing massage to soothe the growing unease in my belly. My nervous system won't shut off, and my brain won't shut up. I can't stop picturing a little dance studio on Main Street in Fortune Falls. And for some reason, I also picture Holden meeting me after work as I'm locking up. Us holding hands, walking down the street with fall leaves blowing at our feet.

Yes. Massage. That's what I'll do now.

I grab my bag and head to the spa.

The spa is tucked away on a lower level of the ship. All soft lighting and eucalyptus air. It's nice. Soothing. This was a great idea. My shoulders drop a bit. See, I'm feeling better already.

A woman in a flowing pink caftan asks for my name, and I tell her, adding quickly, "No couple today. Just me."

Her eyes soften with understanding. "Ahh, yes. This journey is different for everyone. We just had a cancellation, so we can get you set up right now."

She shows me to a small room that smells more of sandalwood than eucalyptus. I change and tuck myself under warm sheets and stare at the ceiling while the room fills with quiet instrumental music that's soothing for the most part, except every now and then there's a loud metal clang in it like a gong.

The massage therapist steps into the room, and holy hell, if he isn't a Chris Hemsworth look-alike. He has a fitted white T-shirt and soft pink pants that are so snug that when he turns to shut the door behind him, the view of his ass should come with a rating.

"Hello. I'm Hans. I'll be your massage therapist today."

And all my brain provides me with is Chris Hansworth. "Hi," I say, grateful it didn't come out of my mouth. "Chloe."

He smiles, and I swear violins play somewhere. "Anything in particular you'd like me to focus on?"

I shake my head, the sound of my hair on the pillow loud in my ears. "No. Just generally stressed. So my muscles have." I squeeze my fist. "Oh, I did have an injury, years ago, so my hip gets a little extra tight."

"May I?" He holds out his hands.

"Yes," I say, closing my eyes. His hands press into my shoulders, and I can feel my muscles actively resisting.

"What kind of injury? If you don't mind me asking?" Hansworth says.

"I was in a car accident. I broke my hip. Well, shattered it really. I had surgery to piece it back together."

"Oh, I'm so sorry. That sounds horrendous." His hands press into the muscles of my arms. "Turn over, please."

I carefully turn, adjusting the sheet with me so I don't flash him. I lay my face in the hole in the pillow, my cheeks smashed, and once again I try to empty my mind. I close my eyes. I breathe. For a moment, it works, and my mind is empty.

My muscles loosen. The soft music playing over the speaker is soothing. This was a good idea. I just need to relax.

Hansworth's hand presses into my back. The one gently works at a knot near my hip, and something in me cracks open. My eyes fill with tears as images of the studio flood into my mind, so vivid and real I can smell the wood polish on the floor, the powdery, sharp scent of rosin, hairspray, and sweat. Sunlight tiptoes in through big front windows. Chubby legs, big tutus, and bigger laughter from the mommy and me class. Toddlers fall more than leap. A hand-painted sign out front is swinging in the breeze. *Blooming Dance Studio.*

Hansworth moves to the other hip. He lightens his pressure, but still, I get a twinge on my left side. A warning. A familiar reminder of my limits. An ache that turns into a throbbing, a tightening that some days causes me to limp. An ache that reminds me *you can love it, but you can't do it.*

My eyes burn, my throat is tight. This is ridiculous. I came on this trip to relax, and all I've done so far is spiral about my future and cry about the past. I move, and Hansworth's hand moves off me.

"Too much pressure?"

I sit up with the sheet wrapped around me. "No. I mean, maybe. I don't know." I wipe my tears, feeling embarrassed to be sitting here naked and crying.

He smiles softly. "We hold a lot in our muscles. It's okay to cry. Sometimes it helps just to let it all go."

So I do. I let the tears fall unbidden. And it's not a pretty stream of tears that delicately falls onto the sheet and makes my eyes shine like the stars. It is an ugly cry.

Hansworth just pats my back and nods.

After there are no more tears to be shed, I say, "Thanks. For the massage and for just...thanks."

He nods. "Anytime." Then he rubs his hand on the back of his neck and bites his lip. "This...I shouldn't ask...but do you want to maybe go for a walk? I have a break, and just in case you're not ready to be alone yet. Or..."

He's stammering like he's nervous, and I can't tell if he's just being nice or if he might actually be interested in me. Either way, I don't want to be alone. "Yes, I'd like that."

CHAPTER 15
HOLDEN

I shouldn't keep pushing Chloe about her dancing. I shouldn't, I know I shouldn't, but part of me is so frustrated with her. I know her injury was awful. There were thirty-seven terrifying minutes where I thought we'd lost her. She hadn't woken up. She was in the ICU. They couldn't tell us much. So when it was a broken hip and some cracked ribs, I was relieved. I feel like such a dick now. When I saw her, I brought a balloon, and she was so quiet. Kyle was trying to make her laugh. She was having none of it. I tried too. And I stupidly said, "At least it's just your hip, not something really important."

Her glare is still seared into my brain. It might as well have been her head to her. What it meant for her dancing, I just didn't process it at the time.

But now…I don't get it. I've seen her move. She runs. She goes to yoga all the time. I feel like she could dance if she'd let herself. It might not be exactly the same, but isn't doing some of something you love better than leaving it forever? Than not having it at all?

Hasn't that been my logic with Chloe all along? I'll be her friend. We'll flirt. I'll get tiny sips of her, and it'll be better than if I really went for it and fucked it up. And lost her forever. Not just her but her whole family. My second family.

I shake my head. Clearly, I should not be dispensing advice. I know nothing.

Instead, I need to focus on getting some beer sent out to the middle of the ocean. I find a sparkly pink attendant. "Hey, I have an emergency back home, and I need to use a phone."

She nods. "Name."

"Hol—Kyle."

The attendant gets on the walkie-talkie, and I can only make out about every other word. "Room...needs help on deck...." She turns to me. "Someone should be with you shortly. Hang tight."

I walk over to the railing, leaning both arms on it and looking out over the vast ocean. What am I even doing here? I should be helping with the Helles. I should be home, working, taking the dog for a walk with grandpa. I should not be out in the middle of this vast blue trying to talk myself out of making out with Chloe and trying to talk her into dancing again.

A hand lands on my shoulder, and I turn to find Gio in running shorts, his shirt spotted with sweat, a wide smile on his face. "Hey, man. Fancy seeing you here."

"Gio." This is it. This is my chance to come clean. I'll tell him I can get him something once I'm home. The logistics are too hard.

"I'm super excited to try your beer, man. Super excited. When did you say it'll be here?"

I smile, and it just comes out. "Couple of days."

Gio gives me a wave and heads off. I have to get this here.

A woman with thick, wavy white hair in a sparkly pink uniform joins me. "Excuse me, sir, were you the one looking for the phone?" She has a packet of paper in her hands and a tattoo of a rose on her forearm.

I show her the one on my bicep. "Hey, we both have rose tattoos."

She lights up. We talk about tattoos for a bit. She has thirteen other flowers on her. I tell her I keep wanting to get another tattoo; it's been a few years since I got one, but I haven't decided what yet. The rose is for my grandma, and was so obvious that trying to find a good reason for my next one has been more of a struggle.

Her mouth falls open. "My rose is for my grandma, too. One of them, anyway, one of them is for my husband."

I shake my head. "That's wild. What are the chances?"

She smiles and shifts her paper and clipboard in her hand. "The phone," she says as if just remembering why she's there.

"Just point me in the right direction."

She sighs. "You seem like a nice kid. I wish I could, but they make it really hard." Her eyes flick to the papers. She gets a pen ready and starts marking things on her clipboard. "May I ask what the phone call is for? Personal or business?"

"I need to get something sent here. Or I guess to our next port."

Her eyes light up. "Oooh, is this romantic?"

"No."

Her brows furrow. "Illegal?"

"No."

She seems almost disappointed by this. "Standard procedure for someone who needs a phone and it's not an emergency—"

"It absolutely is an emergency," I interrupt.

"Not technically an emergency. This paperwork needs to be approved. It's a long process, though. It probably won't happen before we dock in St. Lucia tomorrow afternoon."

My shoulders sag. Fuck.

She lowers her voice. "But if you come with me, and are quiet, and follow instructions, you can use the staff phone."

My heart soars. "Really?" Then it comes back down. "Why? Why are you going to help me?"

She smiles brightly. "Our grandmas are always looking out for us. Don't you think?"

SHE LEADS me through a door marked *CREW ONLY*, the letters sparkling with pink glitter, and points to a locker room.

"Inside, you'll find a shelf with uniforms. Change into one, then head to the third door on the left down the hall. It's the lounge. There's a phone on the back wall."

"Do I have to change into a uniform?"

She shakes her head. "Of course not. Should we go find the paperwork for the phone request?"

I grit my teeth. "Where do I find it?"

"There's a shelf with different sizes near the front. At least there is in the women's locker room. Hopefully it's the same," she says with a bright smile. She gives me a clap on the back. "You'll do great. And if you get caught, don't say my name."

"I don't even know your name."

She nods. "Perfect. Good luck."

I head through the door. There is, just as she said, a shelf of uniforms in different sizes. I find my size and quickly change, shoving my clothes in an unlocked locker. I catch a glimpse of myself in the mirror and stop dead in my tracks. Pink sparkly vest over a white tank top, that if I'm being honest, I don't hate.

I don't hate the tank top, to be clear. The vest is an eyesore. But the shirt actually makes my arms look more muscular. And shows off my rose tattoo. What I do hate are the knee-length matching pink shorts. I'm fucking Pedro Pascal on the red carpet. My vans and crew socks really finish off the look. I check the shelf again, but it's all shorts.

I take one last glance in the mirror. Fuck it. Let's ship some beer.

Heading down the hall, I find the other door marked lounge again in pink glitter. It's kind of nice that they've kept the theme even behind closed doors, so to speak.

Inside, the crew lounge smells like coffee that's lost the will to live. There are a couple of women sitting at a table chatting quietly. They both turn to look at me as I enter, and I give them a solemn nod. For a long moment, I think the jig is up. That they are going to stand and point and scream, "Intruder." But they just nod and turn back to their conversation.

I make a beeline to the pink phone hanging on the wall and dial one of the only numbers I know by heart. No one picks up. I check the time. Fuck. Still too early.

Pulling out my cellphone to get the number, I dial someone else instead. This time it picks up on the second ring.

"Vern. We're closed." Kyle's gruff, sleepy voice comes over the phone. It's around eight in the morning in Oregon, but I knew he'd be there doing something. Deliveries, or the books, or some renovation project.

"Why answer the phone if you're closed?"

"Hey, bud. How's the sun?"

He doesn't bother answering my question, so I don't bother answering him either. "I need a favor."

We talk for a while about the logistics. Kyle is so excited, he said if Ruby wasn't about to pop, he'd fly it down there himself. The tricky thing is where to ship it. And how long will it take?

Kyle searches while we're on the phone, and I pull the ship's itinerary off a corkboard on the wall.

"Okay, I can get it there in three days."

"Three?" My heart is hammering, "That's the soonest?"

"Yep. That's it."

Okay. Three days is fine. We're still on the ship. It's a seven-night cruise. It's fine. "All right. In three days we'll be in St. Maarten."

"Perfect." I can hear Kyle clicking the keys on the other end of the line. "It might get held up in customs if I have the post office hold it. It'd be better if you booked a hotel and I sent it there."

"Brilliant." I pull out my phone and pull up my internet browser. The wheel is just spinning. "My phone is shit here. Can you book me something?"

Kyle clicks away. "Umm…there's only a couple of rooms available."

"A couple. Great. Get whatever. I'm not going to stay there."

He laughs. "At these prices, you might want to."

My stomach sinks. "Shit, really?" This account would be huge. Huge. I tell myself it's worth it. "It's fine. Just get one. I'll pay you back."

"Okay, dude. You're booked at Sunset Beach Club in three days. That's where I'll send the beer."

"You're a lifesaver."

"Don't forget it. Tell Chloe I said hi."

"I will."

We click off. This is going to work. I'll get the beer. Give the sample to Gio. It'll all work out.

I make a couple more phone calls, which makes me feel more like an idiot than this pink uniform. But I think this is a really good idea, so I have to try. And who knows, Chloe might even thank me for it. Or kill me.

I leave the crew lounge on a cloud of hope and send a silent thank-you up to my grandma. On the deck, I run straight into the sunshine and smack dab into a wall of a human wearing a tight white shirt that's blinding in this light.

"Sorry," I mutter as I look up. Walking with the massive trunk of a person is Chloe. Her face is puffy like she's been crying. "Chloe?"

Her mouth falls open. "Holden, what are you wearing?"

I was so caught up in the beer mission, I forgot about my sparkles.

Muscles laughs. "Do you know all the crew?"

My sequins are glinting in the sunlight, reflecting onto his ridiculous pink pants, although I'm not one to talk at the moment. I'm like I'm a walking pink disco ball.

Chloe's eyes are red-rimmed, mascara smudged underneath, and suddenly, I don't give a fuck what I'm wearing or who Muscles is; I just want to know what he did.

"Chloe." I step toward her. "Are you okay?"

She looks at me, and despite looking like her shoulders hold the weight of the world, she smiles. Small at first, but then larger until a full-on giggle escapes her mouth. And now I'm not sorry I'm wearing this stupid getup at all. I'd wear it every day if it kept making her smile like that. I smile. "What?"

"I…It's just…you look ridiculous."

I bow. "Thank you. You look like you could use a drink."

She sighs. "More like five."

Muscles coughs. "I should get going."

Chloe reaches for him, her hands landing on his arms, and fire fills my veins. "No. Why don't you come? We can go to On the Rocks. Dee's probably on by now."

He laughs and places one of his massive hands on top of hers. Who the fuck is this guy? "You really do know all the crew, huh?" His eyes are fixed on her in a way that I really don't like. I hate it, in fact. "I can't, though. I have to go back to work. And we're not really supposed to go to the guest bars."

He gives me a pointed stare. Right. Disco pants.

"But maybe I'll see you around." He squeezes Chloe's hand. "I hope so, anyway."

Oh no, he did not.

He nods at me as he leaves, which I return with a scowl.

I wrap my arm around her shoulder. "Let's get you a big drink, with a little umbrella."

CHAPTER 16
CHLOE

Holden's arm is around my shoulder, which is new for him, but I don't hate it. "Want to talk about why you've been crying?"

I let out a long, slow breath. Where do I even start? "I got a massage."

He laughs. "And it was that bad?"

I nudge him with my shoulder. "No. Hey, where are we headed? I thought we were getting a drink."

"We are, but I thought we could try something not so cave-like."

He leads us to a small bar near one of the pools. Soft steel drums play over the speakers. It has a tiki hut vibe, with a grass skirt awning, but of course, the grass is pink. And pink stools. It's all pink. Holden will blend right in, literally, like camouflage. "Why are you wearing that?"

He pulls out a stool for me. "This ol' thing?"

I shake my head.

The bartender in an almost identical uniform to Holden's comes over with a frown. "Bro, you can't drink here. Staff drinks down below."

"I…"

I cross my legs on my stool, sitting a little straighter. "He's not staff, he had an unfortunate accident at butter churning class, and a very kind attendant lent him this. Should we go back to the room to change?"

The bartender shakes his head, apologizing, and goes off to get us two of his largest strawberry daiquiris.

Holden blows out a long breath. "You are scary good at lying."

I laugh, but it's not true. I'm a terrible liar unless I'm looking out for someone important to me.

Once we have our drinks, I immediately take a sip. The brightness of the strawberry and the bite of the rum taste like a vacation in a glass.

Holden motions to a table in the sunshine. "What do you say? Up for a little vitamin D?"

I choke on my drink. Because no, I'm absolutely not up for vitamin D. Although, as ridiculous as the uniform is, it does look good on him. Snug in all the right places.

Holden pats my back softly. "Take it easy."

I shake my head and point to a table still under the massive pink hut. We move our drinks there and watch as couple after couple walks by in swimsuits, towels draped over shoulders and arms.

"So," Holden says. "What's up with Muscles over there and the crying?"

"Muscles? His name is…" I stop myself because I almost say Hansworth, which isn't his name at all. "It's Hans. The massage was fine, he just pressed on a spot where apparently I have been tucking away all my emotions since 2016."

"A trauma knot. Fun. I keep those in my shoulders."

"Yeah, I just kind of slipped through a time warp, and the past and present loomed in, and it all felt like too much. And then I couldn't get you out of my head."

Fuck. I didn't mean to say that. Especially not like that.

Holden's smile is so wide, it's beaming. "Me? What were you thinking about me?"

"Not you." *Although there were some thoughts of you.* "More what you said about opening a studio."

Holden is sipping his drink, nodding, and his vest has caught a rogue ray of sun. I cover my face.

"That outfit is going to blind me. What happened?"

He laughs. And takes off the vest so he's left instead with a thin white tank top, through which I can see all his tattoos. All his tattoos and his muscles. His rose tattoo is the largest one on his arm.

Without thinking, I run a finger on the delicate lines. "When did you get this one?"

"A couple of years ago. You're changing the subject. We were talking about you opening a dance studio. You should do it. I can help with logistics. Or if you need an investor."

My mouth falls open. He wants to invest? I take another sip of my drink. Then, I set it down a little too hard. "The only problem is I don't dance. So you can't teach dance if you can't do it."

He lowers his voice, his eyes warm and full of concern. "Can you really not do it at all? You seem really active. Is it painful to dance?"

I finish my drink. Wow. That went fast. Holden signals the bartender for two more.

"Honestly, I don't know. I've been too scared to try."

"Okay, so we try." Holden stands, walking off to the bar. He grabs our drinks and leans in to the bartender. They're whispering and looking over at me, and I hate it. What is he doing?

The music turns up, and it's "(I've Had) The Time of My Life."

Holden sways his hips as he walks back to the table with two drinks in hand, and while it's a little off from the music, he's not terrible. He sets the drinks down on the table and holds out his hand to me, all while mouthing the words. I take it and laugh. "For someone who's never seen *Dirty Dancing* before, you sure know a lot about it."

He pulls me into an open space in the sunshine and twirls me around. My blue sun dress spins at my thighs, and I feel like a princess. He pulls me into him. "I've seen it now. Unlike you, sleepy head, I watched the whole thing on the plane."

The beat is strong, and my legs start to move in a Salsa without my permission, really.

Holden follows my lead, even though I should be following his, throwing in twirls every now and then. My heart is pounding, the sun is shining on my face, and the sea breeze surrounds us. It's a perfect moment.

Other couples start to join us, laughing and twirling. Toward the end of the song, Holden whispers to me, "Isn't it time for the big move?"

I shake my head. "I'm not doing that."

"No, I meant me. You'll catch me, right?"

His dimple is popping, his eyes are full of trouble, and I suddenly have the overwhelming urge to kiss the smirk off his face. The song slows down, and Holden pulls me into him. His skin is hot through his thin shirt, and he smells so good. I lay my head on his shoulder. His hand is firm on the small of my back. He leans down and inhales into my hair.

I smile. "Holden Hartman, did you just smell me again?"

"Checking for sunscreen."

I look up into his eyes. "Checking my hair for sunscreen? Wouldn't protection disrupt the full force of the vitamin D?"

The tips of his ears turn pink. "Fuck. I hear it now...I really just meant the actual vitamin."

His smell is too strong. His lips are too close. He's too cute, all flustered in these pink pants and slutty white tank top.

I raise up on tiptoes and lean in, pressing my lips to his.

He's still for a nanosecond, where every nerve ending in my body panics. I read this wrong. I fucked this up. But then he places his other hand on the small of my back and presses me into him, his lips parting as he deepens our kiss. My knees feel weak. All the blood in my body is rushing to my core.

This is ridiculous. I'm throbbing for him after half a kiss. I pull back, bringing my hand to my mouth, wanting to save the feeling while also covering its existence. I kissed Holden Hartman. I kissed my brother's best friend.

"I…lost my head."

Holden drops his hands from my back, but in a lazy way that has his fingertips tracing my hips and sending shivers down my spine. "I didn't," he says in a husky voice.

My breath is caught in my throat. A bead of sweat trickles down my bare back. My mouth is dry, and all I want to do is kiss Holden again, and again, and again. "I need a drink."

I head back to our table, throw the umbrella, and take a large chug of my vacation in a glass. Ah, this one tastes of coconut and bad decisions.

Holden joins me, taking a seat. I sit, too, and fan myself with the drink menu. He smiles. "You can dance."

And in all the excitement, in all the ridiculousness of Holden's pink pants, and having it be the *Dirty Dancing* song, then the kiss, it didn't really sink in. I danced. For the first time, really, since the accident, I danced without pain. I stand and lean my hips back and forth. A little stiff, as always, but no pain.

I sit back down, my eyes wide, and I can feel how huge the smile on my face is. "I danced."

Holden holds out his drink to mine. "You were born to dance. To the soon-to-be studio owner."

I clink my glass to his and take a sip this time. But as I set it down, that familiar unease settles in. I danced one time, to one song, after a massage that probably loosened my muscles. I can't do that every time. What if teaching classes is too much? "What if I can't do it?"

"You can. I know you can. You can do hard things."

His words are so soft, so sincere, so *hot*. He smiles and motions to my daiquiri. "Now drink up. We have therapy in ten minutes."

I HAVE BEEN to my fair share of therapy. But never after two daiquiris. This should be interesting. We make our way through the maze and end up in the pink waiting room once again.

There was no time for Holden to change, so it's pink pants therapy today.

We have a seat in the waiting room, and Holden suddenly turns to me, his face serious. "Give me your hands."

"Why?"

He holds out his hands, and I place mine in them. His palms are warm but not sweaty. He looks into my eyes, and I swear to God my heart skips a beat. Like a large terrifying beat. I don't know who decided heart palpitations were romantic, but it's scary as fuck. I grip his hands tighter.

He says, "You are a really good dancer."

Ahhh. It's our homework. The compliments.

I say, "Thank you." He tries to pull his hand away. "Oh, my turn. Holden Hartman." There's a pregnant pause as big as Ruby. Holden's eyes are searching my face. "You look really good in pink."

He laughs, and I feel it all the way to my toes. "Really good. That's the best you've got? Have you seen my ass in these things?"

My mouth drops open. "You said I was a really good dancer. Is really good, not good?"

"She'll see you now," the receptionist says.

I drop Holden's hands, and he's still chuckling.

We take our seats. Theresa is smiling. "Ah…you two look… happy."

I look at Holden and find that he's looking at me. He does look happy. Relaxed. His shoulders are a little looser, his smile a little wider. It could be the daiquiris. But it feels like maybe it's something else.

She sits in the chair opposite us, crossing her legs, her pink, wide-leg linen pants swishing with the motion. "So, how's it going?"

Holden turns his attention to Theresa, his smirk still fixed on his face. "Really good."

I giggle but try to cover it, and what comes out is an odd bird-like noise. That gets me a quizzical look from Theresa.

She repeats the phrase like she's testing a hot cup of coffee. "Really good?"

"Mmm," Holden says. "Yes."

"And how's the homework?"

"Really good," Holden says.

And I can't. A laugh escapes me. Theresa looks at me, and I try to compose myself into something neutral, serious even. But I feel the smile leaking out of the sides.

"How has the homework been for you?"

All that comes to mind is really good, but I can't say it. I can't. I won't. Instead, I say the only other thing in my brain right now. "We kissed."

CHAPTER 17
CHLOE

Holden turns his head to me, the smile gone.

We kissed. We kissed? I should've just stuck to really good. Really good was going well for us.

Theresa is nodding. "Okay. And is that not something you were doing anymore? You've been together, how long was it again?"

Shit. We're supposed to be a couple that's been together long enough to wilt and instead of parting ways take a cruise to fix it. Of course we kiss.

Holden jumps in. "We haven't been intimate for some time."

I nod, grateful that he supplied some coherent words. Therapy after two daiquiris is probably fine if you're not lying to your therapist, who also happens to be the cruise director that could kick you off the boat and fire your friend's mom.

"And why is that, do you think?" She holds her pen poised to write down why that is.

Why? I look at Holden and he looks at me. His eyes are soft. His face serious, any hint of a smirk gone. He says, "I've wanted you for so long. I didn't know that you felt the same." And then, almost as an afterthought, he adds, "Still."

There is no air in my lungs. In fact there is no air in the room.

Theresa nods, marking some things on her notepad. "Interesting. Say more about that."

Holden tenses. I can feel it even though we're not touching. "When I was younger, I had a crush on Chloe. Who didn't? She was…is…magnificent. Passionate and strong and kind. I kept expecting it to go away. For the feelings to fizzle out, subside. For someone else to make me feel even a little bit of the heart hammering, think I might throw up…"

I make a face, and Holden touches me lightly on the arm. The sensation travels everywhere. My nerves firing.

He continues. "Nausea in the best way. But I dated people, and I never got that feeling. And what I felt for Chloe—what I feel for Chloe kept getting sharper. Like running a blade across a leather strap, each time I saw her or spent time with her. And then we got together and my worst nightmare came true. I fucked it up. Now I haven't just lost her. Ky—I mean, my best friend doesn't look at me the same way either. He's mad at me, on her behalf. He doesn't come out and say it. But there's a distance between us that wasn't there before."

Holden looks me in the eyes. "I always told myself, if I was ever lucky enough to be with her for real, I wouldn't fuck it up." He takes his eyes off me, and I feel the absence like a cold wind. "And yet here we are. So it's the first time we've kissed in a very long time."

I'm lost. How much of what he said was true? Was any of it true or was it just all show, for Theresa, for the cruise.

Theresa nods like this is very normal information to receive at three in the afternoon. "And you?" she asks me gently.

"I…" I have no idea what to say. What's real? What's a lie? I can't keep our fake relationship straight so I just say, "The kiss felt…really good."

Holden laughs, a big belly laugh that breaks through the thick tension in the room. I join in, and even Theresa cracks a little smile.

"This is progress. I have new homework. I want you to keep up the compliments, because clearly it's helping."

We smile at each other.

"Tomorrow the boat docks at St. Lucia. Holden, I want you to plan a date for Chloe. And I want it to be sexy."

She draws out the last word in a way that doesn't feel entirely appropriate.

"No overthinking. No thoughts of past or future. I want this to be a sexy date firmly rooted in the present." Her red lips spread into a smile. "Sound good? And I'll see you back here in two days."

Holden is nodding. We walk out into the hall, Holden walking a little ahead of me as we go. His ass really does look *fine* in those pink pants. He looks back at me and catches me staring. His smirk comes back, dimple popping, sending the butterflies a flight. "You up for a sexy date tomorrow?" He wiggles his eyebrows.

I smile, and in my sultriest voice I say, "I'm up for anything."

HOLDEN IS SHOWERED and packing a backpack when I wake up the next morning, bustling around, his wet hair dripping onto his shirt.

"Did I wake you?" he says when he notices my eyes are open.

I shake my head.

"Well, I'm glad you're up early. That means we can get going on our sexy date."

I bury myself in my pillow. Mostly to hide my cheeks, which are flaming from how much Holden saying sexy while I'm in my pajamas in bed affects me. "We don't have to."

"What's that, muffles?" He grabs the pillow.

I sit up, the blanket falling, and Holden's eyes travel down my body. I'm in my white sleep set with pink bows on them, and I'm fully aware that the fabric is a little sheer in the nipple region.

If I knew we were going to share a room when I packed, I probably wouldn't have brought them.

If it was anyone else, I'd pull the blanket up.

But I like the feel of Holden looking at me. Maybe a little bit too much.

"I said we really don't have to." I don't know what I'm doing trying to talk him out of this date. I want this date. "It's just Theresa wouldn't know. We're already lying to her."

Holden's eyes move from my body and find my face again, it looks like it's a struggle and it sends a happy buzz through my body. "Do you not want to go on a sexy date with me?"

"I do, I just…I don't want you to do it out of some obligation."

"Trust me, I'm not."

There is an energy in the air, so intense part of me wishes we could forget all about the sexy date and just spend that time here, in bed, naked. Get it out of our system right here and now.

I get up before I pull him on top of me. "I'm going to shower."

"Cool. Wear a swimsuit."

THIRTY MINUTES LATER, we walk onto shore for the first time in what feels like an eternity. Holden has a backpack full of, he assures me, absolutely everything we need. So I brought my small leather backpack, which doesn't hold much more than ChapStick and some sunscreen.

My gold flip-flops slap on the ramp, and as soon as we hit the concrete, my legs wobble. I hadn't realized how much my body had become used to the gentle sway of the waves.

Holden grabs my hand. "You good?"

I look at him in his army green shirt that makes his eyes pop and smile. "I'm good."

But he doesn't let go. And neither do I.

As soon as we're off the boat, we're swarmed by taxi drivers and tour companies.

Holden walks up to a man with long dreads holding a sign that says Coki beach $13. "We'll take that ride."

The man smiles and points to what looks to be something between an oversized golf cart and a bus. Already, a few other couples are waiting on benches. We take the seat in the front and then we're off. The air isn't super warm yet, and the wind from the ride is actually a little cold. I'm wishing I brought a light sweater. Holden puts an arm around my shoulders as if reading my mind.

The ride is quick. The bus drops us off near a little hut selling everything from coconut bras to shark floaties. Holden jumps off then offers me a hand down. He smiles, watching as I take the small step, and I'm suddenly happy I picked out this outfit. It's my favorite blue sundress, with little flowers printed on it. Underneath, I'm wearing my white bikini. Sexy date indeed.

Holden talks to someone in the hut and comes out with two mesh bags. He leads the way through the trees, down a small hill, then I see it all. White sand beach, and the clearest turquoise ocean I have ever seen in real life. It's so bright. It's like it's been photoshopped. One of the men from the hut sets up two chairs for us and an umbrella.

We sit and the view is breathtaking. "Wow. This is nice."

"Do you want to sit for a bit?" he asks, then holds up the bag. "Or are you ready to snorkel?"

My stomach flips nervously. "I've never snorkeled before."

He smiles, his dimple popping. "Neither have I. How hard can it be?"

I laugh. "Famous last words."

He hands me one of the bags. Inside are two pink fins, a snorkel, and goggles.

Holden plops down on his chair, but instead of immediately putting on his gear, he scans the beach.

I sit in mine as well, my knees pointing toward Holden.

He points to a couple that have their fins on and are taking large, exaggerated steps into the waves with considerable trouble. "I don't think that's the best way."

I scan the beach as well, spotting a man with a muscular torso with a mesh bag flung over his shoulder. His skin looks like it's been tanned from years living in the sun, swimming in the ocean, being one with the islands. That guy will know what he's doing.

My eyes find his face, and he stares right back at me with a huge smile on his face. Shit. It's Hansworth. He waves, and I wave back.

Now he's walking toward us. Holden is looking in the water. "There, that's the way to do it," he says pointing at an older guy. "Get in the water, then put the fins on."

Hansworth is standing right behind Holden now, casting him in a massive shadow. Holden turns just as Hansworth says, "Of all the beaches in all the world…"

Holden turns back toward me and mouths "seriously," with an eye roll so large it looks painful. I swallow back my laughter.

Hansworth takes a seat on my chair, next to me. He holds out a hand to Holden. "We didn't officially meet. I'm Hans."

Holden takes his hand, a scowl fixed on his face. "Holden."

He shakes it, and I may be imagining it but I'm pretty sure they both wince a little. "You two snorkeling?"

"That's the plan," Holden says, placing his goggles on his head.

"Wonderful. Best snorkeling out here. Did you bring any anti-fog?"

Holden shakes his head. "No."

"You can use mine. Have you ever been before?"

Holden grits out, "No."

"Perfect, I came along when I did. Let's go. The earlier you're in the water, the clearer it is."

I pull my sundress over my head. Two sets of eyes are on me when I throw it on the chair. Yep. This little white bikini was a great purchase.

We follow Hansworth to the edge of the water, and he explains how to walk in and get our fins on without losing one. He also says we'll want to get our hair wet before putting on the mask so it's snug. I'm listening, but I'm also distracted by a couple of kids playing with a shark floatie.

"Are there sharks?"

Hansworth smiles and nods then sees my face. "Not tons. But a few. They're usually near the bottom and don't want anything to do with people."

I nod and look at Holden, who looks as scared as I feel.

"It'll be fine." Hansworth swims ahead, and we follow.

Below us, the world explodes into color—purple coral shaped like brains, a small electric blue fish with a yellow mouth swimming around them. Holden points excitedly, and I smile around my snorkel, sputtering a little and coming up for air to adjust. Holden comes up too. "We found Dori."

I laugh. "How do you even know that movie?"

"Everyone knows that movie."

I arch an eyebrow, and he says, "Some of the guys at the brewery have kids."

Hansworth surfaces and waves at us, taking his snorkel out. "Turtle."

We put our snorkels in and head back under.

Sunlight dances in ribbons across the bottom of the ocean. A school of silver fish passes. We swim to near Hans, and there it is. A massive turtle, floating along, its shell catching the sun beams. It munches on some sea grass then darts ahead, and we follow. While land turtles may be the slowest animal, this turtle is not. It's fast, and it's hard to keep up. It stops again to check out some coral. I'm mesmerized by the pattern of overlapping shapes on its shell and by the gentle curve of its fin, the sharp beak-like nose.

Suddenly, firm hands are on my waist. I'm out of the water and flying through the air. Then hitting the ocean with a splash. My snorkel submerging. I come up for air, taking it out, coughing up water, and Holden's head is above water, too, his arms arcing, slicing through the surface. He motions for me to go. "Swim," he yells. "Go to shore."

CHAPTER 18
HOLDEN

My arms are burning from the hard, fast strokes through the water. I can hear Muscles behind me, but I'm not ignoring him. He probably wants to pet the monster. Chloe is swimming toward shore as well, thankfully. She's quite a few feet ahead because of how far I threw her.

Muscles catches up to me. "What are you doing?"

"Shark," I grit out, not stopping my mission to get to land.

He stops swimming and laughs. Actually fucking laughs. That's fine. Better to die laughing, I guess.

"Wait," he says. Then yells, "Chloe, wait. Come back."

She turns, and I'm about to deck this guy. "Don't have her swim toward the shark. It was giant. We need to get out of the water."

He laughs again, and I stop swimming, my chest heaving.

He shakes his head. "I should've told you." Chloe joins us, her chest also heaving, and in that little white bikini, it is extremely distracting. "It's a statue."

My head snaps to him. "What?"

Muscles is still chuckling. "You really launched her."

"There was a fucking shark."

"Statue," he says. "Shark statue."

"Nope. I swear it was swimming."

"Come on. I'll show you."

We all swim over to where we were. I make sure to stick close to Chloe in case we need to swim away again. There it is, at the bottom of the ocean. A massive shark. My heart hammers in my chest, and I hold an arm out to Chloe, my fingers brushing her stomach under the water.

It moves, and I'm about to launch Chloe again, when the light shifts. It's not moving. It's the light from the waves.

Muscles dives down, swimming like a goddamn merman. He pets the thing, and still it stays put. It really is a fucking statue.

I come up for air, and Chloe does as well, pushing her goggles up and taking out her snorkel. I take all my stuff off, pushing it to the top of my head.

Chloe's smile has taken over her whole face, and I can tell she's dying, trying not to laugh. Her eyes are anime wide as she says, "Oh, Holden. You saved me."

"Fuck off."

She places a hand on my shoulder, and my mind goes back to the feeling of my fingertips on her bare stomach. "No. It's sweet, really. Who knows what that beast could've done?"

I grab her hips, pulling her toward me through the water. Her stomach is flush against mine. Both of our skin is a little cold, but deliciously slick. She doesn't pull away; instead, she moves a little, pressing further into me. "Next time I'll throw your ass to the shark."

She takes her hands and places them on mine, moving them down her back and placing them firmly on her deliciously round bottom. "This ass? You'd never."

And she's right. My hands squeeze, my excitement clearly evident between us. I swallow, looking into her face. I'm so hard it hurts.

I lean down, my lips just brushing hers.

A splash pops up next to us.

"See," Muscles says obnoxiously. "Statue."

Chloe backs up a little, my fingers tracing her hips as she does.

Muscles swims back, an odd expression on his face as he takes the two of us in.

We all put our gear back on to go explore more. We swim out, each of us staggered, but Chloe staying close to me.

The water is refreshing, and the heavy sounds of my breath in my ears are relaxing. It's crazy beautiful. We see tiny yellow fish that look like little lemons with fins. Striped fish dart in and out, their tiny mouths moving almost like they're trying to talk.

We find another turtle, more like he finds us. He's so curious, he swims right up to Chloe and takes a nibble on the end of her hair. Her eyes are full to the brim with panic as she looks to me, and I shrug. She wades back a little, and it swims away. We both move to the surface.

She takes off her gear again. "Holy shit, a turtle just tried to eat me."

I take out my snorkel. "It was making friends."

"Mmm mmm. Friends keep their mouths to themselves."

I swim a little closer, my hands finding her hip again like a magnet. "Is that so? We're friends."

"We are," she says, her voice breathy.

"We didn't keep our mouths to ourselves yesterday."

Her cheeks are a shade rosier than they were a second ago, her breaths faster. "We didn't."

She doesn't move away.

The ocean rocks us gently, lifting her closer on one swell, separating us an inch on the next. My breath feels loud in my ears, like I'm still underwater. Her hand finds my wrist, brushing the inside up my arm, goosebumps in her wake. She moves her hand all the way to my neck, her fingers finding the wet ends of my hair. She moves in close. So close that her lips are a problem now.

I kiss her. I can't not kiss her. It's inevitable. It's all I've wanted to do for years, and here she is on this sun-soaked day, on this beautiful island, thousands of miles away from all the reasons I shouldn't.

She kisses me back. Her lips are salty in the most delectable way. Our kiss is not careful; it's not as tentative as it was yesterday. It's passionate and reckless. Like, at any moment, this spell might be broken.

She makes a small sound into my mouth, and it goes straight through me. It melts me. I am water. I am the ocean. I don't exist anymore. The only part of me demanding attention is my rock-hard cock. Rising up, harder than it's ever been, reminding me that I am still here. It brushes against Chloe's stomach, and even through my swimsuit, the sensation is heady.

I pull back, just enough to rest my forehead against hers. "We should probably take a beat."

She runs her hands down my neck, resting them on my chest, and lets out a little groan. "We've taken a decades-long beat. Maybe..." Her eyes find mine. "Maybe for once, we should give in."

Her hands keep moving down my body, under the water, her fingers toying with the edge of my shorts, and my heart is hammering so fast it's practically making splashes.

Then all of a sudden her hands are off me, she swims on her back away, smiling, her eyes bright, cheeks flushed from more than just the sun. "Think about it."

She puts her goggles back on, places her snorkel back in, and turns, swimming away and giving me a front row view of how amazing her ass looks in that little white bikini.

WE SWIM on the reef opening up like something out of a nature documentary—coral blooming in impossible colors, schools of fish flashing silver—but I can't focus on any of it. All I can think about is Chloe saying *let's give in*. The words echo in my head, drifting in and out with the tide.

I want to give in. I've wanted Chloe for so long. And she clearly wants me. What would be the harm if we both got what we want? If we let ourselves have this. Just once. Before reality comes rushing back in?

After an hour or so, we all head in. Chloe runs ahead to find a bathroom, water streaming from her hair, running down her perfect body in hypnotizing rivulets.

Muscles gives me a slap on the shoulder. "Hey, man, no hard feelings, I hope. I thought you two were on the outs. Wilters."

"Oh, yeah, we are."

He whistles low. "Gotta say, I've done quite a few of these cruises, and I have never, ever, seen Wilters look at each other the way you two do."

I open my mouth to protest, but a more pressing thought comes to mind. "How does she look at me, exactly?"

"The way a kid looks at a piece of cake."

A smile of pure bliss takes over my face.

Muscles lowers his voice. "You two ever think about adding a third?"

"No."

"Cool. Let me know if you change your mind." He winks.

Chloe comes running back, and Muscles says, "Hey, I gotta head back to the ship. But if you're staying for a while, you should check out The Rooster Shack. My buddy works there. Best painkiller in the tropics."

"Thanks, man." I hold out my hand, and we shake.

"See you back at the ship. Remember, we depart at 5 tonight."

"See ya," Chloe says as she plops down on the lounge chair, her long legs stretched out in front of her.

We lounge for a bit, catching our breath. But every time I look over at Chloe—long legs crossed, her bare stomach sparkling in the sun from drops of ocean, her hardly covered chest softly moving up and down with her breaths—my heart races.

I should be looking at the view. The ocean is the deepest shade of aquamarine. The hills beyond are lush and green. It's gorgeous. And it has nothing on the woman sitting next to me.

She catches me looking and smirks. She sits up, turning toward me. "So…what's next for this sexy date?"

"Rooster Shack?"

She puts her sundress over her suit, and it almost physically pains me. "Sure. I wouldn't mind a drink and some food after all that swimming. And nearly getting eaten by a shark."

Her smile is reckless—like our kiss, like both our kisses—and something in my chest aches with it. I swing my backpack on and, ignoring the part of my brain screaming at me to keep my hands to myself, I grab Chloe's hand and intertwine our fingers.

She doesn't hesitate. Her thumb brushes over my knuckles, absent and intimate, like this is the most natural thing in the world. We start walking, our steps falling into rhythm, the heat of her palm seeping into mine.

For a moment, everything feels suspended—the past, the consequences, the rules we're supposed to follow. It's just the sun on our skin, the sound of the waves behind us. I'd love to say that's enough, but I am greedy, and I want more. I want all of her.

She smiles at me, and goddamn, she's fucking beautiful. "Which way to the cock house?"

Her mouth, those perfect rosebud lips saying cock, sends blood rushing straight to mine. I shake my head. "You are trouble."

CHAPTER 19
CHLOE

We walk the short way to the bar holding hands, and my brain keeps repeating that fact like the more I acknowledge it, the more real it will feel. Because honestly, right now this whole day has felt like a fever dream.

How many times have I imagined holding Holden's hand? Kissing him?

The Rooster Shack is a small pink house surrounded by palm trees with no doors. We walk in, and it's just as hot inside as outside. There are beat-up wooden tables with mismatched chairs—yellow, pink, some wood, some metal, some plastic. In one corner of the room is a large Christmas tree with rainbow lights.

In the back is a large plastic shark mounted on the wall with a big toothy grin; one of the front teeth is sparkly gold. I nudge Holden with my shoulder and point to the shark. "Don't throw me across the bar."

He frowns. "I was saving you."

I laugh, but my chest fills with warmth. As completely ridiculous as it was, he was saving me.

We walk up to the bar, and Holden orders two painkillers. I raise my eyebrows at him.

He's usually a beer guy. He smiles, and I swear I feel it all the way down to my toes. "When in Rome?"

I nod. "Or the cock house." I didn't forget the name. I just like to watch his pupils swell when I say the word cock.

"Rooster Shack," he says, his smile growing a notch wider.

We take our drinks to a quiet table in the corner and start talking about all the fish we saw.

I take a sip of my painkiller. It's creamy and sweet, but not overly sweet. It's dangerously good.

So good in fact that I've finished mine before I even notice.

Holden raises his eyebrows. "Another?"

"Yes, please."

Holden grabs my glass and heads off to fetch us two more, and I stare at the Christmas tree. There are all sorts of different ornaments. Little sandals. Mini tropical drinks. A shiny glass sloth.

Holden places our drinks on the table and follows my line of sight.

"Why do you think they still have a Christmas tree?" I ask.

"Why not have a Christmas tree? Christmas is the best holiday," Holden says.

"No, it's not," I say, then scoot my drink while taking another sip.

"You don't like Christmas?" Holden is looking at me with no judgment, just genuine curiosity.

"I do like Christmas. Mostly. I don't know. It's not the same as it was when I was little. My mom really made Christmas special. My dad tries. It's just not the same."

Holden leans in just the tiniest bit. Hardly enough for a passerby to notice, but I do. He's listening. How many times have I talked about my mom with someone I'm dating or trying to, and they backed away? Or crossed their arms. But Holden actually leaned in. His body is still open to me. Not that we're dating.

"Anyway, the best holiday is Halloween. You get to dress up and be anything you want to be."

Holden's smile is wide, his arms flex as he fiddles with a wet spot on the table. "When I was five, I was Ghostface killer from *Scream*."

I sputter on my drink. "That's insane. It's so inappropriate for a five-year-old."

He laughs. "It was, and it was *entirely* inappropriate when my dad took me, a five-year-old, to the theater to see it."

"He did not."

"He did. And he bought me the costume, but in his defense, I begged him to buy it. I was a weird kid."

I reach my foot out, finding him under the table, and run my foot up his calf. "You're still a weird kid."

He presses his leg back into me. "What were you? When you were five?"

Moving my foot off his calf, I say, "I was a ballerina." With a smile, I let the memory wash over me. The scratchy tutu, my favorite pale-pink tights. "I was always a ballerina."

He finds my foot again, placing his next to it. "You like Halloween because of the endless possibilities, all the different lives you could live, and yet every Halloween you were a ballerina."

"It's all I ever wanted to be."

There's a silence that hangs between us, not heavy, not even pensive, just warm. He doesn't try to fix it for me. He doesn't say anything that would make it better because it's not better, and it won't be better. He just lets it be and listens. And in this moment, I have never wanted to kiss him more.

We talk about other costumes, past Halloweens. Holden excuses himself to go to the restroom, and when he comes back, he has a flyer in his hand.

He hands it to me. "We *have* to go to this."

"Did you find this in the bathroom?" I hold it out with the tips of my fingers.

He laughs. "No. There's a community board by the bathroom."

I hold up the flyer and read aloud, "A unique dance experience in the Huntsville botanical garden." He smiles across the table at me. I shake my head. "No. We can't go. We have to be back on the boat at five."

"It starts at four." Holden looks at his watch. He pulls out his phone and starts tapping the screen, his mind seemingly working faster than his fingers. "We can make it there. This botanical garden is not far from the port, so after we finish these drinks, we can get a taxi and go to the garden. See whatever this unique dance experience is, and then head to the boat. It's fate. We have to go."

I sip my drink, still unconvinced.

"It'll be the perfect addition to our sexy date."

I look at the flyer, it's all hand-drawn, but not in a bad way. In a refreshingly human way. In the corner, there's a little rose in full bloom. Maybe it's the two quick painkillers, or my loose muscles from swimming in the ocean, but something about it feels right. "Okay."

Holden smiles, bursting with excitement.

THE TAXI RIDE takes a little longer than we expected. And by the time we arrive at the garden, it's almost 4:30. We head in through a stone path that leads down a set of stairs. With each step, the floral scent gets stronger. It's an interesting mix, and the only thing I can pinpoint is hibiscus.

The stairs open into a clearing, and it's like we've stepped into someone else's dream. The clearing is surrounded by a circle of rose bushes. Honestly, I thought the drawing on the flower was just to signify flowers. I didn't realize roses could grow in the Caribbean. String lights are draped between trees, glowing softly even though the sun hasn't set yet. People are seated on blankets, some on stone benches, some just on the grass, red Solo cups in hand.

Holden and I find an open spot, and he holds up his finger to me, walking through the small crowd of people. He's back in a minute with two red Solo cups and sits crisscross next to me, his bare knee brushing mine and sending an electric pulse up my leg. He hands me the cup. "It's wine."

"Thanks," I say in a whisper as soft music starts to play from two large speakers. The murmurs of the crowd die down. A man at a DJ table turns a few knobs, rose petals surrounding him.

A troupe of dancers enters the garden, feet bare, dressed in black leotards. They move like water, all in sync, flowing this way and that. It's beautiful. The music shifts to something a little heavier, more bass-heavy, and the dancers' movements do as well.

My eyes are fixed. It's magical. The dancers spin and leap, they stomp and roll off one another's backs. They fold into each other, telling a story without words. It's not perfect. Some of the dancers are better than others. One woman laughs a little at her own misstep. It's definitely not perfect, but it is charged and emotional and real. It's human. Like the flyer.

My throat tightens.

Holden glances at me, then back at the dancers. I'm not sure if he noticed the wetness in my eyes, but he gently takes my hand in his and squeezes lightly.

There is a little girl in the troupe, and she is so serious. Each of her movements is precise and practiced. Her mouth is a determined line. And despite the differences in our skin color, in where we've grown up, in who we are, I see so much of myself in her. I want to whisper to her, "Remember *to have fun too. Remember to enjoy this.*"

But what I really want to do is go back in time and tell little me that.

When the music ends, applause erupts. I set down my still full wine glass and stand, clapping so hard my hands sting. Holden joins me and even whistles. The little girl in front beams, like she's just been handed the sun. The dancers bow. A woman grabs a microphone from the DJ, her voice breathless. "Please stay and dance."

More applause. The DJ plays house music, and some of the crowd leave, while others start to dance. Holden places a hand on my hip.

We move to the beat. It's faster than we've danced to before, but he keeps up. I turn my back to him, moving my hips, getting low. When I glance back at Holden, his eyes are fixed on me, dark and hungry. He places a hand on my hip, lightly, enough so I know it's there, but I can still move.

The beat changes to something a little slower. I turn to face him, and he pulls me toward him, his hands on the small of my back. We sway in the sea of people.

"Thank you," I whisper.

He runs his hand up my back, bringing it to my neck, cupping my face gently in his hand. It feels so good. I lean into his palm and flutter my eyes closed. Before they close all the way, I catch sight of Holden's watch, glowing green in the early evening sun.

Fuck. I grab his wrist. "Holden, it's 4:55."

CHAPTER 20
HOLDEN

Chloe releases my hand, and I see she's right. It's 4:55.

Shit.

We have five minutes until our ship departs. I grab her hand, and we run up the stone steps, out of the garden, and down the street.

"How far is the port?" Chloe yells, her flip-flops smacking against the concrete.

I don't want to tell her. It's a mile away. A mile seems really close when you're looking at the tiny map on your phone, but a mile in flip-flops, in the heat, not knowing exactly where I'm headed, feels like an impossible feat. It feels like I'm an idiot and should've never insisted we go to that dance performance.

But Chloe's rapt face as she watched the dancers fills my vision, and I know deep in my soul that it was worth it.

"Not far," I say. "But keep your eye out for a taxi."

Once we're more on the main street, Chloe lets go of my hand and steps out to wave at a passing taxi. It pulls over, and we get in.

"Port, please."

Chloe adds, "Please hurry."

The driver looks pointedly at his clock on the dash and clicks his tongue. Like he knows it's hopeless. But he pulls back into traffic.

"Four minutes," Chloe says, wringing her hands together.

"They probably don't leave right on time."

We hit a red light.

Four minutes turns into three.

Chloe taps her hands on her knees, and I place one of mine over hers.

I say, in as reassuring a tone as I can muster, "It'll be okay."

"We're going to miss the ship," she says.

She's right. And normally it wouldn't matter. Except it does. I need to get that beer sample to Gio. I should've at least gotten his contact info, but I'm an idiot, and I didn't. Me stressing Chloe out is not going to help, though. "We'll figure it out."

She swallows, her breath a little slower.

The light turns green, the driver floors it, and hope blooms in my chest. Maybe we will make it. We weave through traffic. I try not to watch the clock on the dashboard change from 4:58 to 4:59. The port finally comes into view, but it's still so far away, and traffic has slowed to a snail's pace.

Chloe grabs my hand. "Come on. We can run faster."

The line of cars stretches in front of us all the way to the port. She might be right. Either way, it's worth a shot. I hand the driver some cash. "Thank you. We'll just hop out."

He salutes us. "Good luck."

I nod to him, again trying not to look at the clock that now reads 5:03. We run, flip-flops smacking, my backpack thumping with every footfall.

Chloe kicks off her sandals, holding both in one hand, and runs barefoot. She's a fucking gazelle. Long legs moving gracefully, strong and fast. I'm so distracted I nearly run right into a lamppost, dodging it at the last second.

We're still three blocks from the port when the ship sets sail.

Chloe is still running, but I stop, my breath coming out hard and ragged. Clearly, I need to work on my cardio.

She cries out, "No," as she slows down, then finally comes to a stop. Her flip-flops slip out of her hand, hitting the concrete in front of her with an anti-climactic thud.

I walk forward, kneeling to grab them. I think about handing them to her, but she should really put them back on. I take her calf in my hand and slip one on her foot, then the next. My hand runs up her leg, just to her thigh, then I stand.

Her lips are parted, and her face, while still looking completely dejected, also looks maybe just a little bit turned on.

Her words come back to me. *Maybe we should just give in.*

She motions to the ship. "What are we going to do?"

My mind runs through the options. We could leave, catch a flight home, but I have beer coming and I'd really love to make this deal. It could be a solid business relationship that could last for years.

But not if I don't deliver on the very first thing I ever promised —that's no way to operate.

And I can fix this. "We just need to meet the ship at the next port."

She's nodding. Her face serious.

"Come on." I put my arm around her shoulder. "Let's go get some food. And we'll make a plan."

WE FIND a place with outdoor seating right on the water. A server drops a basket of chips and salsa between us, and I dig in like I've been stranded for days instead of mere minutes.

Chloe glares at me. "How can you eat?"

I'd reply, but my mouth is full. So instead, I shrug and pull out my phone and get to work. The server comes around again, and I swallow my bite. "Two margaritas, and I'll have the fish tacos."

Chloe is starting out at the water, tracking *The Shipped Ship* as it slowly becomes smaller and smaller.

I nudge her foot under the table. "Chloe, what do you want?"

"Nothing."

I shake my head. "She'll have the fish tacos."

She sighs but doesn't protest.

According to the cruise schedule online, the next port is St. Maarten in two days. I turn the phone toward her.

"Okay. We just have to meet up with the ship in St. Maarten, so we have tonight. All of tomorrow, and then we meet up with *The Shipped Ship* the following morning."

"What are we going to do until then? And how are we going to get there?"

The server sets down our drinks. Despite everything, Chloe gives him a warm smile and thanks him. I've always thought you can tell everything you need to know about a person by how they treat people when they feel like garbage. Even panicking, even stranded, Chloe is still Chloe. She treats everyone with kindness and grace, always.

I thank the man, too, and then ask in Spanish if he knows a good place to stay.

He does. He pulls off a scrap of paper from his order pad, sketches a quick map, and writes the name in a big looping script.

Casa de Flores.

I smile, sliding it across the table, Chloe. "See? Place to stay. We eat. We sleep. Then in the morning, we'll figure out transportation. Easy."

Chloe still looks skeptical as she eyes the map, but she takes a sip of her drink. "Okay."

The fish tacos are perfect—crispy, limey, delicious. It even seems like Chloe is enjoying them. Her shoulders relax down a notch.

After dinner, we walk the short way down the beach to Casa De Flores. It's a beautiful, large white house facing the water, flanked by smaller bungalows painted sunshine yellow, robin 's-egg blue, rosebud pink. Like giant crayons popping right out of the sand.

Inside, a woman sits behind a small desk. I explain our predicament, the cruise, the running, the general panic and dread.

She nods sympathetically. "Well, as luck would have it, we just had a cancellation twenty minutes ago. Their flight was canceled. Weather. We have one bungalow available."

"Great," I say. "With two rooms?"

She shakes her head, holding up her pointer finger. "One."

I feel Chloe stiffen beside me, but I grab her hand and squeeze. It's fine. We've had one room this whole time, and we've been just fine. No lines have been crossed, in the room anyway. I smile. "We'll take it."

We follow the woman outside to the small pink cottage. Of course. Even off the pink ship, here we are still surrounded by pink. She unlocks the door and gestures us in.

It is a studio, not unlike an apartment I had in my early twenties.

One room.

One bed.

It's a nice big bed, with white linens and pale-pink flower petals strewn on top.

The woman smiles and hands me the key, clicking the door shut on her way out. I look back at Chloe, and her face is as white as the comforter, her cheeks as pink as the rose petals.

I smile and try to lighten the mood. "This is cozy."

She drops her bag on the floor. "That's one word for it."

She pulls her dress over her head, her bare stomach stretched taut. I swallow hard and fight to keep the other parts of me from getting hard as well. She stands there in her white bikini, her face determined.

Fuck me and that tiny white bikini. "What are you doing?"

She throws her dress on the floor near her bag. "We're stranded, but we have a bed, a little kitchen, a shower, and a fucking beachfront bungalow. I'm going to enjoy it. I'm going to swim in the ocean."

Her face is set, like she has decided to have a good time, and by God, no one better stop her. She turns toward the door, and my eyes travel down her bare back to her ass. I've never been so jealous of a scrap of fabric as I have been of her bikini bottoms.

Chloe turns back to me, a smirk on her lips. She caught me looking, for sure. "You coming?"

Yes, nearly in my pants.

I throw my shirt on top of her dress, and we head out the door.

THE SKY IS our own personal light show. Streaks of pink and orange overtake the fading blue beneath. The water is cool, and it feels good after our unplanned run. Chloe and I swim next to each other, treading water. The rosy light on her face makes her look like a painting, and I can't look away.

She catches my eye. "What?"

I shake my head to try to shake off the spell, but it's no use. I've been trying to shake it off for literally years, and it always comes back to this. To me wanting Chloe. "You're beautiful."

She blushes, and it makes me want to grab her even more. "You say that to all the girls you're stranded on a tropical island with."

Then I get an idea. I clap my hands together. "This is the perfect spot to practice the *move*."

Her smile is full of trouble. "What *move* exactly?"

My body reacts to her voice, my swim trunks getting a little more snug. That's not how I meant it. "The one from the movie you love. The lift thing."

She laughs. "You want to practice the *Dirty Dancing* move out here in the ocean?"

"Why not? They used a lake." I motion to the surrounding water. "This is even better."

"Yeah, except this water moves."

There's a hesitation in her eyes. I frown. I don't want to push her, but she thinks there are so many things she can't do anymore, when I think that if she tried, she could. It's not just that either. It's like she doesn't believe in herself. Which is so frustrating because she is amazing. She can do anything. I look into her eyes, the ocean lapping against my waist. "Chloe, you can do this."

Her eyes search my face. I ask, "What's the worst that could happen?"

"My hip could hitch, I could pull a muscle in my back and end up alone in bed for days."

I nod. That does suck. "Does that happen a lot?"

She shrugs. "It's happened a fair amount. Enough that I'm afraid of it."

I sink further into the water. I don't want her to get hurt. "We don't have to. If that happened, though, I'd take care of you. You wouldn't be alone. But I get—"

She's already backing up and squaring her shoulders.

"Let's do this," she says, a spark in her blue eyes. "You ready?"

I'm not. "Yep."

She runs as much as she can through the water that's up to her thighs. Then she jumps, but nowhere near high enough. Her body slams into mine, her stomach pressed against my chest, and her breasts in my face. I grab onto her waist as we both fall back into the water.

If this is how I die, being smothered by her perfect tits and drowned, so be it.

Chloe moves off me, and we both come up for air, her wet hair in her face. She sputters, "You didn't catch me."

"That's not true." I swallow my laugh. "I did catch you. I just didn't stop us from ending up in the water. You didn't jump high enough."

"You're too tall." She laughs.

"Is your back okay?"

She wiggles her hips back and forth like she's testing them. "I'm good. Want to try it again?"

"Absolutely."

We find a different spot where the sand is more level and try again. This time, I manage to grab a hold of her hips, but we still both fall back, her bikini bottoms dangerously close to my face as we sink into the water.

We both come up, water dripping from our faces. We look at each other and laugh.

"Again?" I ask.

"Again," she declares.

We "practice" for a while, until the sunset deepens into a purple bruise.

Then something unexpected happens. My hands find the right spot on her hips, the wet sand under my feet stays steady, I lift, and she spreads her arms. I look up at her face, and her smile is pure joy.

We hold it for a bit, then I gently bring her down, her wet body sliding against mine.

I hold her close, my arms wrapped around her back. Like this is normal for us. Something we do every day. "I'm sorry we missed the boat. It's my fault."

She wraps her arms around my neck. And now we're back to where we were earlier. In this dangerous limbo. "It's not your fault."

"I insisted on going to that dance thing."

She looks into my eyes. "I was freaked out at first. But now that we have a plan, I'm thinking maybe, just maybe it's"—she leans in her lips brushing my ear—"worth it."

Her earlier words come back to me, *just give in*. And I do. I let go. I give in. I lean down and kiss her like there are no consequences.

CHAPTER 21
CHLOE

Holden's lips are on mine, and it is not tentative. It's hot and forceful. I wrap my legs around him, feeling just how excited he is through our swimsuits. Holy shit. How have we not been doing this the whole time?

He moves his hand down to my bikini top and moves it to the side. My nipples that are already pebbled harden at the air, the water, his gaze. He moves his thumb over my nipple, and my core tenses like he flicked my clit.

His palm cups my breast, lifting it up, then squeezing it. The sound that escapes me is somewhere between a cry and a moan. I can instantly feel how it affects him. His mouth moves down my neck, and he puts my nipple in his mouth, his lips hot and wet, his hand firm, still squeezing. I clench so hard it's painful.

My eyes drift to the beach where another couple is coming out of the yellow house. I move us in the water so Holden is in front of me, covering my exposed breast. "Holden, there's a couple on the beach."

He groans. The vibration on my nipple is exquisite, but we can't do this here. He slowly removes his mouth from my breast and places the wet, cold fabric of my swimsuit back over it. I miss his hot mouth on me.

He looks into my eyes. "Can we continue this inside?"

I nod.

Holden's dimple pops as he smirks. "I'm going to need verbal confirmation."

I run my hands down his face, resting them at his sharp jawline. "Holden, take me in that little pink house and fuck me."

I can feel his jaw tick under my fingertips, and he moves toward the shore, me still wrapped around his body.

"Clear enough?" I ask as I run my hands down his chest.

"Crystal."

His feet find purchase in the sand, and he's still holding me. I move to get down, but he grips my ass tighter. "I'm going to keep you right here."

"I can walk. It would be faster."

"I'm not interested in fast," he says in a low scratchy voice that reverberates through my skin. "Plus, I have a little bit of a situation, and you are helping to cover it."

I grind a little on him, right on the rock-hard mound. "You mean this situation?"

He lets out a low grunt. I do it again right as we walk up the beach, past the fully clothed couple having a very civil champagne picnic. Holden grips my ass a little tighter. "You are so going to get it."

I bring my lips to the shell of his ear and whisper, "That's what I'm hoping."

He shifts me in his arm, now holding me up with one hand, and turns the doorknob. Kicking the door closed with his foot.

He sets me down on the dresser, and his lips fly to mine like a man starved. His hands move to my top. He pulls hard. The ties come loose, the whole thing falling to the floor. He backs up, and I immediately miss his lips. I reach for him, but he grabs my hands, holding them out, drinking me. His eyes slowly move over every inch of me until they connect with my eyes. It's electric.

"You have perfect tits."

I smile. "Is this your compliment for the day?"

He lets my hands fall gently as he moves to my breasts, taking one in each hand and squeezing them together. "I don't think I'll be able to stop at just one today."

My chest is rising and falling with my rapid breaths as he squeezes and licks. Then one hand starts to move down. He unties the side of my bikini bottom, his hand moving in, his fingers finding my clit like he had a map.

I reach for him. He's so hard, but he moves away.

"Not yet."

His fingers start to swirl, and oh my God, it feels so good. I scoot closer to the edge of the dresser, seeking more. His hand that was on my breast moves to the other side of my swimsuit and tugs it off. He places a firm palm on my low back as he moves one finger slowly inside. I cry out and grind into him, my hips bucking on their own.

He slips another finger inside, and I clench around him. His eyes swell black as he watches me grind on him.

I reach for his suit and yank. "Take it off."

He finally obliges, pulling his fingers out to adjust the elastic band around his massive erection, and lets the shorts drop.

I freeze. Because holy shit. Holden Hartman is fucking hung.

He blushes. Like, actually blushes. "It's…" he starts.

"It's fucking huge."

He laughs. "We can go slow."

"Condom?"

He goes to his backpack, and I wonder if he always has condoms in there or if this was part of his sexy date plan. I wonder, but I don't ask. Because I don't want to talk. I don't want to break this spell.

He rolls the condom on, and I hop off the desk, taking his hand and leading him to the bed. I lay him down, moving my hands down his body. His eyes flutter close as I get to his cock, and I think of the butterflies that flit about my stomach every time I've seen him for so many years. I don't feel them now. Instead, there is just a deep, pulsing want. I straddle him, placing him at my entrance.

His hand moves to my hips, but he doesn't tug me down; he just grips, his fingers pressing into my flesh. Millimeter by millimeter, I lower onto him, breathing deeply, letting myself expand for him.

"Chloe."

He's said my name a million times, but never like that. My name on his tongue, husky and full of need, while he's inside me, is new, and it feels so right.

I move up and down, achingly slow at first. His grip tightens, but he doesn't move me. He lets me set the pace and the depth. Each time I come down on him, I go just a little deeper, until finally I'm to the base of him and I cry out. It feels so good.

I lean over him, moving up and down. One of his hands finds my breast. He squeezes, sitting up enough to take it in his mouth, sucking on my nipple. My core clenches, and he bucks underneath me. He takes my nipple between his teeth, scraping the edge.

The pressure inside me builds, and his hips buck again.

"Holden."

"Yeah, baby. Say my name again," he says, his mouth still so close to my breast I can feel his breath on my nipple. His hips thrust into me again, and I grab onto him. He sits fully up now, and the change of angle sends a shockwave through me.

He hits a spot I don't think I've ever felt before. It stills me. He looks into my face. "You good?"

"Yes."

He moves underneath me, thrusting into me, and I start to move as well, grinding him. His fingers find my clit, and he swirls, but I move his hand. "It's too much."

He whispers into my ear, "You can take it."

He moves me to the bed, and I lie down as he thrusts into me. I move his hand back to my clit, and as he moves, the pleasure is all-consuming.

His voice is husky as he goes deeper. My muscles tense, while my core melts around him. "That's it, baby. You're doing so good."

"Holden," I cry out this time. "I'm going to come."

"Let go." He thrusts as I move my hips, our rhythm here so much better than our dancing. The pressure builds, and I look into his face, gripping his shoulders. He's watching me intently as I open my mouth, letting out a soft moan as my every muscle tenses. Shock waves ripple through me as I contract and expand around him. He swells inside me, getting even harder, as he cries out, too, fingers digging into my hips. There is a brief moment of overlap, where we are coming together, our bodies fully in sync, and in that moment, time doesn't just stop, it disappears. The world falls away. We are not our bodies anymore. I never broke my hip. Pain never existed. We were always supposed to end up here—two intertwined as one.

And there are no consequences.

<hr>

In the morning, I wake up naked with Holden's arm across my stomach. He is still completely asleep, and I don't blame him. We were up late. It turns out Holden had more than one condom in his backpack—thank God.

My muscles are that kind of sore that is the most delicious. Where they have worked and are happy. My core is also a tasty kind of sore, the kind that comes with flashbacks. Holden's hand on my hips, his mouth on my nipple, his cock deep inside me.

My cheeks warm at the memories. I slip out from under his arm, careful not to wake him. He worked so hard, he deserves some rest. I'll bring us both back coffee.

I locate my discarded bikini. I really need to find some underwear. Then I slip on my sundress. As soon as I open the door, I'm hit with a gust of wind, tiny flecks of rain spattering me in the face.

I step out into the gray day, dark clouds blocking out any kind of sun, and even darker ones looming on the horizon. The sea is churning. The large waves crash one after another onto the shore. It's hard to imagine we were swimming out there just last night. The sea was so calm. The beach is changed as well, now covered in a stinky seaweed that reminds me of discarded Christmas ribbons. I hold my breath until I'm away from the smell.

I walk a little way back toward where we stopped and ate, and find a little general store open. I grab a basket and wander the aisles, past snow globes and palm tree floaties.

They have a small clothing section. The only underwear they have is a matching set of his and hers. Black cotton with white writing on it that says *I'm taken*, then *US Virgin Islands* under that. In the basket it goes.

I find a pair of sweats with a matching hoodie, and of course, the only one they have left in my size is bubblegum pink. And it has *beach bum* printed on the ass. But I'm freezing my *ass* off this morning, so in the basket it goes. After I get a few more things, I ask the nice man working if I can use his dressing room to change. My teeth chatter a little as I do, which I think helps my cause.

Once I'm snug in my new beach bum sweats, I find a small coffee shop and order Holden an Americano and me a latte. While I'm waiting for our drinks, I overhear some people talking. The woman is in a white button-up shirt and a black pencil skirt with a gold name tag hanging from her blouse. The gentleman wearing a branded T-shirt that says *Experience UVI* on it says, "Nah, all the tours are canceled today."

"It's just a little rain." The woman rolls her eyes.

The man shakes his head. "They're saying hurricane."

It's like my heart sucks in a breath. A hurricane? A fucking hurricane. I pull out my phone and go to my weather app. And right there at the top is a small red triangle with an exclamation point, with a 3 next to it.

I click on it and read the advisory from the National Weather Service. Warning one: Rip current remains in effect. Warning two:

high surf advisory. Warning three: Tropical cyclone off the coast of South Carolina is headed south.

No. Why is it that when one thing goes right, three things have to go wrong?

A fucking hurricane.

Come on, Universe. Can't a girl just have a nice time in the Caribbean with an attractive man? Apparently not. Because Holden isn't just any man. He's my brother's best friend. And we've crossed a line, and now the Universe is fucking pissed.

It's fine. We'll figure it out. And it's unrelated, obviously, I'm just projecting.

Right?

It'll all be fine.

CHAPTER 22
HOLDEN

The door opens, and it takes a second for my eyes to adjust to the bright pink. I sit up, rubbing them as Chloe hands me a paper cup that smells like heaven. I set it on the nightstand, then take the other one in her hand and do the same before pulling her onto the bed. "What are you wearing?"

She laughs. "I was cold."

I nuzzle into her neck, kissing my way down. "Thank you for the coffee, you could've woke me up."

She runs her fingertips through the ends of my hair. "You were such a good boy last night, I thought you deserved some rest."

My cock hardens as she says *good boy*. That's a new one for me. My voice comes out rough as I grit out, "Say it again."

She brings her lips right to my ear, her breath a tickle. "Good boy."

I dive into her, my lips finding hers, my hands pulling her cozy new sweats down. When my mouth moves to her neck, she says, "Wait. Holden. Before…" She sighs as my fingers slip beneath her underwear. Her breaths are heavy. "Holden. There's a problem."

"Unless the problem is that my cock is not buried inside you right now, it can wait."

My fingers move, and she leans back. "Okay," she breathes out.

I sit up, taking my hand to either side of her underwear, when I freeze at the printing on the front. Right over where my mouth is about to be. *I'm taken.*

My cock is hard as a rock. "You are fucking taken, by me."

I yank her underwear down to her thighs and use my fingers to spread her open like the petals of a flower. I bring my mouth to her, and she cries out my name. I lick and swirl and suck as her hips squirm with pleasure underneath me. Once her breaths turn ragged, her movements desperate, my hand slips a finger inside her, then two. She's sopping wet.

"Is this all for me?"

"Yes," she moans, her chest heaving.

With my other hand, I reach for her perfect tits. Her nipples are as hard as my cock. She moans out my name, and I can't take it anymore. I reach for the side table and tear the condom with my teeth. I roll it on, my fingers still thrusting into her. My brain is stuck on the printing on her underwear. Yanking off her pants completely now, I throw the damn things across the room. I take her legs in my hands, coming to her core, but not entering.

"Say it."

She moans, her body writhing closer to my cock. "What?"

"Say you're mine. Say this pussy is mine."

"I've always been yours. All yours."

It feels better than it should, having her say that she's mine. I thrust inside her and am nearly blinded with the overwhelming sensation.

It's like she was made for me.

My cock swells even larger. For a moment, I pause, closing my eyes, just feeling her around me. I replay her voice in my head as I thrust hard. *I'm yours.* Thrust. *I'm yours.* Thrust. *I'm yours.*

She moans, running her fingertips down my chest, my skin burning a trail where she touches me.

I want to get it tattooed.

A trail of flowers everywhere her fingers roam.

She moves her hand up, and I catch her finger in my mouth, sucking lightly. Chloe takes her now wet fingers, moving them down and down. Through the center of my pecs, down the abs I've been working so hard in the gym for the past couple years, more for strength than aesthetics, but by the way she's touching them—reverently—I can tell they look good. I'd spend a thousand more hours to have her look at me like this for the rest of my life.

She keeps moving down, past the base of my cock, and to my balls. She cups them lightly at first, studying my face. God, it feels good. I might rethink the whole tattoo everywhere she's touched, though. She gives a small but forceful tug, and my eyes slam shut at the sensation.

I thrust deeper, harder. She lets go of my balls, her hands wringing the sheets in tight fists. She cries out my name as she clenches around me, and it's too much. I let go, crying out, squeezing her legs.

We both fall into a heap on the bed.

Her breaths are heavy, her chest moving up and down, her lips red and swollen. God, she's so hot, it almost gets me hard again.

She leans over to me, propping up on her side. Her perfect tits smashing together. I always considered myself a leg man, but with Chloe, it's everything. I reach out, taking her breast in my hand just to feel the soft fullness fill my palm.

"Holden, there's a storm."

I nod, but I'm mesmerized by her breasts, the way they move under my hand, her nipple pressing against my palm.

She moves to sit on top of me, taking my wrists in her hand and...now I'm hard again.

She leans over me, and I try to catch her breast in my mouth. "I need you to listen. At the coffee shop, people were saying it might be a hurricane."

"I gotta say, putting your tits in my face is not the best way to get me to listen."

"Point taken." She laughs and hops off me, heading for the

bathroom. "Look out the window. I don't know if we'll be able to leave the island today."

This gets my attention. We have to leave the island today. I have to be at that hotel tomorrow. And there's also that thing I arranged for Chloe. We have to go.

I get up off the bed, moving the curtains to the side a little. The ocean looks angry. White caps as far as the eye can see, wave after wave crashing onto the beach. The clouds are so dark, they're nearly black. No.

I call out to Chloe. "I'm going to talk to the front desk."

"Okay, I got you some underwear and sweats, too. They're in the bag."

I open the reusable shopping bag with a sunset printed on the side. Of course, she bought a reusable bag, too, because she's Chloe. Inside, I pull out a pair of tight black boxers that also say *I'm taken*. I slip them on, and the smile that takes over my face is not decent. It's too big. Too corny. But I can't help it. The way my heart fills with love for this woman is—

Wait. Love. I shake my head, slipping on the sweats. I'm getting way ahead of myself. This is a fling. A vacation hookup. What happens at sea, stays at sea. Or on the beach, in this case.

I hear the shower turn on in the bathroom, and I head out the door. The stench is overpowering. Somewhere close to rotten eggs, or putrid fish. I cover my mouth with my sleeve as I head into the main building. The same woman is working, her eyes a little tired this morning. She smiles as I approach. "Good morning, sir. How was your night?"

Flashes of my night come back to me. Chloe's legs wrapped around me, and despite being completely stressed, I smile. A big goofy grin that makes the woman at the counter nod knowingly. "It was great. We were hoping to head to St. Maarten's today."

Her lips turn down, a deep frown etched on her face. "Hmmm, that might not be possible."

My heart sinks, tugging my big-ass goofy grin with it.

She clicks a few things on her computer. "It looks like most of the big flights are either booked or canceled. Oh, well, there is one—"

"We'll take it. Can you book it from there?"

She waves her hand like the so-so gesture, and I'm not sure what that means. She picks up the phone and dials.

After what feels like too long for someone to possibly answer, she says, "Rick, are you flying in this?"

There's a pause, and then she says, "St. Maarten…Okay. Uh huh. I'll ask. I'll call you back."

She covers the phone with her palm. "He says this is going to get a lot worse as the day goes on. But he is willing to fly to St. Maarten as long as it's in the next thirty minutes."

"Yeah, okay. We can do that."

"And it'll cost you."

What about this free trip hasn't? "Understood."

She removes her palm and says, "I'll hand you over."

She pushes the phone toward me and passes me the receiver.

"You the idiot wanting to fly out in this shit?" The man on the other end sounds either drunk, hungover, or still half asleep. Maybe all three.

My stomach clenches. "That's me."

He chuckles. "Well, I'm the idiot who's going to take you."

He takes my credit card information and tells me to meet him at the airport in twenty-six minutes. Twenty-six minutes to pack (easy, we have no luggage) , find a taxi (also shouldn't be too hard), and convince Chloe to get on a tiny plane in the middle of a storm (shit).

CHLOE IS out of the shower by the time I come back, dressed in her ridiculous but absolutely adorable pink sweats. My best bet is just to sweep her up with momentum.

"Perfect," I say. "You're ready. Shoes on. We have to go."

"What?" She slips on her flip-flops at the very least while she asks. "Where are we going?"

"I booked us a luxury hotel." True-ish. "On St. Maarten's. We just have to catch a quick flight over there."

She freezes, one flip-flop on, one still in her hand. "We're flying?"

"Yes." I take the shoe and place it on the ground. She puts her foot in, and we head out the door.

She stops again. "In this?"

"Yeah, it should be good. The real storm isn't for a couple of hours. We'll be fine."

Chloe nods but looks unsure. I don't blame her. Maybe this isn't the best plan. If Rick says it'll be okay, it'll probably be fine. Right?

CHAPTER 23
CHLOE

We catch a cab to an airstrip by the water. It's not an airport, it's just one long runway. And sitting on that long runway is an itty-bitty plane. I look around for anything else that we could be flying in, because there's no way we're going to fit in that. The taxi stops, Holden gets out, but I'm frozen. My hand literally won't open the door.

My eyes scan for something, anything, larger than the plane on the runway. Holden opens my door for me, offering me a hand, and then I find it. Something larger. Almost. The man underneath the plane is twisting a wrench on one of the wheels.

I shake my head as Holden leads me closer to the "plane." He holds up a hand. "Rick?"

"Hey, hey." The man stands, and good lord, he is large. Not fat or anything, just all muscles. "There's my fellow idiot."

I look at Holden, and he shrugs. The man comes over with something in his hands, then lays it down at our feet once he's right in front of us. It's a scale.

"Okay, the plane's ready. I just need you to step on this baby, and we'll be on our way."

A scale?

Holden steps right on, and then it's my turn. Both men are

staring at me. I shake my head. "Why do you need to know my weight?"

"Weight distribution," Rick the Rock Johnson says. "Don't worry. I don't pay attention to the number. It just lets me know where everyone needs to sit."

I'm not particularly self-conscious about my weight; it's more the pulse-pounding fear that it matters. They both continue to stare at me as dark clouds move closer toward the shore, like they're rolling in with the tide. I step on, and Rick claps. "Okay, looks like you're in the co-pilot seat. Let's get a move on, we're burning daylight."

"Co-pilot?" The question comes out as a squeak.

He laughs. "You won't be flying the plane. You just have to sit up front to balance the weight."

Rick opens the side of the plane for me, like this is a normal, everyday occurrence, instead of the start of one of those survival shows.

He gives me a hand in, while Holden enters through the other door and climbs in the back. He sits in the seat right behind me. Once I buckle my seat belt, he puts a hand on my shoulder.

"It'll be okay," he whispers into my ear.

Rick closes my door, and I turn in my seat to face Holden. "I swear to God, if I die on this tiny plane, I'm going to murder you."

Holden doesn't give me any shit, even though he looks physically pained by trying to hide his smirk. "Got it."

Rick gets in, slamming the door shut. "Okay, party people. Let's go."

The plane rumbles to life. The vibration is so strong, I think it may rattle loose the tenuous bolts holding this hunk of metal together.

The dash in front of me lights up. It's covered in knobs and dials, a steering wheel jutting out toward me. I should not be sitting here. There is no scenario where I should be sitting behind the steering wheel of a plane.

The plane scoots down the runway, more like scurries. Bumps along, with spurts of speed. We're headed straight toward a field filled with brown grass and rocks. I slam my eyes shut, bracing for impact. Holden's fingers rest lightly on my shoulder. Then suddenly, we're airborne.

I open my eyes, and we're in the clouds, yet still bumping along like we're on asphalt.

Rick yells, "This'll all even out once we get higher."

Holden squeezes my shoulder, and I yell at him, "Where are your little whiskey bottles now?"

He chuckles, and something in my stomach loosens.

Rick yells, "There's rum under the seat."

Because of course there is.

"I'm okay."

There's a huge bump. Maybe this is really how I go, in this tiny metal can above the ocean. My mind flashes to Holden's hands on my breasts, his lips on mine, his…everything. At least I got to sleep with him before I die. Why didn't we just stay in the little pink bungalow?

Then the plane ascends higher, barreling through the clouds. The sky opens up, and it's blue. So vivid blue. Beneath us, there's a mountain of clouds.

Holden moves his hand, and I instantly miss it. Now that my thoughts aren't torn between fearing for my life and obsessing about Holden, I can just full-on fixate on Holden. What are we doing?

I mean, I know what we did. And I know that I'm the one who was pushing for it with all that *let's give in* bullshit.

But was it bullshit? I have wanted Holden my entire adult life. If I'm being completely honest, I kind of thought that we could get it out of our system, as Dee said. That once we slept together, we'd be good. I'd be cured. No more lusting after Holden.

So far, that is not the case. By the way he took me this morning, I'd say it's not for him either.

It's a weekend thing. A vacation thing. Once we're back home,

I'm sure the spell will be broken. I glance over my shoulder. Holden is looking out the window, a small smile tugging at the corner of his mouth.

He catches me looking, and the smile widens. He throws me a wink, and those damn butterflies are back.

As SOON AS I'm almost used to the jostles and bumps of our flight, the plane plummets.

Not dips, not bounces. Full-on plummets.

Holden grips my seat behind me. "Whoa."

"Ah, yeah," Rick bellows, far too cheerful for the current situation we find ourselves in. "Descent is a little rough. Tighten your belts and hold on to your butts."

I twist around in my seat, my face feeling numb like it's gone to sleep.

Holden leans forward, his breath warm against the shell of my ear, and whispers, "Did he just quote *Jurassic Park*?"

"I…" Another violent plunge swallows my answer and leaves my stomach somewhere in the clouds. I squeeze my eyes shut and pray, something I haven't done since before Mom died.

God, hey. I know it's been a while. This can't be how I die. I know I said it would be okay dying because I finally—finally—boned Holden, and while that is monumentous, I was kidding. I can't die before I've even bloomed. What would Mom say if she were around to say it? I would like to live long enough to make her proud. To find my purpose. And maybe if I'm lucky, bone Holden at least one more time.

Sorry for all the boning talk.

The plane lurches again.

Holden's fingers slide from my seat to my shoulder. I grab his hand, reach behind me, and hold it, our fingers intertwined tightly.

Another massive thud jostles the plane, sending a sharp vibration all the way down to my tailbone. For a brief moment, I think maybe I've been struck dead for talking about boning to God.

The shaking becomes the scream of wheels against asphalt. I open my eyes. The runway rushes beneath us in streaks of gray and the hazy shimmer of heat.

"Here we are. St. Maarten, as promised," Rick says.

I inhale a slow, steady breath. We made it. I'm alive.

My pulse still pounds in my ears as we climb out of the plane and onto the tarmac.

Behind us is a white sand beach, the sea sparkling in the sunshine. The only hint of the storm we left is the dark clouds far off on the horizon. The sun is fierce, hot against my cheeks despite it still being before noon.

On the other side of a chain-link fence, the beach is filled with people. Sprawled on towels. Lounging in plastic chairs. Drinks sweating in their hands. Bobbing lazily in the shallows.

Holden holds out his hand to Rick for a handshake, but Rick pulls him in for a hug. He wraps me in a hug as well, and now we're in an odd sort of group hug that smells like Old Spice, coconut, and rum. "You two be good."

"No promises," Holden says with a smirk.

Rick heads back to the plane, and Holden stares at me.

"You okay?"

My heart has slowed, but I have an odd buzzing feeling. Like, my senses are still on high alert. Like, at any moment, I may still drop from the sky. I bite my lip, assessing. "I'm not sure."

"You look pale."

"Gee, thanks." I frown. Not only do I not feel great, but apparently, I don't look great either.

"No…I mean, do you need to sit?"

"Maybe."

Holden puts his arm around me and leads me to the beach. He finds a pair of chairs not spoken for and guides me to sit in one. He even adjusts the umbrella above it to shade my eyes. "You good? This okay?" Holden asks.

I look out at the expanse of soft white sand and turquoise water. Then at the handsome man asking me the question. This is actually pretty good. I smile. "I am."

"You okay if I make a few calls?"

Calls to whom? That's what I want to say. But what I do say is, "Sure."

Holden steps away while I kick off my flip-flops, roll up my pants, and head to the ocean, stepping in. The water is cool on my toes; the day is really heating up. It's so humid here. I'm wishing I had my suit on underneath these sweats instead of these underwear. Although Holden *really* likes the underwear. The rhythmic lapping at my feet soothes the buzzing of my nerves.

I watch as Holden goes back to the chairs where I put my flip-flops. His face etched with stress lines. I make my way back to the chairs. He smiles at me. "You look like you're feeling better."

I nod. "Should we get suits and jump in the water? Is the storm headed this way?"

Holden points toward the horizon of dark clouds. "It might be. I have a better idea anyway. Come on."

CHAPTER 24
CHLOE

Holden makes catching a cab look easy. He makes most things look easy. The car whirs down the narrow roads, leaving the beach behind and traveling through colorful buildings. Lemon yellow, mint green, powder blue, and pink. It's beautiful. Fortune Falls needs more color on Main Street. Fewer white houses and more pink. I was neutral about pink before this trip, but now I love it. It reminds me of these sweats, the ones Holden so expertly yanked off of me. It reminds me of the ridiculous cruise that forced us to confront what we've been pretending doesn't exist for decades. Our feelings.

Wait, not feelings. Crush. Lust. It's a get-it-out-of-our-system vacation fling. That's it.

We arrive in front of a pale-pink building with large front windows and a sign swinging in the faint breeze with a pair of ballerina slippers on it. Holden pays the cabbie, thanking him in Spanish, and looks at me, beaming.

I look at him, my eyes narrowed. "What's going on?"

His smile grows. "You'll see."

We head in through the open door to a small room with beautiful hardwood floors. And the sharp scent of wood polish and rosin nearly sends me to my knees; it shoots me so fast and far back in the past.

A woman in a purple leotard with braids tied up on top of her head strides out of the back with a wide smile on her face. "This must be the lovebirds."

I look at Holden, and he smiles. Then he holds out his hand to the woman. "Maria. It's so nice to finally meet you. Thank you for being flexible with the day."

Finally? What is going on?

She waves at him. "We're here every day. Made no difference to me."

"This is my fiancée, Chloe." He motions to me, and I'm so lost I feel like Alice falling down the rabbit hole.

I hold out my hand to the woman, and she shakes it, her palm as warm as her smile. "It's so lovely to meet you. We better get moving, though, the kids will start arriving any minute." She looks me up and down, and I can feel the wrinkle on my forehead deepen. Kids? "Are you small or extra small?"

"What?" I mean, I am, but what?

"Leotard, hun."

"Oh, small."

She heads to the back, and my eyes fly to Holden.

He steps closer, whispering, "I told her that you, my fiancée, were interested in opening a dance studio back home and asked if it would be okay if you sat in on one of her classes."

I blink, once, twice, trying to absorb the information, but before I can, Maria is back with tights and a pale-pink leotard draped over her arm. "Here you go. You can change in the back. Like I told Holden, I'm more than happy to have you here, but you gotta work, girl." She hands me the garments, then goes to Holden and turns him toward the door. "And no looky-loos, so, Holden, goodbye. See you in an hour."

Holden throws a pleading look over his shoulder. Pleading for what, I'm not sure. My forgiveness that he made this plan without discussing it with me, that now I'm stuck with Maria and this upcoming class, whether I like it or not. I watch him go.

Then she turns to me. "Change, girl."

I go in the back and slip on the tights, smoothing them over the scar on my upper thigh from the broken glass of the windshield. I slip on the leotard next, and it has the oddest feeling of stepping in the front door after walking in the rain, the smell of fresh cookies baking. It feels like home.

Shrieks of laughter and a chatter of voices come from the front, and nerves fizzle in my stomach. Can I do this? What exactly does she want me to do?

I head out front, and once I'm in the thick of it, there's no time to think. Two little girls run around the space, one in purple, one in pink, both in tutus almost larger than they are.

Maria smiles, placing a hand on my arm. "It's mostly four- and five-year-olds in this class. These are the twins."

The next hour is filled with tutus twirling, pudgy legs running in tights, music, and laughter. At one point, Maria has me demonstrate a grand jete, and the gasp that the girls let out fills my chest with pride. Each girl then gets to take their turn trying it out. It's wonderful, and even though they're all very young, some show real promise. And Maria waters it like they're all her little flowers. Showering each with praise and constructive instruction.

At the end of class, we all sit in a circle and thank each other for the dancing. A little girl places her hand in mine. It's warm and a little clammy, but it's so sweet.

Once all the girls leave, Maria turns to me. "You're a natural."

I smile and blink away the tears forming in my eyes. "Thanks."

"When are you opening your studio?"

"I…" When am I opening my studio? Can I really do this?

Holden walks back in, an iced coffee in each hand. His eyes find mine, and a question hangs there. *Was this okay? Did I overstep?*

I smile at Holden, hoping that my face conveys that it was perfect.

Maria is still waiting for my answer, so I turn to her and the answer comes out of me like it's been nestled in my heart and just waiting for the opportune moment to come flying out. "Hopefully this fall."

And it feels right. Could I have my own dance studio by fall?

Maria places a hand on my shoulder. "It's going to be amazing. Let me know if you have any questions."

I swallow around a lump in my throat. "Thank you…for everything. This was so generous, really."

She smiles, a big, toothy grin. "Thank that man over there."

I use the back room to change back into my sundress, stuffing my sweats and the leotard that Maria insisted I keep into my tote.

When I come out, I take the iced coffee from Holden's hand and slip mine in its place. I take a sip as we walk out the door into the afternoon. It's just a little sweet with the perfect amount of milk. The sky has clouded over, and there's a charge to the air that makes the tiny hairs on my arm stand on end. Is it the storm on the way here, or is it this man next to me?

"How did you arrange all that?" I ask, genuinely in awe of how he put this all together in the middle of the Atlantic.

"That stupid pink outfit was so I could use the staff phone. It was originally scheduled for the day we got into port, but she was able to move it to today. How was it?" Holden asks.

I take his hand and tug him down the street, past somewhere I noticed in the cab ride over. Down a narrow alley, between two colorful buildings.

There's a deep groove between Holden's brows. "Was it not good? I didn't mean to overstep…"

I take his coffee out of his hand and set mine down as well, near our feet.

"I thought it could kind of give you an idea of what could be possible. You wouldn't have to just teach kids. You could do adult classes too."

I back Holden up to a colorfully painted wall, a sweeping mural of a rising tide in blues and greens behind him. Bringing my hands to where his sharp jaw meets his neck, I stand on tiptoe and kiss him. Gentle at first, delicate as a flower petal, softly floating through the air. I whisper as if his lips could hear me, "Thank you."

I go in again, and he meets me, his lips pressing into mine. Hungry. He opens his mouth, and our tongues collide. Like we've both been waiting hours for this. And by the press of his (already) hard length into me, I think it's safe to say we both have.

His hands move down my back, cupping my ass. I bring my mouth down to his neck, and he hoists me up, gripping me firmly. God, I love his hands. They're so large, so strong. But this, right now, is supposed to be me thanking him. So I wriggle down and press him against the wall with both hands, his lips are bee-sting swollen, parted slightly, like they are still searching for mine. I kiss him once softly, and his hands reach for me, but I bat them away. "*Let* me thank you."

I move my hands down, underneath the shorts he must've changed into while I was in class, underneath the boxers, and there he is. Hard as a rock, and all for me. He groans as I touch him. "Chloe. We're tucked away, but anyone could walk by."

I touch him, one long firm stroke, and watch as his eyes flutter. "You'll have to keep watch then." I move his shorts and boxers down as I slowly come to a squat, bringing the tip of his erection to my lips.

Instead of watching the street beyond, he watches me, his eyes fixed on my mouth. I close my eyes and open wide, taking him inside, stroking lightly with my tongue. Teasing.

He lets out a low animal sound, and my core pulses. I start to move, my hand and my mouth in sync, sliding over him, as he gets even larger, his cock swelling in my mouth. I look up at him, and he's still watching me with rapt attention. He tucks a strand of hair behind my ear. I open wider, taking him in deeper, and he moans.

My core clenches again, so tight, then when he tugs at my arm to stand, I don't fight him. He kisses me deeply as I keep stroking him. He covers my hand. "I was able to check in early to the hotel. It's right around the corner."

And for the first time, I notice he doesn't have his backpack. "Let's go."

He puts himself away, using the waistband of the shorts to hide his giant erection. He holds my hand, and we get the coffees, walking down the road, past the colorful buildings toward the beach.

I tug on his arm. "Let's run."

He shakes his head. "This is the pace I have. All my blood is currently occupied."

I laugh. We head down the beach, straight to what looks like a white stone palace. Holden takes my hand, leading me to the road, through the grand lobby, with white marble floors that gleam and a fountain trickling in the middle of the space. But there's no time to stop and gawk. Holden is still tugging my hand, his eyes hungry, and the ache between my legs grows. The woman seated at the desk smiles at us. "Ah, welcome back. Would you like that welcome drink now?"

Holden shakes his head. "No thanks."

"Shall I send some champagne to the villa?"

"Yes, please." He leads me straight out the back to a gentleman waiting for us in a golf cart.

"Villa twelve, please." We sit, and I place my hand high on Holden's thigh. He swallows hard, croaking out, "Hurry."

The wind, as the golf cart moves, rushes my hair back, little drops of rain with it speckling my cheeks.

The ride is quick, and Holden leads me down a stone path into a secluded garden that surrounds me in the fragrant smell of plumeria. My mouth falls open as I take in the large two-story "villa."

Holden takes his finger and turns my face toward him, catching my mouth with his. His thumbs move beneath the straps of my dress, lifting and moving each off, exposing my bikini top beneath. His pupils swell as his hands move to my breast, lifting one out of the triangle and then the other. The sprinkle has turned into a full-on rain, and my nipples pebble as drop after drop hits them, at that and at the way Holden is looking at me.

His gaze tears away from my breasts to my eyes. "Your tits are amazing."

I smile. "You're not supposed to reuse compliments. It's against the rules."

He pulls his wet shirt over his head, his muscles rippling with the motion, and steps closer. "Isn't all of this?"

He pulls me toward him, his slick skin pressed to mine, and kisses me.

CHAPTER 25
HOLDEN

Chloe's mouth is hot on mine, her breasts are pressed against me, and if I don't have her right now, I may come in my pants. My hands move to her back, tugging her dress down the rest of the way. She moves her feet, stepping out of it. The rain is getting stronger, and a large crack of thunder rattles my bones.

As much as I want to fuck her right here, we need to move inside. I take her hand and lead her to the heavy wooden door. And as I shut it behind us, I press her into the wall, kissing her deeply. She moans into my mouth, and it's painful how hard it makes me. I move my thumbs down to her underwear and get on my knees as I pull them down slowly. She watches me, leaning against the wall, her nipples hard, her stomach taut. I want to feel her wrapped around me. But first, I want to make her feel as good as she made me feel outside the dance studio.

I take my fingers, spreading her wide open, then bring my mouth to her. She gasps, I look up, and her hands are on her breasts. It makes me pick up the speed, licking, sucking, and nipping.

She yells out my name, "Holden."

I keep going, sensing she's close.

"Holden, fuck me."

I don't stop.

Then she moans, "Please."

That undoes me. That one little please. I'd do anything she'd ask right now. If I'm being completely honest with myself, I'd do anything she asked anytime, not just like this.

I pull a condom out of my back pocket, then push down my pants and boxers, letting them fall to the floor. Her eyes go wide as I roll it on. "You had that the whole time? We could've—"

I grab her hips, flipping her around, her hands braced on the wall. "I didn't want to fuck you in that dirty alley, where anyone could see you. No one sees these tits but me."

Reaching around, I squeeze one hard as my other hand finds her hip, lining us up. Her back arches, like she's trying to seek out my cock. I enter her, slowly, letting the moment drag like my cock against the walls of her. She cries out, and I keep pressing, pushing into her as she opens up for me.

Once she's almost to the base of me, I pull out quick and she heaves.

My hand finds her ass with a loud smack. "No one sees this ass but me."

"Yes," she breathes out as I enter her again, bit by bit filling her up, until I'm completely inside her. She clenches around me, and I start to move faster, thrusting in and out, deeper and deeper.

"No one sees this pussy but me."

"Yes. Oh, God."

I move both hands to her hips, moving her toward me as I thrust, her hands clawing up the wall, her tits swinging. I watch them bounce, hitting the wall with a smack, and I need her nipple in my mouth. I pull out. Turn her around and lift her up, pressing her into the wall. My cock enters her again as my mouth finds the firm bud of her nipple. I lick then suck.

She cries out my name over and over, and I try, with what little blood is in my brain, to record it. To remember this. My name on her lips. Her.

She clenches around me, so tight I groan. I move my mouth up her neck and pull back, so I can look in her face as she tilts her head back, her ecstasy taking over her whole body, sending shivers through her. It's too much, I can't hold back anymore.

Every muscle in my body tightens as I come. We stay frozen, her still hoisted up against the wall, my arms shaking.

She goes to move out of my arms, but I grip tighter. "Just another moment. I'm not ready."

Her hands trail down my back, fingernails against slick skin, leaving goosebumps in their wake.

Once I've caught my breath, I gently set her down. We both look at each other. Her face is searching mine for an answer I don't know how to give, but it's a question she's not asking. Neither of us wants to break the spell of whatever this is.

"Shower?"

She smiles. "Yes, please."

And there it is again. That lit*tle please* that I want to bite off her lips, like a cat that's been shown too much affection. My heart swells with it. I take her hand again, because I can't stop touching her, and lead her through this ridiculous villa to the bathroom, which is bigger than the one in my house.

WE'RE LYING on the enormous bed, in the silky robes provided, sipping flutes of champagne, candles lit (more due to lack of power than anything romantic, but two birds one stone), and watching the storm roil outside.

Chloe snuggles into me, and I set my champagne flute down so I can pull her in closer, placing my arm around her.

She sighs. "That class was so fun."

The smile that spreads across my face warms me all the way down to my chest. It was a gamble, the whole plan really. It might've failed miserably, and she could've been pissed at me for butting in where I'm not welcome. "I'm glad you enjoyed it."

She looks up at me, the candlelight kissing her cheek. "Do you think I can really do it?"

"What? Have your own studio?"

She nods quietly.

I pull her in closer. "Yeah. One hundred percent. If I can run my own brewery, you can absolutely run your own studio. You're way smarter than me."

And she is. I can picture her now, walking down Main Street in a black leotard and one of her ridiculously large sweaters, fiery leaves falling from the tree behind her, headed for her very own dance studio. Once she's done for the day, the last class taught, all the little ones on their way home practicing their jumps and twirls, she'll head for the bar. She'll come in with a tired smile on her face, happy, fulfilled, exhausted. I remember the feeling well from the first days at the brewery, where it was just me, Granddad, Kyle, and a dream. Kyle helped out so much those first few years.

If this thing between Chloe and me is real, I know Kyle will be okay with it. But what if it doesn't last? I'll lose them both.

"I am *not* smarter than you." She laughs, and I can feel some of the tension leave her shoulders. "You're doing amazing. The brewery is thriving. How many people even work there now?"

I grunt. Because I don't want to argue, and while the brewery is doing good, I tried to grow the beer line too fast, sunk a ton of money into new equipment, and now I really need to pay some of it back. And I really need to pay all those people I employ. Good people. With families of their own. They all deserve raises, bonuses, and better insurance. (Although they assure me the one I picked is great.) And I'd like to expand. Have an actual space and not just a tasting room.

Which is why I need to get that sample to Gio. I wriggle my arm out from under Chloe and head to the window. Rain moves across the waves in great gusts. The waves are huge, pounding the beach one after another. How will my package even get here in this?

Chloe joins me, placing a hand on my back. "Hey, where'd you go?"

I shake my head, not wanting to burden her with my worries. "Just watching the storm."

Her eyes move slowly, reluctantly, from my face to the sea. "Yeah, it's pretty nuts. Are we okay this close to the ocean? I mean, I know we're like hundreds of feet away, but..."

That question is all I need to get going. Something to take care of. Something I can do instead of spiraling about...everything. Exactly what I need. I move to get the sweats that Chloe so thoughtfully got for me.

Her rosebud lips are parted in a small O. "Where are you going?"

"I'm going to ask about the storm and maybe grab us some food. Are you hungry?"

Her mouth closes, and she nods.

"Perfect." I slip on my shoes, moving quickly now. "I'll get us some food and ask about the power and the storm, and then I'll be back."

"Holden, is everything all right?"

No. It's really not. I think I royally fucked just about every aspect of my life up. But I'm not going to make Chloe worry.

A crash of thunder rattles the windows.

Chloe's brows furrow, and she crosses her arms tightly around herself. "I don't think you should go out there in this."

"It's just to the lobby. It's fine." I walk over and place a soft kiss on her forehead, right where her adorable worry wrinkle lives. I want to kiss it away.

But it's still there as I pull back. It's still there when I turn to look at her as I walk through the bedroom door.

***

THERE IS no golf cart waiting to take me to the lobby. I duck my head against the wind and the rain, shove my hands into the pockets of my sweats, and march on. What am I going to do? Even if Chloe and I keep this casual, which we have to, I'm going to have to tell Kyle. It'd be so much worse if he found out another way.

I squint against the relentless spray of water to my face. What am I even doing? I stop walking and take a deep breath. I am seeing if my beer can still get here. I am making a plan for how I'm going to tell my best friend I slept with his little sister, and then I'll figure out how to tell Chloe that our vacation fling has to stay on vacation. What happens at sea, stays at sea.

Easy. Right?

Fuck.

I start to walk again when a sudden sharp pain erupts on the side of my temple.

CHAPTER 26
HOLDEN

My hand flies to my head as I watch the coconut that just hit me fall to the ground and roll away on another gust of wind.

Just what I need.

I make it to the lobby, soaking wet. Behind the desk, the woman's mouth falls open, and she rushes over, the radio behind her crackling. "Sir, you're bleeding."

I bring my hand down, and sure enough, my hand is covered in blood. I knew it was wet, but I thought it was the rain. My knees wobble at the sight of it, and the woman pushes me to a chair. She's back a moment later with a towel.

I hold it to my head and try to find my thoughts. The package, the storm, the ocean. "I have a package coming."

She shakes her head.

I pull out my phone to show her the tracking number, but I can't pull up the email. There are absolutely no bars of service, just a small SOS in the corner of the screen. I can't even pull up the email with the tracking number, let alone track the package.

The woman sits in the chair across from me. "No packages are getting here in this.

I look out the window. The palm trees are bent at a stiff angle.

"Are we okay this close to the ocean?" I ask.

She sighs and motions to the radio. "It should pass in a day or so. Everyone is saying it's just a tropical storm, the hurricane is going to miss us. We should be fine. We look closer to the ocean than we are. There's a cliff, the actual beach is a trek. We'll be okay."

In a day or so.

"We're supposed to meet up with our ship. We were on a cruise and we—" Fucked around and found out. Missed the ship. And instead of flying us home, I brought us here. To get the beer sample that may never arrive. God, what a mess.

The woman is shaking her head, again, and I wonder how much bad news she's had to give today. "I can try to call, if you like, but I'm pretty sure they'll divert to another port."

I'm not sure what my face is doing besides bleeding, but I must look pitiful because she gives me a very sad smile and rises.

"I'll see if I can get anyone. The phone lines are still working, so that's good."

"Great."

I hold the towel up to my face. It's all just great.

She speaks in impossibly fast Spanish on the phone. I can only pick out words here and there, but what I do understand is no bueno.

After a few minutes, the woman sits across from me again, this time looking less sad and more businesslike. Like her phone conversation gave her confidence. Much like this little mission was supposed to do for me. "Sir, The Shipped Ship is diverting to Grand Turk. After that, they head back to Old San Juan. They said you are welcome to meet up with them there or they can ship your things to you, free of charge, of course."

Of course.

Fuck.

Then I remember my other mission—food. "What about food? My…" I can't bring myself to say fiancée. I can't keep pretending. "Chloe is hungry."

She smiles. This one seems genuine and warm. "The fridge should be fully stocked, as well as the pantry. Is it not?"

I haven't checked. The champagne was in an ice bucket on the counter, two glasses next to it. "I'm sure it is. We…" We were too busy screwing to notice. Too brain-dead from multiple orgasms to even think to look.

"If it's not, just let me know. We're not using the golf carts in this. Are you okay to walk back? Would you like me to get someone to walk with you?"

I shake my head, moving out of the door just as two more rain-drenched guests are coming in, their faces falling when they clock the closed bar. Another problem for the woman with the sympathetic face to fix.

I head back out in the storm, the rain cool on my face. It actually feels nice. My temple throbs from where the coconut hit me.

What am I going to do? Gio's going to write me off as a flake if I not only don't deliver the sample but am never to be heard from again.

Wait, the phone. The landline. Maybe I can call Gio and explain what happened. It's funny, really. Except I don't know his number.

But Chloe's bartender friend would. And Chloe might have her number.

The walk back feels like it takes twice as long. When I finally trudge up the stone walk to the villa, the sky is dark, not just from clouds. Night has settled upon us.

The villa glows a warm, inviting orange. I open the door. There is a fire in the hearth, and Chloe is in the kitchen, something fragrant sizzling on the stove top. She is dancing around the kitchen to a song that must be in her head, humming lightly, peering into an open cupboard that, as promised, is filled with food.

I can't help but smile. She's so freaking cute.

She turns and catches me staring, with this big-ass goofy grin. "What?" she asks.

"Nothing." I shrug.

She motions to the kitchen. "I found food. And the fireplace and the stove all work. They must be gas."

I nod. "Must be. What are you making? Omelets?"

A tomato is lobbed in my direction. "Oh, my God. Stop." Then her eyes find the side of my head. I thought it was mostly cleaned up. Guess not. "What the hell happened?"

She flies into my arms, her finger gently finding the tender spot on my head. I flinch. "It was a coconut."

"Are you okay?"

I bring my hands around her waist, pulling her closer into me, my rain-soaked sweats getting her satin robe wet, but I don't mind. I hope she doesn't either. She wraps her arms around my neck, her fingertips finding the edge of my jaw, the ends of my hair. Her touch is feather-light and full of care. My voice is husky as I say, "I am now."

She brings her lips to mine. The food can wait. The plan, the beer, the making sure this all stays on vacation. It can all wait.

I sink into her, her breath mingling with mine. I switch off the stove, then hoist her up onto the counter. She lets out a little "oooh" as her ass hits the marble.

I fiddle with the sash of her robe, untying it slowly. "I got your robe all wet."

She breathes out a little laugh. "That's not the only thing you got wet."

She draws out the last word like one long stroke, and it makes me instantly hard. This woman is going to kill me.

I pull off the sash and throw it to the ground, opening up her robe. I run my hands over her perfect tits. God, I can't stop looking at them. I take one in each hand, lifting and squeezing. She moans, throwing her head back, her hair cascading in a wave over her shoulder.

I move my hands, taking down one shoulder then the next, removing her robe. I stand and look at her, unable to comprehend how lucky I am that I get to touch her.

I stare for so long she shifts on the counter, and the robe falls to the ground. "Are you just going to look…or…"

A smile tugs at my lips. "Do you want me to touch you?"

She nods.

"Show me how."

Chloe moves her hands to her breasts, tentatively at first, just a light touch. Then she squeezes them together, her nipples trapped between her fingers, her chest rising and falling with her breath.

I take off my wet sweatshirt and kick off my wet sweats while I watch her. She moves one hand down her stomach slowly. Spreading her legs on the marble counters, she brings her hand between her thighs and starts to swirl.

My cock is throbbing. I push my boxers down, letting them fall to the floor.

She puts one finger inside and cries out, "Oh God."

I clench my jaw. I need to touch her, to be inside her, to feel her around me. I grab my cock and stroke. The condoms are in the other room. I point at her, squinting. "Don't move. I'll be right back."

She gives me a devilish smile, moving her finger in and out. "Not even like this."

I run, full-on run, despite my giant erection. The condom is already on by the time I get back to the kitchen, and she's moved. But I'm not mad about it.

She's standing next to the counter, bent over, her fingers still working between her thighs, her pert little ass just waiting for me.

I come up behind her, putting my hands on her hips, running one over her smooth ass. I move her hand to stop her from pleasuring herself. All the pleasure will come from me now. I place her hands on the counter and bend her over, until her tits are smashed against the cool marble.

"I told you not to move." My voice is rough, gravely.

"I didn't obey," she says, looking back at me, a spark in her eye. This woman.

"Naughty girl." I take my hand and swiftly smack her on the

ass. She moans, and it's smooth and velvety. The sound does something to me, and whatever control I had is gone.

I line myself up with her entrance and thrust inside all the way to the base as she cries out, "Holden."

My name on her lips is a gift. I grab onto her hips, bringing her against me as I push into her over and over. It feels so good. But I want more. I want her body pressed into mine. I'm jealous of the counter.

I pull out, and she whines. I turn her around and lift her up, pressing her body into mine. It feels like sweet relief. She wraps her legs around me, and I walk us by the fire. I sit on the couch with her on my lap. She moves a little, and we adjust, finding just the right spot, as she lowers onto me. I run my hand down her back. I let her set the pace. I realize with blinding clarity that I have no control over this. No say in how much I love having her body wrapped around mine, her skin touching my skin.

This doesn't feel like a vacation. This—her—feels like home.

CHAPTER 27
CHLOE

Holden's eyes are dark as I lower onto him, over and over. His hands wrap around my hips, his fingers brushing my ass.

I've never been this needy. I want his hands everywhere all at once. I want him to fill me up. I never want him to stop. His gaze on me is too much. I have too many questions when I look into his eyes. I move off of him, and he groans. "Where are you going?"

I turn around, taking a shaky breath, giving him a view of my ass as I bend over. "I'm not going anywhere."

I stare at the fire as I brace my hands on his thighs and lower onto him from behind. His hard length moves inside me, and his groan tells me he likes the new angle.

I lower onto him over and over, the flames from the fire dancing.

Holden calls out my name. His hands grab my hips. He spins me around and places a hand on my face tenderly.

His eyes are unavoidable. I stare into them. I'm lost. He holds me close as he rocks into me. The friction of my body moving on top of his hard length inside me sends me over the edge. I still, pulsing around him and he groans out my name over and over.

I can't help thinking how much I'm going to miss having him say my name like this. Getting to have him like this.

Once we are back in silky robes, lying by the fire, I'm watching the flames again, and he's tracing a line down my hip. There's an odd energy to the air, something more than the electric charge of the storm. While we were having sex earlier, something shifted. I can't describe it. It was tender. It was emotional. It sounds so sappy to say, but it really felt like we were making love.

This thing between us feels a lot like love. It's a ridiculous sentiment...or is it? Maybe, just maybe, this vacation fling between me and Holden could be something real.

I turn around, tracing the opening of his robe, my eyes finding the cut on his temple. "What happened again?"

He chuckles, his hand moving toward it. "A coconut."

I laugh. "It hit you from the sky?"

"Yes, it did." Something in his face changes. "There was some other news..."

I sit up, wrapping my robe tighter around me. "News?"

Holden sits up too. "Yeah, so it turns out the ship isn't stopping here."

I feel like I misheard him. "What?"

"The Shipped Ship was diverted to another port because of the storm."

I laugh. This is crazy. "You're kidding."

He shakes his head. He's fidgeting with the end of his robe, and he almost seems nervous. I wonder if he thinks I'll be upset. I put my finger under his chin, bringing his eyes to meet mine. "Hey, it's fine, right? I'm still having a great time on this vacation. We don't need to be on the ship to have fun."

I waggle my eyebrows up and down, and he cracks a smile, but there's still something going on.

"Did you leave something important on the ship?"

He shakes his head. "They'll mail us all our stuff. I guess this kind of thing happens a fair amount. Once the weather clears, we can fly home from here. The thing is, there's this guy..."

My stomach sinks. What is he talking about? "What?"

"No." He holds up his hands. "God, you're looking at me like I owe a card shark or something. He's the man who picks the beer the ships serve. They have this cruise in the Caribbean, but they also have an Alaskan cruise near us."

I nod and start to move to the kitchen. We still haven't eaten, and I should make something. "Cool."

Holden follows me. "Yeah, so I was trying to get him a sample of Woodshed. If he selected us, it could be big. That kind of contract could really put us on the map."

There's a tightness in my chest, and I'm not sure why. I get out the tofu to fry up. Holden is still explaining, his words getting faster the more he talks.

"That's why I had this hotel booked. I was going to ship the beer here."

This hotel was not a romantic plan for me. I'm so stupid. Of course it wasn't.

Holden clears his throat. "With the storm, though, it can't get here."

"Right," I say.

"Do you have that bartender's number? The one you made friends with."

My mind is still trying to catch up. "Who was shipping the beer?"

"Kyle arranged it, with some of the guys from Woodshed."

I slice the tofu. "How?"

"When I used the staff phone."

It's stupid. It's childish. But my heart squeezes. He didn't put on that silly pink outfit and sneak around to use the phone for me. It was for work. Apparently, he's been working this whole time.

It's fine.

Of course, it's fine.

He owns his own business, he has to work all the time. Will it be like that when I own my own studio? Probably. No time to stop and enjoy someone's company. My focus will always be divided.

"So," he says, coming to sit on one of the barstools. "Do you have it?"

"Dee's number? Yeah." I grab a zucchini from the fridge and slice it. A tofu vegetable scramble it is. "Do you think cell phones will work in this weather?"

"No," Holden says, then goes to look out the window. "Maybe in the morning the storm will have cleared, and they will. Or we can use the phone in the lobby?"

"Sounds good." My tone is clipped. I can hear it. But there's not a damn thing I can do about it. I find a pepper and slice it.

Holden turns back to me, his eyes wary. "Are you pissed?"

I frown. I am pissed. I have no real reason to be, but I am. "No," I say.

Holden chuckles. "Yes, you are."

"No, I'm not."

"Chloe, your body is tense, and you're slicing that pepper like it personally wronged you. What is it? Would it be weird to call your friend? I hate to ask, really. I just don't want to seem like a flake to this guy."

I nod. That all makes sense. Why *am* I mad? "I can call Dee, it's fine."

Holden comes over and wraps his arms around me, kissing my neck. "Thank you." He turns me to face him, his blue eyes blazing into mine. "You are a really good friend."

I laugh. "Is that your compliment for the day?"

He smirks, moving his hand under my robe and giving my nipple a playful pinch. "You said I couldn't use tits anymore."

A small laugh escapes me as I turn back to the stove. I try to relax. To let my muscles relax. To enjoy his mouth on my neck as I fry us up the most basic stir-fry, but there's this shadow now over the whole thing. We're going to head home in a few days, and he will once again be all consumed with the brewery. And I will be back to being his best friend's little sister.

THE STORM HAS EASED. The wind has died down completely, and the landscape looks different with the palm trees upright and the ocean calm. I let Holden sleep in, and I'm headed to the lobby to call Dee, since my cell phone still doesn't have any service.

The lights are on in the lobby, so the power must be back. The woman is very kind when I ask to use the phone. She also points out a desktop computer on a small desk in the corner that is free for guest use. I thank her and sit, pulling out my phone to get Dee's number.

It picks up on the second ring, and I tell her it's me. "There you are. I thought you died. Where have you been? Wait, don't answer that, I have theories."

"Hi to you, too." But I'm interested. "Okay, what are your theories?"

"Okay, first guess, you and Holden have been holed up in your room, not faking a damn thing."

I laugh. "You're half right. We're not in our room."

"What? Where the hell are you?"

"We missed the boat. We're in St. Maarten staying at the Sunset Beach Club."

Dee whistles, and the sound crackles through the receiver. "Wow. That place is fancy."

"Yeah, it really is."

Dee sighs. "He must've really wanted to impress you."

The noise that leaves my body is somewhere between a scoff and a laugh. "No, that's not what this was," I tell her everything. About us the past few days, about the compliments, and the kisses, and the dance studio. Finally, I explain about the beer sample and ask if she can get a message to Gio. But my tone must give me away somehow.

"I can talk to Gio, that's no problem. I can also give you all his contact info to give to Holden. Gio won't care if he gets a sample now or in two months. He just cares about the beer. Can I ask, why after having what sounds to me like an amazing time with a hottie hot man, you sound like you're on your way to your own funeral?"

Aren't I? Maybe not my funeral, but whatever this thing between Holden and me is. We'll head back to Fortune Falls, and all of our steamy times will stay here to wither and die, to live only in our memories. But I don't say any of that to Dee. Tears prick the back of my eyes, and an unfiltered sob comes out. "I don't want to lose him. But he's been working on this deal the whole time, behind my back, it feels like maybe I never had him to begin with."

Dee's voice comes over the line as a low rhythmic "hmmm." A full minute of silence follows. It stretches on so long, I wonder if we were disconnected.

"Dee?"

"Yep. Thinking how to put this without hurting your feelings."

Oh no. My muscles tense. "Me? What did I do?"

"Look, hun. I'm the last person that should be doling out relationship advice, but you need to actually talk to Holden and tell him how you're feeling. About all of it. About him. About you and him. About him and his work. You need to tell him what you want. If you don't speak aloud what you want, you'll never get it."

Her words hit me like a rogue wave. But what do I want? Like, really want?

We say our goodbyes and make a tentative plan for her to come visit when she has a break next. As soon as we're off the phone, I walk out of the lobby and to the beach. There are men in striped shirts and white pants cleaning up all the seaweed that washed up.

The sky is a dark purplish blue. Like a bruise. The sea is a deep blue. Should I talk to Holden? What would I say?

Holden, when we go back home, will you be my boyfriend?

It sounds so stupid.

Holden, back in Fortune Falls, can we keep fucking?

Nope. That sounds even worse. And it's not truly what I want.

I want to be with him, for real. I want him to hold my hand down Main Street. I want him to bring me flowers on Valentine's. I want him to put his hand on my thigh while we sit at the Vern, in front of all our friends. In front of my brother.

I want us to be in love, out loud.

Off in the distance on the horizon, a small rainbow appears above the water. It's faint, but it is there. I look back toward the beach. Off to the side, Holden comes running down the steps in hotel issue gym shorts and no shirt. His fists are pumping at his sides.

He spots me, and his face lights up. The butterflies are back, swarming my chest, flooding my stomach.

He runs toward me, out for a morning jog, and I run toward him like a woman who just figured out what, and who, she wants in life.

When we meet, I jump into his arms, wrapping my legs around him. I kiss him deeply, passionately. Gathering all my bravery. I'm going to tell him I love him. That I've always loved him.

When our lips part, he sets me down gently. "Well, hello to you, too," he says with a smirk. "Did it go well with Dee? You got Gio's number?"

My bravery sinks like the tide into the sand, disappearing, burying itself deep underground. I can't tell him. That's not what this is for him. Instead, I try to smile, not sure if it works. It feels odd on my face. "I did. It'll all work out."

CHAPTER 28
HOLDEN

The internet comes back the next morning, and the first thing I do is step out onto our porch and call Gio. He's super cool and gives me a PO Box he checks regularly where I can send the beer sample. The next thing I do is book our flights. The soonest we can get out is tomorrow.

Then I call Kyle to see if he can pick us up.

He answers his cell on the third ring. "Hey, man, let me call you back."

He calls back twenty minutes later. And he sounds bone tired as he says, "What's up?"

"Hey, we're headed home tomorrow, wondering if you could pick us up. We get in really late, so I can always—"

"Not a problem. Did you take good care of Chloe?"

Flashes of me taking care of her fill my mind, and guilt slicks my stomach. "I tried my best. What's going on there? You sound stressed."

Kyle laughs, but there's a crack to it. "I'm going to be a terrible father."

"What? No, you're not. That's crazy."

We talk for an hour. Kyle says all the ways he's worried he'll mess up. I tell him all the reasons that's impossible. He's going to be the best dad. The more we talk, the worse I feel about keeping this huge secret between us. My dad left when I was young, and I tried to have a relationship with him for a long time until it became very apparent that he's toxic. Always a nasty thing to say about what I'm doing and who I am. Mom moved to Arizona about ten years ago. My granddad died a couple of years after that. And my grandma died two years ago. Kyle is literally my family, and sometimes it feels like my only family.

"You're going to be the best dad. Because you are strong and dependable. You got this."

He laughs. "Thanks, dude. For always being there."

We say goodbye, and I make a silent vow to always be there. Whatever this is between Chloe and me, we have to leave it here.

We can have one more beautiful night, and then go back to being friends. It's what she wanted from the beginning anyway.

I head back inside and find Chloe curled up on the couch with a book. When I show her the flight information on my phone with a smile on my face, she frowns but says, "Oh great."

"Did you want to stay longer? I mean, we can't stay here longer." I literally can't afford it. "But I could get us a room somewhere else?"

Could I? I'm not sure. I could probably change the tickets. Except, I don't really want to. I'm ready to go back home. See how they're doing with the Helles. Sink back into my routine. As much as I want to stay in this island paradise with Chloe longer, I'm ready to be back home.

She shakes her head and closes her book. "No, this is great. It's been fun, but it's time to go home. I should pack."

I grab her hand before she can go. "Can I take you to dinner tonight? Somewhere special. One last night."

Her gaze levels me. "One last night."

She walks into the bedroom, her book under her arm. I know she meant the trip. Part of me has this sinking feeling that she meant—that maybe we both meant—us.

I call every nice restaurant on the island. They're all booked.

So instead, I enlist the help of the amazing people at the resort. They help me set everything up, including getting an outfit for me, a white button-up shirt and gray pants, and a dress for her. It's light blue. Just like her sundress, but it's a bit more sheer and a lot lower cut.

Chloe is quiet all day. Reading. Messing around with her phone. I let her know we have plans at five, and she nods at me. I let her know there's a dress in the bathroom for her. And she nods. I try pulling her leg, literally, toward me on the couch. She pushes me off and says, "I'm going for a walk."

I don't want to push any more than I already have, so I work. Now that the internet is back, I can check up on emails on my phone. Chloe comes back a while later, and I wave at her, but I'm deep into draft two of an email to our current distributor.

Around five, she comes out of the bedroom, wearing the long blue dress. My phone slips from my hands, falling to the throw rug with a thud. She looks amazing. The low neckline kisses her collarbones, just the way I hope to later. The blue brings out the blue in her eyes. I stand. "You're gorgeous."

She gives me a tentative smile, motioning to my ratty shorts. "I feel a bit overdressed."

Shit. I got caught up. "Give me two minutes."

I run to the room and get dressed faster than I ever have. Once I emerge, she's staring out the window. I come up behind her, placing a hand on her hip. She flinches. Jumping away.

She covers it with a wide smile, but it was there. "You look very handsome."

"Thanks." I offer her my hand. "Shall we?"

We walk toward the main building and have a seat at the bar. This is the first part of the plan. Drinks at the bar. She orders a large glass of red wine, and I order the IPA they have on tap.

She swirls her wine in the glass and takes a sip. "It's funny, if someone back home had handed me a glass of cold red wine, I would've handed it right back. But I'll miss it."

Chloe's eyes sparkle in the low light as her words hang

between us. She'll miss it. She'll miss us. But she's right, we agreed to leave this on vacation, and vacation is almost over.

The server shows us to our table, which I had them set up on the beach. It's more beautiful than I even imagined. Tiki torches surround the table, the tide moves in and out, glowing with the stars, and a few long-stemmed candles flicker in between the place settings. It would be perfect if it weren't for the faint smell of rotting seaweed. The staff has cleared it all away, but a faint smell remains.

We order, the catch of the day for Chloe and a steak for me.

Chloe smiles at me, and this time it looks genuine. "This is really beautiful."

I heave a sigh of relief. "I was hoping you'd like it. I wanted to make this night special."

"Our last night." The sadness is back in her eyes. She looks at me and takes a deep breath. "Someone told me recently I need to be more clear with what I want."

I shake my head. "It's okay. I know."

She tilts her head to the side. "You do?"

"I think so. I think we both want the same thing."

Her eyes narrow. "Let's say it at the same time, then."

"What we want?"

She nods. "One, two, three."

As she says, "I want to try this for real. I want to be with you in real life."

I say, "This, us, has to stay on vacation. We have too much to lose if it weren't to work."

Her mouth falls open. How did I read this so wrong? We can't. I can't lose my second family. I can't fuck this up. We can't be something back at home.

"Chloe, I...It's too much to lose. I can't—"

She stands. "I understand. Really."

Then she walks off down the beach. I follow her. "Chloe, wait."

She doesn't stop.

"Chloe."

She starts running, and she is fast, but we can't leave it like this.

I run, giving everything I've got, and catch up to her. Touching her shoulder. She turns to me, and there are tears streaming down her face.

"Holden. Just give me some space. You didn't do anything wrong, okay? We said this thing between us would stay out here in the Caribbean, and it will. I want something more, and you don't. It's fine."

"It's not fine." I wipe a tear away, and she moves out of reach. "It's not that I don't want…"

"Me," she says. "You can say it. You don't want me. And that's okay."

"Chloe, it's not that I don't want you. It's that I'm terrified I'll mess it up. Like today, you were pissed at me all day. I don't even know why."

"It's stupid." She shakes her head.

"I'm sure it's not."

"I was upset you booked all this for a beer sample and not me."

My jaw clenches. She's right. I did. But at the time, we weren't a *we*, not like now. "That is kind of dumb."

Chloe turns to leave, and I gently touch her arm. "I only meant when I booked this, we hadn't slept together. If you want a luxury hotel that I book just for you,"—I pull out my phone—"I'll get us a different one right now." My credit card winces at this declaration.

She laughs, and it fills my chest. "It's okay. You're right anyway. This fling would never work in real life. We'll leave it on vacation."

I take her hand, and we walk back to our dinner. It should feel good. We made up. We've agreed. We both want the same thing, but instead, it feels like there is a hole in my chest.

CHAPTER 29
HOLDEN

The airport is crowded. We check in for our flight with no bags to check because they're all still on the cruise ship. We breeze through security. Our flight is a long one. We leave at 5 p.m. here, and even though we'll travel back in time, it'll still be after midnight when we get there. By the time we make it to the gate, we have a little over forty minutes until we board. I watch as people head to a swanky marble bar and order fancy-looking drinks.

I motion to it. "Should we get a drink and some food? It's a long flight."

Chloe nods. "Sure."

We take a seat at the bar. I order a burger, and she gets the fish tacos. We sit in silence, her eyes glued to the television in the corner showing *Magnum PI*. Once the bartender hands us our drinks, I hold mine out to her for a cheers. "To an amazing vacation."

She smiles, but there's a sadness to it. She brings her glass to mine and clinks lightly. "To an amazing vacation."

I sip, the IPA trickling down my throat. It's delicious, but does nothing to ease this tightness in my chest. "What are you most excited for when we get back home?"

She sets her wine down and crosses her hands. "Setting up my dance studio. I'm thinking of calling it Bloom Studio."

The smile that blossoms on my face is wide. "That's a perfect name. I'm serious about helping, too. If you need anything. Help with the paperwork, or the money stuff, or shit…If you need someone to install mirrors and clean the windows. I'm your man."

The last words linger on my tongue, and I like the taste.

Chloe's eyes are searching my face, and she has that sad, sweet smile again. "That's very kind. You're so busy, though. With the brewery. You don't have time to be *my man*. And you don't want to be. Kyle can help me. And I'm sure if he needs you to pitch in, too, he'll let you know."

Kyle. Right.

We are leaving this—us—here.

But this gnawing hole in my chest won't go away.

"Chloe." My hand finds her knee. She's wearing those pink sweats she picked up in St. Thomas. She looks cozy, adorable, and resolute. "We could try…at home. This could be real. You and me."

My words are all jumbled. What I really want to say is buried somewhere in the pauses, the stutters, but not coming out. *I love you. I don't think I can leave us behind.*

She places her hand on mine and squeezes. It's polite. It's a *no, silly man, we can't.* "It'll be better this way. Stick to the rules. What happens on vacation, stays on vacation."

"We made the rules. We can break them." Rising panic tightens my chest even further. This can't be it.

"I'm not sure we did." She picks up her glass, taking a sip, shifting her knees away, and my hand falls.

The plane is delayed and delayed again. I text Kyle and tell him we'll find our own way back. Finally, we board the plane. My jaw is clenched so tight it's starting to ache. We're all the way in the back. It was the only seat available on such short notice.

Across from us is a family with a baby that's already crying, snot running down its face in green rivulets.

They run through all the safety precautions. Chloe watches it intently. When the plane rumbles down the runway, picking up speed, she flinches, but she doesn't reach for me. I want to comfort her. I want to make her feel better. I grab her hand and hold it tightly in mine. She catches my eye and smiles, this one real, this one genuine. She's looking at me how she looked at me on St. Thomas. And it hits me just as I slam back in my seat, the plane taking off, I don't want her to ever stop looking at me like that.

Once the plane is on an even keel, the seat belt sign clicks off, and Chloe lets go of my hand. She mutters "restroom" as she unbuckles her seat belt and moves the short distance from our seat to the bathroom.

I wait a full minute, all the while fighting with myself about whether or not I should follow her. Stupidity wins out, or maybe it's not, maybe it's something else. I just want to touch her again. I just want to make her feel good. I knock lightly on the restroom door, and when she slides it open, I step in quickly, her eyes going wide with shock.

"Holden, what?"

I bring my mouth to hers and kiss her with all the passion building inside me. When our lips part, I say, "Technically, we're still on vacation."

She nods. "So true."

Then her mouth is on mine, her arms wrapped around my neck. The back of my calves hit the toilet. I slam the lid down and take a seat, bringing her with me. Her legs are straddling me, her crotch finding me already hard, and she grinds against me. Her soft moan is hot on my ear.

I squeeze her ass, taking it in both my hands, moving her harder against me.

There's a sound outside our little room. She breathes out. "We have to be quick. Do you have a condom?"

I don't want anything about this to be quick. But she's right. I move a little, and she hops off me. I take a condom out of my back pocket while she unzips my fly, tugging my jeans down, then my boxers. She bites her lower lip like I'm the most delicious thing she's ever seen. It makes me grow larger right before her eyes. She runs a hand lightly over my cock. "So ready. Good boy."

I need to be inside her right now. I roll the condom on as she turns around and lowers her sweats, taking her underwear with them, exposing her bare ass. I take a handful and squeeze. "Your ass is perfect."

She turns around and smirks at me. "Is that my compliment for the day?"

She grabs my cock and lowers onto it as I watch. Her pace is quick, chasing her own pleasure, and I love every second. Her breaths start to get ragged, her movements fast, and I grab her hips, slowing her. "Turn around."

"I'm so close."

"Please." I'm begging now. This is what it has come to. "I want to see your face."

She stops and turns around, lowering onto me again, achingly slow. My hands move under her sweatshirt, up her back, holding her close. I want this moment to last forever. As she lifts and lowers, her hair falls in my face. Lavender and honey.

I inhale deeply as she clenches around me, the pressure too intense to stop. A massive wave crashes over me, and all thoughts leave my brain as I squeeze her tight and she whispers my name softly, "Holden."

I want to snatch it from the air. I want to bottle it and keep it forever. It's all over too fast. She moves off me, adjusting her clothes, washing her hands. Throwing me a wink before slinking out. I sit there for a few more minutes. Letting my breath slow, my heart rate returns to a normal range. I run some cold water on my face and catch my reflection in the mirror. That right there is a happy man.

How can I go back to a world where I don't get to touch

Chloe? Where having her lavender and honey hair fall into my face isn't a daily occurrence?

I head back to my seat, trying to ignore the pointed looks from the flight attendants in the galley. Even if they kicked us off the plane mid-flight, what just happened in that tiny bathroom would've been well worth it.

Chloe moves to give me the window seat. She holds up her phone. "Ruby says they're picking us up."

"Yeah, I talked to Kyle yesterday. But with the flight being delayed, it's going to be too late. I'll rent a car. Tell her no need."

Chloe laughs. "You try telling her no."

I sigh. Because she's right. Ruby is a force. There is no telling her no.

Chloe is staring at her screen. "She says it'll be fine. Kyle's driving."

The tension in my jaw is back. The tightness in my chest. Kyle is driving. Reality rushes back in with the force of a storm.

Chloe looks at me, and I see it in her eyes too. Vacation is over. This—us—is over.

CHAPTER 30
CHLOE

It's pitch black as we stumble outside the Portland airport. The air is cold, and the sidewalk smells faintly of urine. A far cry from the tropical paradise we just left, where the air wrapped you in a warm hug and smelled of plumeria. Most of the time anyway.

I'm so tired. I didn't get any sleep on the plane. I kept looking at Holden, trying to memorize the lines of his face. Trying to hold on to the feel of his lips on mine. Not that I won't see him when we get back, but it won't be the same. Despite my exhausted state, the sight of Kyle's truck parked at the curb sends a rush of adrenaline coursing through my veins. He flashes his lights in case we didn't recognize it was him. Will they be able to tell? Will Kyle look at me and Holden and instantly know that we slept together? A lot.

Holden reaches the truck first and throws me a wink. "It's going to be okay."

I give him a half smile. He opens the door for me, and I crawl into the back of the truck, Holden climbing in after me. I say, as brightly as I can muster at one in the morning, "Hey."

To which Kyle immediately shushes me, pointing to Ruby sleeping in the passenger seat, her hands on her belly and her head leaned against the window. Kyle whispers, "She tried to stay up. The baby had other plans."

I smile, a warmth spreading through my chest as I picture Kyle and Ruby holding their little bundle of joy. I say, "That may be a theme for a while."

Holden quips, "Like the next eighteen years."

Kyle chuckles. Then asks, still in a whisper, "How was the trip?"

Holden's eyes find mine in the dark cab. His pinky brushes my thigh, and all the times we were naked together flash through my mind. My cheeks burn, and I'm grateful it's so dark in here that Kyle can't see me blush.

At the same time, we both say, "Good."

THE NEXT MORNING, I wake up in my bed, at my dad's house, and the smell of coffee brewing in the kitchen. I'm still so exhausted from the trip, but I'm also too excited to sleep. Today I have plans to make. I have a goal to achieve. Actually, several goals. Open my own dance studio and find my own place.

I hop out of bed and go to get my running gear on, but instead I dig out one of my old leotards and tights and make my way downstairs. Dad smiles at me when I walk in the kitchen, his eyes widening just the tiniest bit as he clocks the leotard. He pours me a cup of coffee. "Ahh, there's the world traveler. How was the trip?"

I take the coffee from his hands with a grateful smile, as I consider the question. *How was the trip?* Memories flood my vision. Omelets, and painting classes, and finally the dance studio —Holden at each one.

But we chose to leave it there.

I can do this without him.

"Transformative," I say.

Dad smiles behind his coffee mug. "Like the outfit."

"Thanks. Do we still have the bar set up in the garage?"

"Sure do. I'll have to move a few boxes. That's no trouble, though." He heads toward the garage door. "I'll move them right now."

"I can get them, Dad."

"You sure?" His eyes look wary.

"Yeah."

The first few boxes are easy, but the last one is really heavy. I think about getting my dad, but I can do this. I'm a strong, capable woman. I take a deep breath, bend, and push. My hip tightens, and my back spasms. The box moves, though.

I run my toe over the floor, testing the water, and with each arc, my back screams at me. My breaths are fast, my heart racing. No. This can't be happening. I move to the floor and stretch. My back locks up completely, the pain is intense. It's so tight, I don't think I can get up off the floor.

I attempt to leverage myself with my arms, but it's too painful. I need help. Shit.

"Dad!"

Music is playing from my phone. He can't hear me inside. I try calling out to him a few more times, but it's no use. I roll myself to the ground and lie facing the ceiling, my knees up in the air. The rafters are dusty, as are the boxes stashed overhead. I see one labeled in scrawling Sharpie that says *Christmas decorations*. I think of that crazy Christmas tree in the bar. I think of Holden. I think of my mom. Tears stream down my face in salty rivulets.

That's how Dad finds me.

"Peanut? What happened?"

"I hurt my back."

Dad helps me up. He wants to put me in the car and head straight for the hospital, but I convince him there's no point. This has happened many times before. I can just message my doctor. He nods, helping me into bed with an ice pack and a sparkling water with fresh lemon.

"Thank you, Dad."

"Literally anytime."

"Could you hand me my laptop?"

He frowns. "You should just rest."

I smile. "I can rest with my laptop."

He shakes his head, but hands it to me.

At least I can work on my business plan some more. When I wrote it, I was going through a particularly low time, and it helped to have something to focus on. But then I abandoned it. Every time I thought about actually teaching the classes, my heart raced, and I felt like I wanted to crawl out of my skin.

But now, I'm excited about teaching. I just don't know if I can do it. I moved one stupid box, and I'm laid up for the rest of the day. On top of that, I'm not even sure this plan is any good.

I make an appointment for Monday at the bank. Eventually, I have to put the plan away, because the muscle spasms seem to throb out, *You can't do this. You're too broken.*

Stuck in bed with an ice pack and Tiger Balm, my thoughts flit back to the Caribbean. The trip feels like a dream. Each day that passes makes me feel more and more like I made it all up.

I sleep a lot. I catch up on episodes of *Survivor*. The white sand beaches that they run around looking for idols on remind me so much of Holden that it takes my breath away.

Finally, when Monday arrives, my back spasm has subsided, and once again I can walk like a somewhat normal person. I am still hopeful I can open my studio; it might just take some adjustment and some built-in rest time for my body.

My appointment with the bank is today. I shower and put on a nice pair of jeans and my most professional-looking sweater with a stretchy back brace underneath it for a little extra support. I borrow Dad's truck, my business plan on the passenger seat.

I arrive five minutes before four. Early as usual. I sit in the cushy chair provided until a gentleman in a plaid sweater vest calls my name.

"I'm Greg. I'll be assisting you today. What are we working on?"

"I want to open a dance studio in town." Chills tingle down my arm. It's the first time I've said it so concretely. So casually. It fills my chest with pride and a deep sense of peace. I *want* this. With every fiber in my being.

We sit at his desk, and I look at the little knick-knacks while he looks over my business plan. There's one of those lucky cats with one paw up. There's a picture on his desk with a small child and another handsome man, a little taller than the gentleman I'm sitting with, all smooshed together in an embrace at a pumpkin patch.

He glances up and catches me looking. He smiles warmly and turns the photo toward me. "This is Nate, and this little lady is Maribelle."

"You have a beautiful family."

"Thank you. You know Maribelle has been wanting to take a dance class. We'll have to go to your studio once it opens."

My heart soars. "I'm approved for the loan?"

The smile falls from his face. "Oh, no. Sorry. I was getting ahead of myself." He turns to his computer and asks me some questions about myself. He nods as he scrolls the mouse. Nods and frowns.

He lets out a long, heavy breath. "So, there are a few things. First." He smiles, and it's warm, and it's genuine, and I want him to stop there. Leave it at first. But he keeps talking. "You've written a beautiful plan. Really nicely done. But it is missing a location. We need a location because it'll give us a better idea of what mortgage payments or lease payments will look like. Also, it'll give us a better idea of the renovation budget."

I pull out a notebook and start writing, *Location!* I can do that. Kyle used to be in real estate, and he still has a lot of buddies who are.

Greg says, "So the second, slightly larger problem is your credit score. It's lower than we like to see."

The credit card that my last boyfriend and I took out together was so that it would be easier to pay rent together. But he also used it to pay for plane tickets for trips that weren't even with me. I canceled the card as soon as I found out, but not before it tanked my credit score, apparently.

I close my mouth and shut my notebook. "Is there anything I can do?"

Greg nods. "You can get a co-signer."

My entire body feels heavy. "A co-signer."

Greg smiles. "It's really not uncommon for small businesses, especially ones opened by young people"—thirty is the new seventeen, I guess—"to have co-signers."

He hands me a folder with his card in it. "Don't hesitate to call with any questions."

I thank him for his time, then drive the truck down the block and park across the street from the Vern. I can't drink with the amount of ibuprofen I'm taking at the moment, but I want to feel the familiar stool under my butt. And I want to see my brother.

The tables are nearly full, and then I remember: it's trivia night. Just my luck. When I want to wallow on my own, the place is packed.

Ruby waves to me from a barstool. It's odd to see her in front of the bar. I head over and try to wrap my arms around her for a hug, but she's too wide. We laugh at my efforts, and I end up giving her back an affectionate pat instead. "You're still pregnant?"

She shakes her head. "Nah. Too many tacos. You want a pint or a glass of wine?"

She moves to stand, and Kyle is over in a heartbeat, like her stool had an alarm on it. "Sit down. I got it. Or she can get it herself. You are not allowed behind this bar."

I laugh. "Ruby, what did you do?"

Kyle says, "She has been having contractions all day, and she won't let me take her to the hospital."

He then goes to help a couple waiting to order.

My mouth falls open. "What? Isn't your due date like last week?"

Another gentleman walks up to the bar, empty pint glass in hand.

Ruby shakes her head. "It's the twenty-first. It's an entire week away."

I shake my head and move behind the bar, grabbing the guy's glass. "Another?"

He nods. "Pabst, please."

I turn my attention back to Ruby as I pour. "People have babies early all the time." A couple of people hop in the back of my line, while a few make their way to Kyle's. "Where's Darla?"

Darla is their other bartender and the whole reason I thought they didn't need my help at the moment.

"Quit," Kyle says while pouring some whiskey into a glass.

"What? Why didn't you call me?" I take the next order for two margaritas and start to make them, grabbing the mix.

"We thought you needed a rest after your vacation," Ruby says, and there's a twinkle in her eye that makes my pulse hammer on the side of my neck. Do they know? Have they talked to Holden?

I laugh, but even to my ear, it comes out nervous and high-pitched. "Why would you think that?"

"Holden told us all about it. Sounds wild." Kyle reaches over me to grab a lime.

The room is spinning. They know. My overprotective brother knows that I slept with his best friend, and he's cool with it? I'm about to say something when the back doors come swinging open.

Kyle hands his drink over. "Ah, speak of the devil."

CHAPTER 31
CHLOE

Holden walks through the door, a metal dolly in hand, wearing a Woodshed Brewing t-shirt.

"Hey," he says with a warm smile as his eyes find mine behind the bar.

"What are you doing? Aren't deliveries below your pay grade?" Kyle asks with a chuckle.

"Nah, you know better than most that when you own the business, nothing is below your pay grade. Rob's sick."

"No," Kyle says.

I hand over my drinks and get to work, grabbing the next few beers, my head still swimming. How is everyone so cool? Was I worried about nothing? "Kyle was just saying you told them *all* about our trip."

Holden's face goes pale, his eyes wide. "Not all. Not everything," he says a little too quickly.

Both Kyle and Ruby perk up, their eyes switching back and forth between Holden and me. Ruby says, "What else happened?"

Holden makes desperate eyes at me while I get the next order.

He clears his throat. "I told them about missing the boat, and the storm, and having to fly back early."

Kyle nods, his voice gruff. "What didn't you tell us?"

There it is. I wasn't overreacting. My brother would not be okay with Holden and me being together. I jump in. "Umm, did you tell them about the sparkly pink uniform you wore?"

Ruby laughs then clutches her belly. She bites her lip. "Oh."

Kyle hops over the bar and is by her side in an instant. Ruby says, "I think my water broke."

"We need to go. Now." Then, in his booming voice, he says, "Folks."

I cut in, "I can run the bar. You don't need to close."

Kyle looks at me, all the patrons still staring at him. "You sure?"

Holden takes off his flannel. "I can pitch in."

"Okay. Don't stay open all night. Just close after trivia." Kyle turns to the customers and, with a wide smile, says, "We're having a baby."

The bar erupts in applause and whoops.

Ruby throws me a wink. "Don't do anything I wouldn't do."

Holden steps behind the bar and starts taking orders and pouring pints. For the next two hours, we're slammed. We move past each other, our fingers brushing every now and then, and each time I feel it down to my toes.

The trivia players are thirsty. Holden moves to get some limes, and he casually puts a hand on my hip as he scoots past. I nearly combust. My cheeks flame, a heat that travels all the way down to my chest. I look up to meet his eyes, but he's focused on slicing a lime. Does he feel it too? Or is it really over for him?

After trivia wraps up, most of the customers trickle out. At around ten, Holden clears his throat. "We're closing early tonight. Thanks for coming in, but it's time to go, friends."

There is a collective "boo" from the handful of stragglers left. I text Kyle to see how things are going and to tell him we're closing up. The rest of the customers leave once they've finished their drinks, without more reminders. I close the till while Holden locks the door.

"Whoo, it's been a minute since I've been behind the bar." Holden sits on a stool, stretching his neck.

I count out our tips from the till. "We made great tips, though."

I hand him his stack of bills, and he shakes his head. "Nah, you keep it. You were working harder."

I hesitate, but then take the cash and put it in an envelope. "I'm going to need it."

"Are you?"

I nod and hold up an empty beer glass to Holden.

He nods. "Yes, please. Why do you need cash?"

I sigh as I pour him a large pint and me a club soda with lemon. I take the stool next to him. We'd been so busy, I forgot I came to wallow. "I talked to the bank today about getting a small business loan."

Holden's eyes light up. His whole face lights up, in fact, his smile beaming. "That's amazing."

I shake my head, blinking back tears. "I have bad credit. Or not bad…but not great. I had this shared credit card with my last boyfriend. Anyway, it doesn't matter. It's not going to work."

"You could get a co-signer. I would be happy—"

I snap. "How will that work, Holden? You're going to co-sign my loan and what?" I throw up my arms. "How will we explain that to Kyle? To anyone. That there's absolutely nothing going on between us and yet we're signing paperwork together."

His eyes look wounded as he turns them back to his beer, his jaw clenched.

"You heard Kyle when he thought something was going on between us?"

"I heard. You're right." He slams the rest of his beer and stands, throwing his flannel back on.

Maybe I shouldn't have been so harsh. I was hoping that he would push back. And say, *who cares what Kyle says. Who cares what anyone says? Let's be together for real.*

But he didn't.

I check my phone, and there's a picture of a tiny squishy baby face on it.

Kyle: Meet June Papadopoulos

I squeal and then show my phone to Holden. "I'm an aunt. Well, again."

Holden smiles, but it's sad. "Congratulations."

"Let's go," I say, grabbing my purse.

"It's a family thing." Holden shakes his head. "I have more deliveries. I'll catch up with them tomorrow. Do you need a ride? I can drop you."

A family thing. I want to say, but you are family. But he's not. And he has work to do. Again.

"I got it."

Holden nods and heads out the back. I follow, turning the lights off as I go. He gets in the Woodshed delivery truck, and I walk across the street to where I parked the truck, but it feels like a piece of my heart went the other way. Holden meant it when he said it was a vacation romance. He doesn't want to be with me for real.

Anything romantic is really, truly over between us.

***

I TEXT my dad to see if he wants me to pick him up. He texts back that he's already at the hospital. When I arrive, he opens his arms out wide, and I run into them.

"It's a perfect day," he says as he wraps me in his arms and picks me up off the ground, spinning me in a circle the way he used to when I was little.

When he sets me down, tears are silently streaming down my face.

The wrinkle between his brow appears, the one I know so well. If I'm good at anything in this life, it's making my father worry.

"Honey, are they happy tears?"

I smile, but I can feel it waver. I wipe one tear away. "That one was."

He chuckles and leads me to a pair of empty chairs in the waiting room. "What's going on?"

I inhale a shaky breath and wipe away another tear. "It's just..."

How to explain? I went on an unexpected vacation, had the best sex of my life, and now I'm in love. But I didn't fall in love on the trip, I've been in love—for years—with Holden. One of the only men in this whole town that's off-limits.

Or how about: I finally figured out my passion in life, or not really figured it out. Dancing has always been my passion, but I let myself love it again. I let the dream change and become something new. Something that could be sustainable. Only I can't do it because I've made too many mistakes in my life. I'm not a safe bet.

I run my hand on my jeans. I can't say any of that to Dad. Instead, I say, "I finally figured out what I want in life, and it turns out I can't have it."

Dad sighs. "Oof. That's a big one. Is this a what? Or a who?"

"Both. I figured out what I want and who I want, and I can't have either."

"Yet." Dad looks at me, his eyes warm. He puts an arm around my shoulder and pulls me in. "I don't know the particulars. Care to share?"

I shake my head.

"Fair enough. You know your mother used to make sand castles."

I nod. I've seen the pictures and heard the stories. I think I even remember helping once, but it's fuzzy. I close my eyes. Salt air. Sun on my shoulders. Scratchy sand between my toes. Cold water ran over my fingers as I filled a little pink plastic bucket with water straight from the foamy waves.

"Every year, the designs she picked would get more intricate. She was always pushing herself, expanding her skills. But every year when she was practicing, she would come to me and tell me, 'I'm going to change it. It's too hard. What was I thinking? I'll just do another turtle.' And every year I would say, 'Or you could try again tomorrow and just see.' Tomorrow would come, and she'd try a different way. She'd add more water or more sand. She'd come home and tell me it needed more water. Or I wasn't compacting the sand at the right angle. She'd try again, and I won't say without fail, because there were many, many fails, but eventually she would figure it out. It just took time, patience, and sometimes a new approach."

I let his words sink in like water into one of my mother's sand sculptures.

He clears his throat. "Without knowing any of the details, I can say this, you have time. Whatever the what is, if it's something you really want, you can work towards it. Bit by bit. Spray by spray. One grain of sand at a time if you have to. Sometimes you just have to be brave enough to try another way. Just because one way didn't work out doesn't mean it's a lost cause."

I nod and lean into him.

"Now the who..." He chuckles. "I have a feeling that one might work itself out."

He would say that. He met Mom in high school, and they were instantly head over heels for one another. But it's all said with love.

"Thanks, Dad."

He stands. "Let's go snuggle that baby."

THE NEXT MORNING IS GORGEOUS. Sunshine streams in through my window. And it feels like a day to chase a dream. While I was holding my new baby niece and smelling her perfect little head, my dad's words were ringing through my head.

All I need is a new approach. I have time.

And I had an idea.

I get on some leggings and a cute top, grab my mat, and ride into town, straight to the yoga studio on Main. I'm fifteen minutes early for the 8 a.m. vinyasa with my favorite instructor, Ahn.

The room is packed, but there's a few spots in the front. I set up my mat, and as I stretch out my hamstrings before class, I practice my speech.

Ahn's partner Michelle owns the studio, but they essentially run it together. The class is wonderful. It feels good to move my body with a group, in this gorgeous light-filled studio instead of our dusty garage.

After class is over, I speak with Ahn, and she calls for Michelle. "This lady wants to teach a dance class," Ahn says with a big smile.

"Oh," Michelle says. "That's fun."

We all head to Story Club Books for coffee and talk for a solid hour about the idea. When we part, I feel like I've made two new friends, and we have two classes on the books. Both of which will start in two weeks. Beginning ballet for ages 6-12 and a hip hop class for adults.

I ride my bike back home like it has wings.

I'm so excited, I can't sit still. After a shower and a bagel, I get to work cleaning the garage. My goal is to make it less dusty and more studio-like. I move all the boxes to the side. I sweep. And I make a plan to put down a hardwood floor square in front of the barre already installed. While I'm cleaning, I find some bags of potting soil, and it gives me another idea.

I borrow my dad's truck and head to the hardware store. I get the supplies and some seeds. The front flower bed has been empty for years. If I'm going to stay—which I need to save all the money I can, and it's nice being close to Dad—I'm going to make this feel like my home too.

CHAPTER 32
HOLDEN

My delivery driver, Rob, has shingles. I brought him some beer, some doughnuts, and told him to take all the time he needs. But that means that on top of everything else I need to do, I'm the delivery driver and have been for almost a month. Our orders have been insane. Which is great, but it means I'm spending a lot of time in the truck.

Currently, I'm driving up the coast on my way back from Coos Bay, music playing softly over the stereo. The road stretches out in front of me, and all I see is Chloe.

I can't stop thinking about her.

Her hair. Her legs. Her laugh. I miss her. It's fierce and constant. Like missing my own arm.

When I helped out at the bar a few weeks ago, part of me thought—hoped—that maybe we would pick up where we left off. But she's right. Kyle sounded pissed when he thought something might've happened between us.

And I can't risk messing everything up.

God. I feel like a piece of shit, keeping it from him.

I visited him, Ruby, and June at the hospital, and I could tell he knew something was up with me. I brushed it off. Said it was work stuff. Which is partly true. Work has been crazy. I sent a sample to Gio and am waiting to hear back. The Helles is going great, actually, and I started a new beer.

It's pretty rare these days that I brew on my own, but this one I did. I couldn't sleep the night June was born. Or the next night. Or the next. My mind keeps replaying my hands on Chloe's hips as I moved past her behind the bar. My hands on Chloe's back, dancing in that beautiful garden. My hands on Chloe's bare skin in that little bungalow by the sea. And then it would get stuck on her face when she talked about Kyle and how he wouldn't be cool with us being a couple. One night last week, I gave up trying to sleep and went to the brewery.

It's a special beer. One of the most personal ones I've brewed in a long time. I haven't made a beer for someone since my granddad passed. But this one—this one is for Chloe.

Even if I never tell her. Even if no one ever knows.

It's hers.

My phone rings over the Bluetooth, and I answer it. "Yeah."

"Hey," Kyle says over the phone, his voice gruff.

Panic shoots to my chest, my heart racing. He knows.

"Hey, dude. What's up?"

"I—"

He stops for so long, I think maybe he hung up.

"Kyle?"

He lets out a breath into the phone, the buzz of it filling the cab of the truck. "I'm not good at this."

"Good at what?" At telling your friend to stop lusting after your little sister? I think, but don't say.

"Being a dad," he chokes out. "I'm just as bad at it as I thought I'd be. So at least there's that. At least I was right."

I feel like a real dick. Here I was making this all about me. It's about him. And I've been a shit friend. "Dude, you just started. You can't be an expert already. And I'm sure you're doing great."

"No. I'm not. Ruby is amazing. She's feeding the baby. They have this boob thing going on. And they're both girls. It's like she knows instinctively what to do. She bounces and shushes and makes all these noises, and June eats it up. Then she looks at me like, " Who is this guy? He does not know what to do. He's got no milk. He doesn't smell as nice."

I laugh. "You're not wrong there."

"I just don't know what to do. I can see Ruby is tired and frustrated sometimes, but I just…" He sighs. "I'm trying."

"Kyle, bud. She knows that. She does. Look, I'm about an hour out of town, then I'll head over. Okay?"

"Okay."

I TEXT ONCE I'm at Kyle's place so I don't wake up June. Kyle answers the door in sweats covered in stains. "Hey," he says, and he sounds half asleep. "Come in, have a seat. Want coffee?"

"Sure." I head into the living room, while Kyle shuffles into the kitchen, moving one tired foot at a time, almost zombie-like.

Ruby is in the living room, *The Great British Baking Show* on television, folding laundry, in similar sweats. At least it looks like she's folding laundry. Once I come in and have a seat as per Kyle's instructions, I can see that she's just folding and refolding the same scrap of white fabric. "Hey, Ruby."

"Mmm."

"Need a hand?" I ask, holding my palm out for the laundry.

Tears well up in her eyes, and she throws the fabric to the ground. "The corners won't match up. And as many times as I fold these burp clothes,"—she hits the tower next to her, sending the whole thing toppling onto the couch—"They're not any easier to store. They just fall apart like I didn't even fold them. Same with the onesies."

"They look great."

Kyle comes in holding two mugs of coffee, which he instantly puts on the coffee table and gives me the death glare. "What did you do?"

I hold up both hands.

"He offered to fold laundry," Ruby cries.

Kyle's brow furrows. He sits next to Ruby, rubbing her back.

"Is that a bad thing?" I mouth to Kyle.

He frowns and mouths back. "I'm not sure."

Out loud, I say, "I'm sorry. I was just trying to help."

Ruby sniffs and then wipes her face with one of the burp clothes. "It's okay."

"We're not sleeping much," Kyle offers, which earns him a glare from Ruby. He whispers to her, "Hun, we're not."

I take my mug and blow on the steam. "Look, I have an idea. My house is open, it's quiet. Why don't I watch June for a couple of hours, and you two go take a nap? I'll fold the rest of the laundry."

"Yes," Kyle says while Ruby says, "We couldn't."

They look at each other and have a hushed conversation.

"Have you ever watched a baby before?"

"Yes," I say. And I have. My cousins were all younger than I was. It's been years, and they were all more like one when I watched them, but I have. It can't be that different.

Ruby whispers to Kyle and then goes to the kitchen. Kyle says, "We're just going to talk it over."

I nod, setting my coffee down and picking up the laundry. "Sure."

They come back a few minutes later, and Ruby says, "She's sleeping. She just went down, so she'll probably be asleep for two hours. Then she'll want the bottle in the fridge."

She shows me how to use the bottle warmer and how to test it on my arm, and she shows me the baby monitor camera.

Kyle pulls me aside. I hand him the key, and he says, "Thank you."

"Of course, dude. Anytime. Really." Which isn't true if I'm being honest. But I don't have any other deliveries today, and even though I should check on my secret brew, it'll wait. This is more important. I smile at Ruby. "I got this."

They leave, and I fold the rest of the laundry, putting the neat little stacks on the chair. Then I move on to the sink full of dishes, *The Great British Baking Show* still playing in the background.

Maybe I should make them something. Not the overly complicated tart that the Welshman on the screen is making. But maybe some chocolate chip cookies. Ruby is always sharing her baked goods. It'd be nice to make something for her. Once the dishwasher is loaded and running, I find the bowls and pull them out, getting started on some oatmeal chocolate chip cookies. Why oatmeal? Because it's the recipe I know I can find, right there on the side of the canister.

The batter is easy to mix. Then I find the baking trays in the drawer under the stove and pull one out. It's stuck on another tray. I tug and it comes loose then it slips through my fingers and falls to the floor with a clatter. I hold my breath, as if now it's my own breathing that is going to make a difference. That's what will wake up June.

One second passes, then two, then three, and I think I'm in the clear. But there's the scream. And oh what a scream. I run to the nursery, and June's little face is scrunched up, her mouth open wide, her cheeks red. I scoop her in my arms. "You've got quite the voice on you."

I cradle her to me and bounce a bit. The screams die down a bit, but she's still audibly annoyed with the situation. I try the rocking chair, and I hum a tune. It's not until June's head starts to get heavier on my shoulder that I realize it's that stupid song from *Dirty Dancing*. The one Chloe and I danced to on the ship. It hits me with the force of a Mack truck.

I miss Chloe so much.

There's an audible gurgle from June and then a huge toot. My hand is wet where I'm supporting her little tush. My shirt is getting wet, too, and the smell is alarming. June starts to wail again, and I hold her out a little. She has pooped. Somehow through her diaper.

I do *not* got this.

The doorbell rings. I cradle June back to me, trying to soothe her. "Don't worry." I bounce her, and the doorbell rings again.

Okay. I got this. I'm fine. I'll open the door, the smell alone should drive whoever is there away, then change June, then change me. Then she can help me make the cookies. Four-week-olds love cookies, right?

I open the door, and Chloe is there. In a pale lavender leotard, with a matching skirt made out of some kind of transparent fabric. She's also wearing a black band around her hips. Her hair is down, and it cascades over her shoulders and down her back. She's holding a tray with aluminum foil on top. "Holden?"

"Hey."

I move inside, and she comes in as well.

"What are you doing?"

I laugh. Bouncing June, who's still poopy and not happy about it. "We have a little situation."

"I can smell that," she says with a smirk. She disappears into the kitchen, and I take June into the nursery, laying her on the changing table. I unbutton the snaps, but if I pull the onesie up, poop will end up all over June's mad little face.

Chloe comes and joins me. She stands so close to me that I get a full whiff of her hair. Ooh, how I've missed that smell. She looks at me. "You okay?"

I laugh and shake my head. "I've been better."

"Mind if I?" She motions to June, and I step out of the way.

She takes the onesie down from the top by moving the sleeves over June's little arms. Smart. As she leans over, I see a speck of dirt behind her ear. I reach to brush it off.

Chloe stands straighter, her hands still busy cleaning June.

"It was dirt," I explain.

"Oh." She blushes, and I want to kiss each cheek. "I was planting some more things in the garden."

"Planting." It's nearly mid-May. "Isn't it a little late?"

She smiles, picking June up and carrying her to the bathroom as I follow. "I planted late bloomers." She points to the little plastic bathtub, and I understand. I grab it and start filling it with water. "It seemed only fitting."

I laugh. Once the tub is filled and Chloe makes sure it's the right temperature, she places June inside. June coos and taps at the water.

"You know," I say. "I've been thinking about that."

"About what?" Chloe asks as she runs a washcloth over June's belly.

"You." *And nothing but you*, I think but keep that part to myself.

Her mouth ticks to the side with the hint of a smile. "Me?"

"Yeah. You and the whole late bloomer thing. You asked me once about my tattoo. I got it for my grandma after she passed. She had a huge garden, her roses still bloom every year, even when I had no idea how to take care of them. She loved those roses. Part of the reason she loved them was that they bloomed year after year. Not like her dahlias. Every spring, she'd be out there planting new bulbs. She'd be covered in dirt and she'd say, 'All this trouble and those roses just bloom. Season after season.' I've even seen a bud or two during some warm winters."

Chloe motions to a stack of towels. "Could you hand me one of those?"

I go to grab one and hold it out. She lifts June out of the water, and I wrap it around her. She puts June in my arms, and I bounce her. "I don't know what I'm trying to say—only maybe there is no right time to bloom. Maybe we're like roses and we bloom and wither over and over. Season after season."

Chloe is nodding slowly, her eyes warm. "You might be onto something there."

CHAPTER 33
CHLOE

I help get little Junebug dressed while Holden showers. I bring her into the kitchen to warm up a bottle, and there's a batch of cookie dough on the counter. It smells delicious. The man can bake, too. Is there anything he can't do?

Then my mind wanders to all the things I know for a fact he can do to me. My cheeks flush, and I push the thought away.

"Let's bake these," I tell June as I bounce her and she gnaws on my hair. I heat up her bottle and preheat the oven. While the bottle is warming, we scoop some dough onto a tray, and I think about what Holden said. Maybe he's right. Maybe I've been thinking about this wrong. I don't have to find a forever path, just my path for right now. And honestly, the classes at the studio have been going so well, I'd love to move into my own studio soon. I've even found the perfect space. It was an old mechanic shop, but it's big, and clean-ish. With a large rolling door that we could put windows in to let in even more light. In the summer, we could even open it up and let in the breeze.

It's perfect.

Except there's the pesky money issue. The owner wants to sell, not lease it. And with everything it would take to renovate it, if I put in all my savings, I still need around fifty thousand dollars.

I pop the cookies in and grab the bottle, testing it on my wrist, while I tell June, "Money is the worst."

"Why do you say that?" Holden comes into the kitchen, his hair wet, in a soft gray shirt that has big print that reads *Promoted to Daddy 2026*. "I mean you're not wrong. Just wondering why?"

"Promoted to Daddy, huh?"

He stiffens when I call him that. I laugh.

He smirks, his cheeks pinking. "We can't all pull off a leotard the way you do."

My stomach tightens at his words. There's an energy hanging in the air between us while we're both silent, eyes drinking each other in.

Holden clears his throat. "It's all I could find without digging through Kyle's stuff too much. What's with the money troubles?"

I let out a large sigh and debate telling him. It's not really his problem. And I wouldn't unload all my life's problems on him before. But honestly, there's no one else I'd rather talk to about it, any of it. Anything really. I've missed him so much. And not just the kissing, although I've missed that too. I've missed talking to him. Just being in his orbit.

So, I do it. I pop the bottle in June's mouth and tell him everything. About how well the classes have been going, about my ex and the credit card that killed my chances at the loan, for now. I even tell him about the space for sale. June finishes her bottle and falls asleep on my shoulder. She sleeps through the timer for the cookies.

"Chloe, that's amazing." Holden takes the cookies out of the oven. "I know you weren't into the idea before, but I'd be happy to co-sign the loan."

I shake my head. "No, I couldn't..."

"I understand." He holds up both hands. "What about a Kickstarter or something? When the brewery was first getting started, we had one to get a new FV, and it went really well."

"I have no idea what an FV is, but a fundraiser isn't a bad

idea." It's not. I can see it now. "It could be kind of a talent show. That way, my little class could perform."

They've been asking about it. It could be really fun and raise some money. I could add it to my savings and just hope no one else wants to buy the mechanic shop until I can raise the rest of the down payment.

Holden's eyes are sparkling. "Oh, that could be fun. My buddy's grandma manages the community theater, I could have him talk to her about using the space. They have a concessions stand in the lobby, and Woodshed would be happy to provide beer and snacks. Should I talk to him?"

"Yeah, that would be amazing."

Holden smiles. "Can he give her your number?"

"Yes. Absolutely." My eyes flick to the time on the stove clock behind Holden as he puts another batch of cookies in the oven. I have exactly fifteen minutes to get to my class. "I gotta run." I head into the living room, trying to find my bag where I dropped it, as Holden follows me. "I have class."

Holden comes to me. He smells amazing. Sweet and spicy. Our skin brushes as we transfer June from my arms to his. His eyes find mine, and my dad's words come back to me. *If it's something you really want, you can work towards it…One grain of sand at a time if you have to. Sometimes you just have to be brave enough to try another way.*

We were talking about the dance studio. But maybe it applies to people too. Maybe Holden and I could really work. Maybe we just need to be brave enough to try at all. Except that's not what he wants. He said so that night on the beach.

Holden's eyes move to my mouth, then back to my eyes. "Chloe, I've miss—"

The front door opens and Ruby rushes in, with Kyle right behind her. She stops in the doorway and sniffs loudly. "Are those cookies?"

"Is that my shirt?" Kyle laughs, but he looks suspiciously between Holden and me. "What have you three been up to?"

"Gotta run."

I give Ruby a kiss on the cheek and Kyle a hug, then swoop up my bag and run out the door.

***

A FEW DAYS LATER, an older woman named Maureen calls and says the theater would love to help with a local fundraiser. We talk for nearly an hour and set the date for Friday, June 5. Which gives me about a month. Not a ton of time, but enough. In class, we work on a routine. Even my adult hip hop class wants in on it.

I make flyers and a link to the sign-up sheet. I'm calling it *Fortune Falls' Got Talent*. All the proceeds go to opening Bloom Studio. Within the first two days of the flyer going up, the sign-up sheet is almost full. This is going to work.

A week later, after my class gets out, I'm sweeping the studio. My phone rings. It's Holden. I stare at the screen, my heart in my throat. What does he want? I've gone back and forth in my mind a million times since we took care of June. We should just tell Kyle and let the chips fall where they may. And if we don't work out, we'll cross that bridge when we come to it. And then I think there's no way. He doesn't want me. And I couldn't make Kyle choose between us.

The call is just about to go to voicemail when I pick up.

"Hey, it's me. Holden."

"Hey," I say and sit on the hardwood floor, my legs suddenly feeling very jelly-like.

"I just wanted to talk about concessions," he says. "I've seen the flyers; they look great."

Right concessions.

"Do you think? Um…" Holden is stammering. "Would you want to discuss it over dinner? Tonight?"

I blow out a breath. I do. And I don't. "Holden, I'm not sure that's such a good idea."

"It could be…"

"Holden—" What do I even want to say? "Sure."

"Sure?" His voice is laced with excitement.

"Yeah. Name the place."

"I was going to make us something. Is my house okay?"

Me and I. At his house. Alone. The butterflies swarm my chest like a plague. "Okay."

"Seven?"

"Sounds great." It does. And it doesn't.

God, what am I going to wear?

I SPEND the rest of the afternoon working on the fundraiser. Reaching out to people who have signed up. Seeing what they are going to perform, how long the act is. Then, make a tentative schedule. A few people dropped out, so there are a couple of spots still open, but even if we don't fill them, the schedule is good. It'll be fun.

It was a nice distraction from dinner tonight.

Then I get a text.

Dee: Hey I'm in your town. Surprise.

I nearly drop the phone. We've been talking and texting regularly, and she didn't mention she was visiting anytime soon. Last I heard, which was just a couple of days ago, she was going on a trip with the scuba instructor.

Me: Fortune Falls?

Dee: Yes! Are you busy?

Me: I have a thing tonight, but come over!

I text her my address. She's there in fifteen minutes. I half expect here to show up with who we've been calling Scuba Steve.

"Where's Scuba Steve?"

She shakes her head. "We didn't work out."

"No."

She sighs and plops down on the couch. "Let's just say he was exploring the other fish in the sea. With his mouth."

"No."

"Yeah. That's all right. A friend was headed this way, and it means I was free to come see you."

I tell her about the phone call. "We're meeting for dinner tonight."

"Ooh." Dee claps. "Let me see the outfit."

"I haven't picked it yet."

Dee looks at her watch. "We'd better get moving."

I put on a pink polka dot dress. It gets a thumb to the side from Dee.

Then I change into jeans and a black shirt. It gets a thumbs-down.

I gasp.

"The jeans are too baggy. Show off those stems, girl."

I laugh, but she's right. Holden is an admitted leg man.

Finally, I change into the blue sundress with little flowers that I know he likes. Dee approves.

"Where are you staying?"

"At the Fortune Falls Inn."

"Want to meet up later?"

Dee shakes her head. "Hopefully, you'll be busy all night. Let's meet up tomorrow."

If I wait to get on my bike any longer, I'm going to be late. We hug and she gets in her rental car, while I hop on my bike, flicking on the light and adjusting my helmet, and start to pedal.

With each push down of my foot, I feel a little more excited. This feels right. Holden and I. Planning something together. Being there for one another. Spending time together in real life and not just on vacation.

I know the way to Holden's grandparents'. When he moved there in his teens, I used to ride by. Trying to catch a glimpse of him. Pathetic, I'm aware.

I ride to the little red house with white trim, the roses out front are already starting to bloom, their petals catching the light of the moon. But that's almost the only light. The moon, the street lamp, and my bike light.

There are no lights on in the house.

I lean my bike against the porch, and the porch light comes on. Relief washes over me. He's here. It's fine.

I climb the steps and knock. I wait for a full minute, then knock again. This time I wait for two minutes. I'm so still, listening for any noise from inside that the porch light goes off.

I wave my arm, and the light goes back on. It's motion activated. And I'm an idiot.

Holden isn't here. He stood me up.

I check my phone. No texts. No missed calls.

I stare at the little doorbell with a camera on it. He can watch me stand here and wait for him for far too long. This was a terrible idea anyway. He must've realized it too.

I lean into the camera. "You're right, Holden. This was a bad idea. I'll see you around."

And with that, I get back on my bike and ride away. I feel even worse than I did as a kid when I was trying to catch a glimpse of him with no luck. So much worse. There was a second there where I really thought I could have everything I wanted.

CHAPTER 34
HOLDEN

My phone buzzes in my pocket, but Gio is mid-sentence, and I don't want to be rude. It seems Gio is always mid-sentence.

I watched June again this afternoon. It's become a bit of a weekly routine. I come over, and Ruby or Kyle, whoever is not at the bar goes to nap. After I gave little June back to Ruby, I finished up some errands and then headed back to the brewery. I intended to help close up, then head to the store for supplies to make pasta, some wine, and some flowers. I had just enough time to stop at the store and take a quick shower before Chloe would be at my doorstep.

But as I walked into the brewery, sitting there in the tasting room, looking around with narrowed eyes was Gio from The Shipped Ship. He got my sample, and he loved it. *Loved it.* He wanted to see what else I had.

And he insisted he couldn't drink alone.

That was over an hour ago. I let all the other guys leave; their shifts were well over. After working all day, skipping lunch, and just being bone tired, I am feeling the beers.

I look at the time. Fuck. It's past seven.

I hold up my finger. "I'm just going to head to the restroom. Here, have a taste of our double IPA while I'm gone."

I take my phone out. The buzz was a notification from my porch camera. Shit.

I don't waste time watching the video; I dial Chloe.

It rings once, twice, three times. Voicemail.

I hang up. I dial again. Once. Twice.

Okay, I'm going to have to leave a voicemail.

Three times.

"Chloe. It's Holden. Something came up. I'm so sorry I didn't call sooner." Shit. Shit. Shit. Did I just slur sooner? "Let me make it up to you. Tomorrow? I could make you breakfast. Or wow, that sounds presumptuous." I smile, remembering us making breakfast at the resort. Me putting her up on the counter, her legs wrapped around me, her hair in my face. Lavender and honey. "Your hair smells great. It's one of—no, I take that back—it is my all-time favorite smell. And you have smelled that way for…for so long. Is it shampoo? You know what don't tell m—"

The voicemail cuts me off.

That was hands down the worst message I have left, for anyone ever. *Man.* I am drunker than I thought.

I go to the video from the porch camera and press play. Chloe stands at the door and waits. My heart sinks. How did I lose track of time like this? She should not have had to wait for me. The porch light goes off, then comes back on. She leans in, her hair falling in front of her shoulder, her cleavage looking amazing in that dress. She says into the camera, "You're right Holden. This was a bad idea. I'll see you around."

Fuck.

I head back to the bar, and Gio smiles at me, then sees my face and frowns. "Everything all right?"

I pour myself a large IPA and sit on the stool next to him. "I fucked up."

"The beer?" His alarm is almost comical.

I shake my head. "No. That's the only thing I'm not fucking up."

"A woman." Gio states it as a fact, not a question.

I sigh. "A woman. The best woman. I don't deserve her. And honestly, I can't have her."

Gio sips his beer, his eyes thoughtful. "She doesn't feel the same way for you that you feel for her?"

I search my body for any truth in this statement. Scanning through memories. It's not true. "I'm pretty sure she feels the same for me as I feel for her."

Gio nods. "And you love her?"

There's no doubt about it. "Yes."

"Then you can have her. And she can have you. You love each other. Any other obstacle can be surmounted."

"Surmounted." I roll the word around. It's a mouthful, and I'm not sure if it's true. If things didn't work out, I'd lose Kyle, and Ruby, and now little June. "I'm her brother's best friend. He's… he's family. It's a huge risk, if I ever lost her, I'd lose everything, everyone."

"Ahhh. Well, to love is to risk. There is no other way to do it."

His words settle around me like an early morning fog.

He smooths his mustache. "Do you think you can live a happy life pretending you don't love her?"

I shake my head. "No."

"Then you must risk it all."

He's right. It's so clear now, if I don't give my all to this, the way I have for the brewery, I will regret it the rest of my life. And what's even worse, so scary it takes my breath away, I will lose Chloe for good.

I've got to fix this. It's time to make a plan. Well, sober up, then make a plan.

THE SUN COMES UP TOO EARLY, BLASTING its way through my curtains. I'm surrounded by little scraps of paper. I fell asleep making notes. Making a plan for how I'm going to fix things between Chloe and me. Gio was very happy when he left the brewery. He wants to order a couple of different beers for each cruise line. It's huge. He's in town for a bit, so we can hash out all the details "whenever," as he put it.

I get up and shower and make myself a huge cup of coffee. This morning is a big scary day. Phase one of my plan. Come clean with Kyle.

Once the coffee is drunk, I get in my truck and pick up some doughnuts and some to go coffees from the corner store. A peace offering.

I knock on the door. It's just after nine. That's a reasonable time for a pop in, right? I was worried that if I called or texted, I'd chicken out.

Kyle answers the door, wearing June on his chest in a little carrier thing. He smiles widely when he sees it's me, and my stomach sinks. I'm a piece of shit. I should've told him about my feelings a long time ago. I should've asked for his blessing before falling in love with his sister. Although, that's not really how love works. It doesn't wait for permission. But I could've had his blessing before acting on it.

"Hey," he says, lifting up June's little feet to her delight. "Is it nap time already?"

"No." I laugh and hold up the box in one hand and the drink carrier in the other. "I have doughnuts. And coffee."

Kyle leads me into the living room.

Ruby bustles in, kisses Kyle on the cheek and then June, a yoga mat under her arm. "I'm off."

Kyle catches her and kisses her full on the mouth for so long that I look away. Ruby heads out the door with a little sigh. Kyle sits, with June still strapped to his front.

I clear my throat, my palms sweating. I rub them on my jeans.

Kyle opens the doughnut box and grabs an apple fritter. "Dude, what's going on?"

I shake my head. "Huh?'

"You're wiping your palms off on your jeans. You only do that when you're nervous. What's going on?"

"I…" How do I start this? I wipe my hands off again. June is staring at me with her big blue eyes. Maybe it's a good thing he's wearing June. He can't kill me in front of his daughter. "I wanted to talk to you about something."

"Okay." Kyle sets the doughnut down.

I lick my lips and resist the urge to wipe my hands again. "It's about Chloe."

"Okay." Kyle lifts June out of the little carrier and lays her on a colorful mat with little toys hanging over it. Still close enough, though, that he probably won't murder me. "What about Chloe?"

"Right. It's about Chloe and me."

Kyle takes off the carrier, his arms flexing as he does. Has he been working out? That's all I need right now is for him to be stronger. Kyle nods slowly. "You and Chloe?"

"Yeah." I swallow hard. I just have to do it. Rip off the Band-Aid. "I love her."

June's little coos are the only noises in the room.

"We all love her, dude. She's the best."

I clench my fists. He's not getting it. "No, I'm *in* love with her."

Kyle freezes. Maybe this was a bad idea.

Then he cracks a smile and laughs. Actually laughs.

"No, I'm serious."

"Oh, I know." He's still laughing. He wipes a tear away. "It's just hilarious that you think I didn't know that. That we *all*"—he motions around the room like it's full of people—"didn't know."

I sit back on the couch, all the tension leaving my muscles. "You knew?"

"I'm not blind." Kyle has composed himself. "I mean, I knew

you had feelings for her. Love, though? That's big. Have you told her?"

I shake my head. "No. I actually kind of fucked things up."

Kyle's jaw clenched. "Please don't make me hurt you. What did you do?"

I tell him about all of it. Well, I leave out anything graphic because it's still his little sister. And it feels good to talk to him. I've held on to this secret for so long. It feels good to finally share this with him. Then I tell him about last night.

He swoops up June off the floor and nods. "Yep. You messed up. So, now you have to fix it."

My whole body feels a little lighter. "You think I should? I mean…you approve?"

He chuckles. "Are you asking for my blessing?"

"Yes," I say without a hint of a smile. Because I am. I should've asked for it before I crossed any line at all.

Kyle smiles. It's warm and genuine. "There's not a better man she could be with, in my humble opinion. But my opinion isn't the one that matters. So, what's the plan?"

"I actually was thinking of something, but I need a little help."

CHAPTER 35
CHLOE

There is so much to do to get ready for the fundraiser. Dee is a huge help. Still, every night I fall into bed completely exhausted. Kyle and Ruby are handling the concessions. Holden still offered to, and that's the only text I have responded to with a quick *no need*.

And there isn't any. In fact, I don't need anything from Holden at all. I can be just like him and throw everything I have into my work. And I do. I hardly eat. I can't sleep; I lie awake at night, staring at my ceiling and thinking about Holden. Then I force myself to think about something else, the talent show.

Until finally the day arrives. Friday, June 5. The day of the talent show.

I wake up early and get on my leotard, heading straight for the garage, even before my coffee. I'm too nervous not to dance. I warm up, stretch, then I put on some Olivia Dean and let loose. "Ok Love You Bye," comes on, and I feel the rhythm in my bones. I move with the beat, letting it sweep me away.

The chorus echoes through my head. "Ok, love you, bye."

Our situation is not unique. There's plenty of people who love each other and are better off not together. A world full of passionate, incompatible people.

I know I love him. That I know. And I think he has real feelings for me. It might even be love, but it's not enough. We don't work. And there's too much at stake if—no—*when* it all falls apart.

After I've danced myself into an exhausted calm state, I shower and pour myself a big cup of coffee. My dad is in the kitchen, puttering around with his sourdough starter. Not puttering exactly. It almost looks like he's practicing something. Some complicated footwork, and whoop—there's some hip action. He notices me and jumps, taking out an earbud. "Hey, didn't see you there. Can I make you some eggs?"

I shake my head, my eyes narrowed. He's up to something. "I'll grab a bar."

He looks concerned, but he doesn't push.

"I'll see you tonight?" I say as I give him a kiss on the cheek.

"Six p.m. I'll be there." He smiles, and there's definite mischief to it.

I don't have time to figure it out. I have two classes to teach today before I can head to the theater and start setting up. "See you then."

The classes are fun. We run through the routines for the talent show. It's going to be an amazing night. And so far we've already made a big chunk in reaching our fundraising goal.

By the time I get there, Dee, Ruby, and June are already decorating the theater, June strapped to Ruby's chest, kicking her feet. There are huge paper flowers everywhere. It's a floral explosion in here. And it's beautiful.

We work together, hanging floral garlands, and then we set up the items for the silent auction in the lobby. Nearly everyone in the whole town donated something. The artist retreat that happens every fall at the camp by the falls had some of its artists donate works. There's a gorgeous painting by Zara Ashford—it's a reflection of a dancer, the focus is on the wooden barre, and the dancer herself is blurry. I would bid on it in a heartbeat if I weren't saving every penny. Story Club Books, the bookstore in town, donated a huge book bundle, including a signed first edition of *Vex*. Anh and Michelle donated a year's membership at the studio. Kyle even donated a private party at the Vern.

I'm overwhelmed by the generosity of this town.

Kyle comes in a bit later, bringing a keg of beer. "Refreshments are here."

Ruby lets out a whoop. Then asks, "Did you bring all the treats too?"

"In the truck, hun."

She kisses him on the cheek.

"What's on tap?" I ask.

Kyle smiles, and it's full of mischief. It seems like everyone is up to something. "You'll see."

"Or, you could just tell me."

He shakes his head.

I let out a frustrated sigh. The front door swings open, and my hip hop class comes bustling in wearing matching-ish black outfits and sneakers. There's too much to do, so whatever surprise Kyle has with the concessions, I'll let him have it.

More performers roll in. One after another. My ballet class comes all wearing giant sparkly tutus, some of them clinging to their moms for dear life. I let them know parents are more than welcome on stage for the performance, and if any little one really isn't feeling it, they don't have to perform. No tears at this talent show.

By the time 6 p.m. comes, the auditorium is full. Not an empty seat in the house.

I walk out onto the stage, the lights bright.

"Hello. I'm Chloe Papadopoulos, and I'm the future owner of Bloom Dance Studio."

The auditorium erupts into thunderous applause. The lights are so bright in my eyes. I signal to Ahn up in the booth, who so graciously volunteered to run them, to turn them down just a bit. My eyes scan the crowd of faces as I give my little prepared speech. Looking at who's here. But really searching for Holden.

He's not here. At least not anywhere I can see.

I thank everyone again and tell them to enjoy the show. The first act is Hank, the persnickety old man from the Vern, juggling. And he's good. At the end, he even lights his batons on fire, much to my alarm, because that was nowhere in his proposal, but he pulls it off and doesn't catch himself or the theater on fire. He even gets a standing ovation. It's a perfect way to start the night.

All the acts are amazing. I go onstage for our hip hop performance, and we nail it. Then after a few acts I'm back on stage with the little ones for our ballet performance. We are the last act before intermission.

We show off some of the things we've learned, and only one girl, our littlest, comes out holding her mom's hand, who does the dance as well. Then we have a free dance to the song "Sunbreak." The girls twirl and leap and jump. Our precocious four-year-old in the group twerks. Everyone cracks up. It is funny, and honestly excellently executed. That girl can move.

We end the dance by joining hands and dancing through the audience to a standing ovation. Anh announces the intermission. The girls squeal and jump in the lobby. Their parents rush out, giving hugs. I give some of the girls high fives.

Kyle comes out from behind the counter and hands me a red Solo cup as the auditorium fills with people. I try to hand the cup back. "No thanks."

"You should just try it. Take a tiny taste. It's a special brew." Kyle points to a sign hanging from the concession stand. It has light-purple lavender on it, covered in butterflies and bees, on a honey-yellow backdrop. In a luscious green font is spelled out *Budding*. Underneath it says, *A hopeful, lavender honey blonde ale made for Chloe.* The Woodshop Brewing logo is right in the corner.

I look around again for Holden, but I don't see him anywhere. I take a small sip. It's light, crisp. The malt of the honey is balanced with the floral notes of the lavender. It tastes like spring in a cup. It tastes like hope.

The sign, the label says the beer is for me. And Kyle handed it to me. Does he know about Holden and me?

Kyle is standing behind the counter handing a cup to a customer. I walk over, and he smiles. "What is this?" I hold up my cup.

"Beer."

"Right." I'm not sure how to approach this if I got it all wrong.

"You should give him another chance. He's a really good guy."

My heart stops. He does know. I'm at the same time relieved and panicked. "But…you…"

Another customer orders a beer and one of Ruby's famous brownies. He grabs them, all the while talking to me. "Don't be mad he told me. He needed advice on how best to apologize."

"I'm not mad. You're not mad?"

Kyle lets out a large breath. "Chloe, I've known you two had eyes for each other for a long time."

"But you're not upset? What if we don't work out? What will happen?"

Kyle hands another beer to a customer then turns to face me, making the rest of the line wait. "Chloe, we could all die tomorrow. When Mom…" he stops and swallows hard. Then lets out another deep breath. "It wasn't her time. None of us knows how long we're here for." He finds Ruby across the room, bouncing June. "I loved Ruby for years before I told her. I was scared, too. I was scared of what would happen if it didn't work. But look at all the amazing things that have happened because it did. And if I had let the fear win, I wouldn't have June. I wouldn't have Ruby. I wouldn't be who I am right now. I'm a *fucking* dad."

I smile. "You're a fucking dad."

He turns back to the customer and grabs them a beer, but keeps talking to me. "Just keep an open heart. Don't worry so much about what couldn't go right. Maybe, maybe this once, it'll all work out."

"Is he here? Holden?"

Kyle bites back a smile as he shrugs.

He is. But where?

CHAPTER 36
CHLOE

After the intermission is over, the acts continue. They're all amazing. I check the schedule, and we're just about to wrap things up.

I head to the stage with my microphone. During one of the acts, I changed out of my leotard and into my blue sundress, and it swishes around my legs as I walk on stage. My cheeks are tired from smiling, but my heart is full.

I hold the microphone to my mouth. "Thank you all so much—"

"Hang tight. There's one more act," Ahn says from the booth.

One more act? My thoughts go to my dad dancing in the kitchen. Did they set something up? I start to walk off stage, but Anh comes on again. "Stay put, Chloe."

Someone runs out and grabs my microphone.

Holden walks out on stage in a leather jacket, a black button-up shirt, not buttoned all the way, and fitted black pants. He takes off his leather jacket and tosses it to the side, to the applause of the audience. He holds out his hand to me. "May I have this dance?"

I look at him, my lips curling up into a smile. "We haven't practiced."

He pulls me close, and the lights go low. He whispers, "We can figure it out as we go."

Music comes on, and I know it from the first note. It's "(I've Had) The Time of My Life." The *Dirty Dancing* Song. A spotlight finds us on stage, and we move together. It's not the exact dance, it's our own, and it's messy in spots, but it's heartfelt and genuine.

The song reaches a crescendo, and Holden smirks at me and gives me a wink. He jumps off the stage, full-on jumps. I laugh. The auditorium lights go up, and he dances through the aisle, and it is spot-on, Patrick Swayze's dance. He must've practiced a lot. As he moves, people start getting up and dancing to the end of the aisle. My dad joins them, Ruby wearing little June, Kyle comes in from the lobby, Dee is even in on it. Along with a bunch of guys from the brewery and some of the women from my hip hop class.

It's a full-on flash mob. They all dance their way back down the aisle toward the stage. I swish my skirt. I can't believe Holden put this all together. The audience is going wild, clapping along to the beat of the song, and some are even dancing in their chairs. My ballet class is going bananas in front of the stage, giggling and twirling.

Holden dances his way to the stage and gives me a hand down. "We don't have to do the move."

I look at him, this beautiful man who arranged all this for me, and I think of all that practice as the waves moved around us. "We're doing the move. Go back to your spot."

He smiles and squeezes my hand rushing back across the aisle.

Butterflies fill my chest as he mouths at me, "You sure?"

I nod. Then take a deep breath and run, full speed toward Holden. The crowd stops clapping; it's like the whole room collectively sucks in a breath. I hold in my core, spread my arms out wide, and Holden lifts me high above his head, like I'm light as a feather.

The applause is so loud it thunders in my ears. From up here, I can see Ruby dancing with Kyle, laughing, as June kicks her little feet. Dee is dancing with an older gentleman with a mustache, and it looks like maybe they're doing the twist. Anh has even come down from the booth and is slow dancing with Michelle, cheek-to-cheek. The room is filled with so much love. And so is my heart. It feels like it may burst.

Holden brings me down, and my body skims his on the way. I wrap my arms around his neck, while people all around us dance. Everyone is getting out of their seats now and getting in on it. The song ends, but it goes right into Stevie Wonder's "Signed, Sealed, Delivered," and people keep dancing.

"You finally did it," I say.

Holden brushes some hair out of my face, tucking it behind my ear. "Did what?"

I lean into the palm of his hand, savoring the feeling of him. I've missed being close more than I even admitted to myself. "You flash mobbed me."

"Life goal accomplished." He laughs. "I know you love them. And I know you're not the hugest fan of beer, but I had to make that brew for you. I couldn't get your scent out of my head, and brewing is my love language."

I smile. "I tasted it. It's good."

"There's some chilled Tempranillo behind the concession stand, too."

"Oh my God, thank you."

He laughs.

I nuzzle into him. "It is good, but it is still beer."

He mimes a dagger plunging into his heart. I laugh. Then he leans down and kisses me. It's soft and sweet, and full of all the things we've wanted to say for years.

When he pulls back, he says, "I love you, Chloe."

"I love you."

"I hope you don't mind, I talked to Kyle about us."

I nod. "Yeah."

"But only because I want us to really be an *us.*"

"Me too."

He picks me up and spins me around, my skirt swishing. The

room spins, and I can practically see the butterflies in my chest swirl all around us.

I WAKE up the next morning, wrapped in Holden's arms, tangled in Holden's sheets. We don't have the final numbers yet from the auction, but the preliminary figures look really good. Like nearly forty thousand dollars good. A huge chunk of it came from a massive bid on one of the paintings, the one of the dancer.

The light is sunny this morning. Summer is ready to arrive, and it's going to be great. I stretch my arms, a little sore from all the dancing last night, and all the dancing in general with my classes. I'm honestly pleased, though, with how well I've been doing. I was so scared that my body would give out. Or I'd have another injury. Or I just wouldn't love it as much as I did, since I can't quite do it the way I used to.

But I was wrong. It is different. I have to warm up more. And more of my own workout time is focused on strength training. Even though it is different, I still love it.

Holden nuzzles into me. "It's too early."

He's right. Monday morning, I need to see a man about a building, but today is Saturday. So I snuggle back into him. He rolls over on top of me, and he's already hard. "Well, good morning to you, too."

He kisses my neck, his lips moving down my body. Down, down, down to my breasts. He takes my nipple in his mouth and sucks. I moan as his fingers move down. He finds me wet, and he brings his head up.

"Good morning to you, too." He smirks.

Then he moves his head all the way down as I lie back on the pillows and let the sensation of Holden between my legs overtake me. It feels like a dream, a fantasy, too good to be true. But it is. He's here. With me. And we are a us.

MONDAY FINALLY COMES, after a weekend spent mostly in bed. Kyle comes with me to my 3pm appointment with the owner to put a down payment on a beat-up old mechanic shop.

The final total from the fundraiser was $47,216. It's bananas. I sign the paperwork, get the keys, and then head out into the sunshine. Kyle gives me a big hug.

"You did it."

"We did it. I couldn't have done any of this without all your help. Everyone's."

He smiles and pats my shoulder. "We're just thrilled you finally let us."

I walk to the shop, it's just about four blocks away from the bank, and open the door, switching on the lights. It's going to take a lot of work, but it's going to be amazing.

I lay out a blanket, sit on the floor, and look around the place. It's dirty now, but what I see is gleaming hardwood floors, mirrored walls, with a barre. I see kids running around in tutus and soft lighting. I see rolling up these doors and setting chairs out for summer performances, and maybe even some barbecues.

I'm so lost in thought, I don't hear him come in, until he's sitting right next to me. Two glasses in one hand and a bottle in the other. Holden sits with a little grunt. He holds up the bottle of Cabernet. "Champagne would be more fitting, but I remember you saying on the ship you don't like it."

My heart melts into a puddle on this grease-stained floor. He remembers the little things. I smile and scoot closer to him. I place my legs on either side of him, taking the glasses and the bottle out of his hands and setting them down.

I take his face in my hands and lean in and kiss him. When I pull away, I hold his hands as they rub my legs. "I realized I owe you—"

He shakes his head. "You don't owe me anything."

"Let me finish," I say, covering his mouth playfully. "I owe you some compliments."

I can feel his lips turn up under my palm.

"You are brave. You started your brewery with a hope and a prayer and hardly a lick of money. And that, I see now especially after working on this, is brave.

"You are kind. You're loyal to your friends. And you see what people really need. Like when Kyle and Ruby needed a break. Or when I needed a little push. Like when you set up that job shadow, basically, on a tropical island. With no phone service. How did you do that?"

He shakes his head. "I told you. That sparkly pink uniform had magic powers."

I smile. "You are magic. You're steady and patient." I motion to the room. "All this is because of you."

He shakes his head. "I know the rules. I'm supposed to accept the compliments. But all this…" He gestures around, then places his hand back on my legs. "All this is because of you. You brought people together. Your passion for dance, for people, for life—it's infectious. You've made a dancer out of even me."

I smile, but I notice the wrapped paper package by the door that wasn't there before Holden came in. "Uh huh. And you had nothing to do with any of it, huh? What's that?"

"It's a congratulations present."

"It wouldn't happen to be a painting of a dancer's reflection in the mirror, would it? A little something you picked up at an auction?"

"Maybe…"

"Holden." I swat at him. "How can you afford that?"

He smiles wide and bright. "We got the cruise contract. Gio especially likes Budding Ale."

Excitement bubbles up in me. It's too many good things. I kiss him, full on the mouth, and he rolls me onto the blanket.

He runs his hand through my hair.

"I love you, Holden Hartman."

"I love you, Chloe Papadopoulos."

We kiss, and everything melts away. We are here, living our dreams, being brave. Trying a different way.

CHLOE: A LITTLE OVER A YEAR LATER

The Fortune Falls Fall Festival is at the end of the week, and I'm exhausted. Three of my classes are giving performances at the studio, and we've been practicing. On top of that I've been making the decorations for the studio and also helping to make some for Woodshed, which is unveiling its new tap room at the festival. Room is a funny thing to call it. It is a full-on bar, with wood-fired pizza and a large outdoor space with corn hole and bocce ball, and a gorgeous garden. Holden's been working so hard, I wanted to help, so I said I'd make his decorations too.

A car pulls up to the house. I can hear the gravel crunch. I check out the window, and it's Ruby. I run out and am just locking the door behind me when another truck pulls in beside Ruby.

Holden hops out. "Hey, baby, where are you off to?"

I smile, my arms full of craft supplies. "It's Tuesday. Margs and Meg night."

Holden joins me on the porch. "Margs, Megs, and crafts?"

"They're going to help me with the decorations."

He smiles and nods, taking the things out of my hands and setting them down. He pulls me into a hug, nuzzling into my neck. "I was hoping we could have a little alone time."

Ruby honks and hangs out of the truck. "Come on, lovebirds. Meg waits for no one."

I smile and kiss Holden. The butterflies beat wildly in my chest. I thought after I moved in, they might calm down, but they're as strong as ever. "Later," I whisper into his ear and give it a little nip.

I pick up my stuff, and Holden playfully swats me on the ass, then I get into Ruby's truck. We drive to Dee's cabin. She's visiting for the week, but the Inn was full. So she rented out a rustic cabin near the waterfall and seems to be loving it. The early evening sun spears through the trees and lights up the orange leaves.

When we get to Dee's, the door is open, and she is setting up pillows on a blanket spread out on the side of the house. Ruby parks, and we hop out of the truck.

Dee smiles, her pink hair tied up in a messy bun. "I thought we could have movie night under the stars."

The blanket is set up with snacks and a bottle of wine, and there's a projector on a table behind it. It's beautiful.

"Where did you get all this stuff?"

She laughs. "It was included in the house."

Ruby plops down. "Will we be able to see to cut the leaves out?"

That's the decorations they're helping me with. Cutting tissue paper leaves. I want to say, *oh, it's fine either way*, but I really need the help.

Dee smiles and holds up three headlamps. Now it's perfect.

Dee throws on *When Harry Met Sally*, Ruby pours the wine, and I hand out the tissue paper, stencils, and scissors.

We work all through the first movie, the sun goes down, and the stars come out, then we watch *You've Got Mail*. By the time Shopgirl meets NY152 in the garden, all the tissue paper I brought is cut into delightful leaves, the wine is gone, and Ruby has a new plan for Dee.

"You should try online dating. Look, it worked for Meg."

Dee is shaking her head. "I'm fine. I'm happy without a man.

What I really need is a change of scenery. I love this cabin, but I still feel like I haven't found a home, you know. *The Holiday.* If I'm going to emulate any movie, it's going to be that one."

Ruby claps her hands together. "Oooh, a little life swap. Leave it to me." Then she looks at me.

I laugh. "Don't look at me, I'm not swapping lives."

She lays her head on my shoulder. "Of course you're not, your life is perfect."

I'm about to protest when I stop myself. Nothing is perfect. But my life is filled with passion—in my work and at home— good friends, and love. So much love. It's not perfect, but it's as close as I've ever felt.

I smile. "It is pretty great."

THE FESTIVAL IS about to kick off, and I'm just putting the finishing touches on the studio. It's a gorgeous fall day and a little on the warmer side, so the doors are rolled up. We've got bobbing for apples out front. And I'm setting up the chairs for our performances. The four-fives class is going first. They're going to be fall fairies and show us what they've learned over the past couple of months.

I'm just placing the last chair when I smell him. It's the same scent that's been driving me wild for years. Spicy and sweet. Ginger and toffee, and something a bit boozy underneath.

Holden places a hand on my waist, and I turn. He's holding a bouquet of roses, and I can tell they're from his grandmother's bushes out back. They're gorgeous, some pink, some soft orange, and it reminds me of the sunset on St. Thomas. Him hoisting me and dropping me in the ocean over and over again until we got it. And then it turned into something so much more.

I smile, and he wraps me in his arms. "Thank you. Shouldn't you be at your grand opening?"

He nods. "I had to come to wish you luck, and I needed a kiss."

He leans down, his lips pressing into mine, and I melt into him. The roses slip from my hands as he lifts me up. I wrap my legs around him, my hands on the back of his neck, as he starts carrying me toward my office. I pull my lips away. "Do we have time?"

"I'll be quick," he says in a gruff tone that sends tingles all the way to my toes.

"That'll be the day."

He kicks the office door closed with his foot and places me on the desk, pulling my leotard down from my shoulder. "I'll be quick-ish."

We are not quick, and by the time we come out of the office, you can hear music from neighboring businesses and murmured conversations of people enjoying the festival. But we're not late. Or at least I'm not. Our performances don't start for another forty minutes. Kids should start arriving in twenty.

I adjust my leotard, and Holden runs a thumb over my lip.

"Lipstick." He smirks.

I do the same to him. He wraps me in his arms again and looks into my eyes. "Blooming looks real good on you."

I smile. "Is that your compliment for the day?"

"No. I'm going to give that later." He nips at me, and I squeal.

Ruby and Kyle come walking up, with little June Bug toddling up in a little orange tutu that is so precious I could die.

Kyle says, "Break it up, you two. There are children present."

Ruby makes a fart noise. "Let them kiss."

Holden laughs, moving his hand from my waist and grabbing my hand. "Like she doesn't see you two kiss all the time."

"That's different," Kyle says.

Holden turns to me. "I'd better go. I'll see you later at Woodshed?"

"You know it."

He winks at me, and my heart soars. I watch him leave, his ass looking mighty fine in his threadbare jeans. Ruby comes to stand next to me and bumps my hip with hers.

I sigh. "One day, I'm going to marry that man."

Ruby's face falls. "He already asked? He was supposed to wait till later. I was going to film it."

My eyes go wide, and Ruby's cheeks turn white as a ghost.

"You were going to film…what?"

Ruby clamps her mouth shut. Her lips are in a tight line. Tears well up in her eyes. "I can't believe I said that."

Then a small sob escapes her. Kyle rushes over and levels me with a death glare. "What did you do?"

I hold up my hands because if anyone didn't do anything here, it's me.

Ruby sniffs. "I told her about the proposal."

Kyle covers his mouth.

Ruby lets out another sob. "It's pregnancy brain."

Kyle hangs his head and shakes it.

"What?" I say, my shock doubling. What in the fresh hell is happening here? Holden is going to propose, and Ruby's pregnant. "You're pregnant, again?"

Kyle's shoulders are shaking, and when he uncovers his mouth, he's laughing.

Ruby pushes his shoulder. "It's not funny."

But Kyle is cracking up, then I start in on it. Because it actually is pretty funny. Then Ruby starts laughing. Little June Bug toddles over, and she laughs, too.

Kyle is the first to compose himself. "Oh, man. You spilled every last bean."

Ruby hangs her head. "I can't be trusted."

"When are you due?" I ask.

"It's still early. I'm not due until April." Ruby picks up June and snuggles her on her hip.

"And when is Holden going to propose?"

Kyle steps in. "You have to act surprised. We"—he gives Ruby a loving but pointed look—"were sworn to secrecy."

Kids start showing up, running up to me in their adorable fall fairy outfits. Orange, yellow, and rich-brown tutus with matching wings. People arrive, and we go through our steps, to much applause from families and community members, but my brain is elsewhere. My thoughts are firmly stuck on one thing: Holden is going to propose.

After the last performance, I put away all the chairs and dump the water from the bobbing for apples bin. The sun has set, but there's still a golden line on the horizon, like it can't quite let the day go yet. Stars dot the sky. I lock up and grab my bag, wishing I had thought to pack something else to wear. But who wouldn't want to be proposed to by the man of their dreams in a fall fairy costume?

I walk the short three blocks to the brewery's new space and walk back to the garden entrance. It's gorgeous. Bulb lights hang, crisscrossed from poles on the edges of the fence. The tissue paper leaves are hanging from the string of the lights, making a pleasant orange glow. The flowers in the garden are still in bloom. The wooden picnic tables are filled with people enjoying beers and pizza. There's a small stage near the building of the brewery where a live band is playing "Sally, When the Wine Runs Out."

I spot Kyle and Ruby, holding hands with June, dancing in a circle. Dee waves at me as she dances on stage with the band.

Ruby spots me, and waves, then makes a very loud, "Caw, caw."

Like a bird.

Holden comes out on stage just as the song is finishing up, and the band takes a break. Dee jumps off the stage and into the crowd.

Holden takes the microphone, and his eyes find mine across the crowd. He motions for me to come up. "I want to thank you all for being here. I'm not much for speeches."

I make my way to the stage, and Holden gives me a hand up.

"So, I'm going to make this short and sweet." He turns to me, and my heart flutters. "Chloe, I love you. You are the most amazing woman, and I know you've done a lot of soul searching these past couple of years…"

Boy, that's the truth.

"I'm so proud of you for finding your passion and going after it with all you've got. Even before that, you were…are…the most amazing woman. I love you not because you're an excellent dancer or a hard-working entrepreneur. Which you are both those things and more. But I love you simply for being you. Chloe."

Holden kneels. My heart squeezes. He pulls a ring box out of his pocket and snaps it open.

It's a gorgeous gold ring with a solitary diamond.

"Chloe, will you be my wife?"

Time stops. I look around at the faces in the crowd. Ruby is tucked into Kyle's arm. My dad is holding up June, beaming. Dee has her hands clutched at her heart.

I find Holden's eyes. Warm and soft. The corners of my mouth turn up, and I say, "Yes."

The crowd erupts in applause. Holden throws down the microphone and swoops me up in his arms, spinning me around. He sets me down and brings his forehead to mine. "Yes?"

"Yes. A thousand times, yes." I take his face in my hands. There's so much I want to say. He's my world. I look at him, and I see my past, but I also see my future. I see us, our wrinkled hands clasped tightly as we board a cruise to celebrate our fortieth wedding anniversary. We have time to say all that later. For now, I say the most important thing. The only thing that really matters. "Holden Hartman, I love you. And I'd be honored to be your wife."

He kisses me like no one is watching, even though half the town is. And I swear, the butterflies in my chest take flight, swirling around us all in the amber glow of the twinkle lights. Holden grabs my hand, and we jump off the stage, running through the crowd.

"Where are we going?"

Holden smiles at me. "I'm taking you home."

ACKNOWLEDGMENTS

Thank you, reader, for joining me for the fourth and final Fortune Falls book. (Although you may see some of these characters again in a different series.)

This book was so much fun to write. And while it was truly a blast, it was also cathartic. While I was never on the track to become a professional dancer, I did break my hip ten years ago, and I deal with some chronic pain issues from that and arthritis. It was healing for me to write a character also dealing with chronic pain and finding ways to still pursue her passions. I hope it resonated with some of you as well.

I'd like to thank my romance girlies, Stephanie Paul and Robin Blackburn. Thank you for all your insight, your quick critical reading skills, and your friendship. You make this all so much more fun.

I want to thank my sister, Alaina for always being there to bounce ideas off of and talk books and just hang out. Love you.

I want to thank Andy for encouraging me to pursue this dream. And Aggie, for being a constant joy in my life. You make me want to be the best me. Love you both.

I want to thank my indie author buddies. You all have taught me so much. It's been a long time since I've felt like I have "my people," but I feel like I've found it now.

I want to thank Alanna and Tessa for working their asses off for the indie author community. Book'd, and Tatt'd was my very first event as an author, and it's still the most fun! I love the unhinged chat. The community you two have built is really special. Thank you for letting me be a part of it.

I want to thank my editor, Andrea Holland. I love working with you! Can't wait for our next project.

And I want to thank you, dear reader. Thank you for being here. I hope you loved it

ABOUT THE AUTHOR

I received a BFA in mixed media studio art. With a degree in the arts and no solid plan, I've had the opportunity to hold many different jobs: video store manager, barista, photographer's assistant, toy store clerk, and yoga instructor at a retreat in Puerto Rico, to name a few. Hands-on research for her books.

Currently, when I'm not writing, you can find me working at a Title I elementary school library, crafting with my little girl, or hosting the podcast, *So I Wrote a Book…Now What*, where I interview fellow authors about their revision process.

Want to join my newsletter?

instagram.com/ncbartonwrites
tiktok.com/@ncbartonwrites

ALSO BY NC BARTON

Fortune Falls Series

The Now in Forever: A Small Town Second Chance Romance

The Art of the Meet Cute: A Small Town Found Family Romance

The Road Not Taken: A Friends to Lovers Christmas Roadtrip Romance

Love on Location Series

Meet Me at the Loch: A Grumpy Sunshine Celebrity Romance

Meet Me at the Villa coming this July.

If you're a fan of thrillers I have a pen name NC James that writes mystery-thrillers.

In a Dark and Lovely Wood